WELCOME TO THIS COLLECTION
of stories about Kaya, a Nez Perce girl growing
up before America became a country. As Kaya
prepares to become a leader for her people,
she has no idea what lies ahead—that white
people will soon change Nez Perce life forever.
The Nez Perce people have lost much over the
last 200 years, but they have never lost their
spirit. Because of the tremendous strength,
courage, and will to survive of girls like Kaya,
Nez Perce children today are still learning their
own language, listening to legends, dancing in
traditional dress, and proudly riding beautiful
horses that look just like Kaya's own Steps High.

Together in this special edition, Kaya's stories
will capture girls' imaginations for years to come.
Step inside Kaya's world of daring adventure
and deeply held traditions, and be inspired all
over again.

Kaya

STORY
COLLECTION

BY JANET SHAW

ILLUSTRATIONS BY
BILL FARNSWORTH

★ AmericanGirl®

Published by American Girl Publishing, Inc.
Copyright © 2004, 2008 by American Girl, LLC

Questions or comments? Call 1-800-845-0005, visit our Web site
at **americangirl.com**, or write to Customer Service, American Girl,
8400 Fairway Place, Middleton, WI 53562-0497.

Printed in China
08 09 10 11 12 13 14 LEO 10 9 8 7 6 5 4 3 2 1

PICTURE CREDITS
The following individuals and organizations have generously
given permission to reprint images contained in "Looking Back":
pp. 395—*The Long Trail* © Proferes 1999, www.proferes.com; pp. 396–397—
photo by Kathy Borkowski (Wallowa Valley); Sakakawea Statue, C1106,
State Historical Society of North Dakota, Capitol Grounds, Bismarck, ND
(Sacagawea statue); National Numismatic Collection, National Museum
of American History, Smithsonian Institution (peace medal); Idaho State
Historical Society, Boise (MS2/1053/3, 6) (drawing of Nez Perce spiritual
images); pp. 398–399—Courtesy Sid Richardson Collection of Western Art,
Fort Worth, TX (*Trouble on the Horizon*, Charles M. Russell, 1893); photo
courtesy of National Park Service, Nez Perce National Historical Park (Nez
Perce chiefs); pp. 400–401—photo courtesy of National Park Service, Nez Perce
National Historical Park (Swan Necklace); *The Long Trail* © Proferes 1999,
www.proferes.com (painting); pp. 402–403—Idaho State Historical Society
(MS2/1053/3, 6) (drawing of warriors); MSCUA, University of Washington
Libraries (NA 878) (Ollokot); Idaho State Historical Society (MS2/1053/3, 6)
(drawing of Nez Perce women); Smithsonian Institution (NMNH 2987B1)
(Black Eagle); Bettmann/Corbis (Chief Joseph); pp. 404–405—Lewiston
Tribune, Lewiston, ID (park ranger with tepee); photo by Antonio Smith
(girl dancer); © Chuck Williams, Mosier, OR (girl on horseback).

Vignette Illustrations by Susan McAliley

Cataloging-in-Publication Data available from the Library of Congress.

Kaya and her family are
Nimíipuu, known today
as Nez Perce Indians.
They speak the Nez Perce
language, so you'll see
some Nez Perce words in
this book. "Kaya" is short
for the Nez Perce name
Kaya'aton'my', which means
"she who arranges rocks."
You'll find the meanings
and pronunciations of
these and other Nez Perce
words in the glossary on
pages 406–407.

TABLE OF CONTENTS

KAYA'S FAMILY AND FRIENDS

page 1
MEET KAYA

Kaya's boasting gets her into
big trouble and earns her
a terrible nickname.

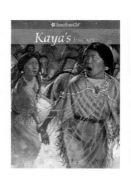

page 63
KAYA'S ESCAPE!

Kaya and her sister Speaking Rain
are captured in an enemy raid.
Can they find a way to escape?

page 129
KAYA'S HERO

Kaya becomes close friends
with a warrior woman named
Swan Circling, who inspires Kaya
and gives her an amazing gift.

page 197

KAYA AND LONE DOG

Kaya befriends a lone dog,
who teaches her about love
and letting go.

page 271

KAYA SHOWS THE WAY

Kaya is reunited with
Speaking Rain, who has a
surprising decision to share.

page 337

CHANGES FOR KAYA

Kaya and her horse, Steps High,
are caught in a flash fire.
Can they outrun it?

LOOKING BACK   395

KAYA'S FAMILY

TOE-TA
*Kaya's father, an
expert horseman and
wise village leader*

EETSA
*Kaya's mother, who is a
good provider for her
family and her village*

KAYA
*An adventurous girl
with a generous spirit*

BROWN DEER
*Kaya's sister, who is
old enough to court*

WING FEATHER
AND SPARROW
*Kaya's mischievous
twin brothers*

**KALUTSA
AND AALAH**
*Toe-ta's parents,
who teach Kaya
the old ways*

**PI-LAH-KA
AND KAUTSA**
*Eetsa's parents, who
guide and comfort Kaya*

STEPS HIGH
Kaya's beloved horse

SPEAKING RAIN
*A blind girl who lives
with Kaya's family and
is a sister to Kaya*

SWAN CIRCLING
*A strong warrior woman
whom Kaya admires*

KAYA'S FRIENDS

RAVEN
*A boy who loves to
race horses*

FOX TAIL
*A bothersome boy
who can be rude*

LONE DOG
*A special dog who
becomes Kaya's friend*

TWO HAWKS
*A ragged and angry
captive who becomes
Kaya's friend*

WHITE BRAIDS
*A kind woman who saves
Speaking Rain's life*

TO THE NEZ PERCE
GIRLS AND BOYS,
MOTHERS AND FATHERS,
GRANDMOTHERS AND GRANDFATHERS,
UNTO THE SEVENTH GENERATION

MEET

Kaya

LET'S RACE!

When Kaya and her family rode over the hill into *Wallowa*, The Valley of the Winding Waters, her horse pricked up her ears and whinnied. Answering whinnies came from the large herd grazing nearby. Kaya stroked the smooth shoulder of her horse.

"Go easy, Steps High," she said softly. "We'll be there soon." But Steps High whinnied again and began to prance, stepping high just like her name. Speaking Rain's old pony whinnied, too. A sickness in Speaking Rain's eyes had caused her to lose her sight, so Kaya held the lead rope of her pony.

"I hear so many horses!" Speaking Rain said. "What do you see, Kaya? Tell me." Because

1

Speaking Rain's parents had died, she'd lived with Kaya's family and was a sister to her.

Kaya studied the white-peaked mountains, the broad valley, and the shining lake so she could share the beauty of this beloved place with her blind sister.

"The snow's still deep on the mountains," Kaya said. "The lake reflects the green hills and the blue sky. The river's full of red salmon and running higher than I've ever seen it. The tepees are set far back from the bank."

"Where is everyone?" Speaking Rain asked. She held her buckskin doll against her chest.

"Some men are spearfishing in the river," Kaya said. "Some little boys are tossing up a hoop and trying to shoot arrows through it. Little girls are playing near the tepees, and all along the shore women are cleaning and drying salmon."

"I've smelled the salmon for a long time," Speaking Rain said. "It's a powerful scent! The men must have a big catch this year."

It was midsummer, the season when the salmon swam upstream to the lake to lay their eggs. Many

bands of *Nimíipuu* gathered here each year to catch
and dry the salmon. Kaya and her family were
traveling with several other families from Salmon
River Country to join the fishing. Her family was
also visiting her father's parents. Kaya loved these
reunions with her grandparents and her many other
relatives, old and young—all the children were just
like brothers and sisters to each other.

Kaya's mother and her older sister, Brown Deer,
rode just ahead. Her mother glanced back over her
shoulder, then reined in her horse and motioned for
Brown Deer and Kaya to do the same.

"What is it, *Eetsa?*" Kaya asked her mother.

"The bundles on my pack horse have slipped a
little. They'll rub a sore spot if I don't balance them
again," Eetsa said. "I need to retie them."

Eetsa and Brown Deer quickly slipped off their
horses and began untying some woven bags from
a pack horse. Wing Feather, one of Kaya's twin
brothers, had been riding behind Eetsa's saddle.
The other twin, Sparrow, rode behind Brown Deer's.
It had been a long journey, and the little boys
were restless. Kaya helped the twins down so they
could stretch their legs. The boys giggled as they

scampered to hide behind a travois and peeked over, their dark eyes gleaming.

travois

"Look after your brothers well," Eetsa told Kaya, as she always did. Eetsa and Brown Deer hung several woven bags of dried roots and dried buffalo meat on their saddle horns.

As they worked, they glanced eagerly at the tepees along the river. Kaya smiled to herself. She was thinking that Nimíipuu loved to travel, but they loved the excitement of arrival even more. Already her grandfather and two of her uncles were riding out to greet them.

"I'm so glad we're here!" Brown Deer said. She smoothed her buckskin dress and touched the abalone shells she wore in her ears. "Remember what fun we had the last time we visited?"

Kaya nodded. *"Aa-heh!* I remember what fun you had dancing every night! I wonder which boys will serenade you this time," she teased. After the hard work came hours of trading and games. There would be feasting, singing, and always dancing, with the beat of the drums echoing down the valley.

Kaya turned and saw her father gazing at the

4

herd of sleek horses, some of them spotted, in the wide meadow. Perhaps *Toe-ta* was thinking of trading for some of the horses, or of the races they'd have. He was an expert horseman. Often he won races on his fleet-footed stallion.

Kaya was certainly thinking about horse races. For a long time she'd imagined being in one on her adored Steps High. She knew Steps High was fast, but also young and untested. Toe-ta had told her that Steps High wasn't ready to race yet.

When Eetsa was satisfied that everything was in order, she and Brown Deer mounted their horses. Kaya helped the little boys climb back onto the patient animals and take their places again.

When Kaya turned to Steps High, the horse tossed her head and pawed the ground. Kaya rubbed her cheek against Steps High's soft muzzle. "If only we could race I know we'd win!" she whispered as she climbed into the saddle.

"Did you say something to me?" Speaking Rain asked, as Kaya took her pony's lead rope again.

"I was talking to Steps High," Kaya said. "I told her that when we race we'll beat all the others!"

Eetsa turned to look Kaya in the eye. "I've told

you before not to boast," she said firmly. "Our actions speak for us. Our deeds show our worth. Let that be your lesson, Kaya."

Kaya pressed her lips together—she knew Eetsa was right.

"Come, let's meet the others," Toe-ta said, and led the way on his stallion.

When Kaya and her family rode up, her grandmother, *Aalah*, and one of her aunts were waiting at the doorway of their tepee. Aalah stepped forward. Her face was creased with age, and little pockmarks, like fingerprints, covered her cheeks.

"*Tawts may-we!*" she said. "Welcome, my son! Welcome, all of you!" Smiling, she hugged Kaya and Speaking Rain as soon as they climbed off their horses. Then she took the twins into her arms. She kissed their chubby cheeks and tugged their braids.

"Tawts may-we!" Eetsa said. As Toe-ta and the others dismounted and shared greetings, she took the woven bags from her saddle horn. "We brought these for you," she said, offering their gifts with pleasure—it was an honor to give them.

6

Aalah received the gifts with thanks. Then Auntie put one hand on Kaya's shoulder and her other hand on Speaking Rain's. "You've grown! Are you hard workers like your sister, Brown Deer?"

"Aa-heh! We are!" Kaya and Speaking Rain said at the same time, and giggled.

"*Tawts!*" Auntie nodded. "You girls help Brown Deer unpack the horses and bring your things inside."

Kaya and Brown Deer carried their bundles into the tepee and placed them across from where their grandparents slept. Speaking Rain stacked the bundles neatly along the wall of the tepee. It was

tule mats

always packed full when they gathered here. But Kaya liked it crowded and cozy, and the tule mats that covered the tepee let in cool breezes and light.

After the women and girls had put everything in order around the tepee, Eetsa allowed Kaya to take Speaking Rain and the little boys to play. "Remember, it's your job to look after your brothers carefully," she reminded Kaya.

Kaya knew there were dangerous animals about. She also knew about the Stick People—small, mischievous people who might lure a child to wander too far away into the woods. "Aa-heh," Kaya said. "I will."

She led Speaking Rain and the twins to a group of boys and girls gathered in the shade beside the river. Raven, a boy a little older than Kaya, was playing a game with a length of hemp cord.

"Here's what happened when Coyote went to put up his tepee," Raven said. The twins watched, wide-eyed, as Raven's fingers flashed, weaving the cord into the shape of a tepee. Then, with a tug, he made the tepee collapse. "Coyote worked too fast!"

8

he said. "He didn't tie the poles properly, and his tepee fell down on him!" Everyone laughed and the twins squealed at the fun.

Raven leaned back on his elbows in the thick grass. "I see you have a new horse, Little Sister," he said to Kaya. "She's a pretty one."

"She's the prettiest horse in the whole herd!" Kaya said. She couldn't disguise her pride. Steps High wasn't large, only about thirteen hands high. She had a black head and chest, a white rump with black spots on it, and a white star on her forehead. "She's fast, too," Kaya added. *That wasn't boasting,* she thought—just saying what was true.

Fox Tail squatted beside her. He was a bothersome boy who could be rude. He always followed Raven, trying to impress the older boy. "Your horse looks skittish to me," he said to Kaya. "Why would your father give you a horse like that?"

"Toe-ta didn't choose my horse," Kaya said. "My horse chose me."

Fox Tail laughed and slapped his leg. "Your horse chose you? How?"

"One day I was riding by the herd with Toe-ta,"

Kaya said. "A filly kept nickering to me. So I whistled to her. She followed me. She came up to me and pushed her head against my leg. Toe-ta said that meant she wanted to be my horse. He worked with her so I could ride her."

"Is that a true story?" Fox Tail demanded.

"Ask my father if that's true," Kaya said.

"I believe you," Raven said. "But you say she's fast. Should I believe that, too?"

"I haven't raced her yet, but I've run her many times," Kaya said. "She glides over the ground like the shadow of an eagle."

Fox Tail jumped to his feet. "Like an eagle—big talk!" he said. "Let's race our horses and see if yours flies like you claim she does!"

"Yes, let's race!" Raven got to his feet, too.

Kaya had an uneasy feeling. *I shouldn't have boasted about her speed*, she thought. *I've never raced her*. "My horse is tired now," she said hesitantly.

"She's not too tired for one short race," Fox Tail insisted. "Maybe your horse isn't so fast, after all."

Kaya felt her face grow hot. Her horse was as swift as the wind! She was sired by Toe-ta's fine stallion, Runner.

Kaya stood up. "Speaking Rain, could you take care of the twins for me?" she asked. "I know it's my job, but I want to race."

Speaking Rain was braiding strands of grass into bracelets for the little boys. "I'll try, but sometimes they play tricks on me."

"I'll only be gone a little while," Kaya assured her.

Kaya, Raven, and Fox Tail got on their horses and rode up to the raised plain at the end of the lake. Often people held celebrations and races here on the level ground, but today Kaya and the boys were alone.

Now that she'd decided to race, Kaya was eager to begin. Steps High seemed eager, too. When Fox Tail's roan horse came close, Steps High arched her neck and flattened her ears. When Raven's chestnut horse passed her, she trotted faster.

Raven reined in his horse. "We'll start here. When I give the signal, we'll race until we pass that boulder at the far end of the field." He held his hand high. Then he brought it down and they were off!

The boys took the lead, stones spurting from under their horses' hooves. They lay low on their horses, their weight forward. They ran neck and neck.

Steps High bolted after them but swung out too

11

wide. Kaya pressed her heels into Steps High's sides. Then she gave Steps High her head, and her horse sprang forward.

Kaya thrilled to feel her horse gather herself, lengthen out, and gallop flat out! She was running as she'd never run before. Her long strides were so smooth that she seemed to be floating, her hooves barely touching the earth. Her dark mane whipped Kaya's face. Grit stung her lips. She clung to her horse, barely aware that they'd caught the other horses until they passed them. She and Steps High were in the lead!

Then, suddenly, Steps High began to buck! She plunged, head down, heels high. Kaya grasped her mane and hung on. She bit her tongue and tasted blood. Steps High bucked again!

Raven spun his horse around. He was beside Steps High in an instant and grabbed the rein. He pulled the horse sharply to him, and, in the same motion, he halted his own horse. Steps High skidded to a standstill, foam lathering her neck. Kaya slid off.

Steps High's eyes were wild. For a moment she seemed never to have been tamed at all. Kaya's legs were shaking badly, but her first thought was to

Kaya clung to her horse, barely aware that they'd caught the other horses until they passed them. She and Steps High were in the lead!

calm her horse. She began to stroke Steps High's trembling head and neck.

Fox Tail came galloping back. "I knew that horse was skittish!" he cried. "She just proved it!"

"She proved she's fast, too," Raven said.

Kaya wanted to thank Raven for coming to her aid, but her wounded pride was a knife in her chest. She could hardly get her breath. Leading her horse slowly to cool her down, Kaya silently walked away from the boys.

When Kaya had rubbed down Steps High, she turned her horse out to graze. Then she started back through the woods, heading toward the river.

Her feelings were all tangled up like a nest of snakes. She was excited that Steps High had run so fast, but she was disappointed that her horse had broken her training. She was relieved that she hadn't been bucked off, but she wished the boys hadn't seen her lose control. She knew she shouldn't have boasted, but she also wished she could have made good on her boast and won the race.

When Kaya glanced up from nursing her hurt feelings, Fox Tail was coming down the trail toward her on foot. He stopped right in front of her. "You told us your horse chose you," he said with a smirk. "Would you choose her after the way she tried to buck you off today?"

"She's the best horse ever!" Kaya said. "She can run faster than your horse, and I can run faster than you, too. Want to race me right now?"

Fox Tail cocked his head. "The first one to the riverbank wins!" he cried. He turned and sprinted away down the path.

For a little while Kaya was right on his heels. Then Fox Tail left the path, leapt over a fallen log, and took off through the woods. *He must know a shortcut,* Kaya thought. She followed him.

But she couldn't keep him in sight because he jagged in and out of shadows. Was that his dark head beyond the bushes? Now she was uncertain which way to go. She stopped to listen for the sound of the river as her guide.

She stood in a gloomy clearing surrounded by black willows. She listened for rushing water. There was only silence. No wind blew in the leaves, no flies buzzed. All she could hear was her heartbeat.

Then a twig snapped behind her.

She whirled around. Did something just duck behind that tree? The shadows around her seemed to waver and sway. Was it the Stick People? Had they led her to this part of the woods?

Kaya held her breath. She knew the Stick People were cunning and crafty. They were strong, too. She'd heard they could carry off a baby and leave it a long way from its mother.

A flock of jays cawed—or was it the Stick People signaling to her? They seemed to be saying, "Forgot! Forgot!" Kaya shivered. What had she forgotten?

Then she gasped. She'd forgotten her little brothers! Kaya should never have given her job to Speaking Rain. The little boys were four winters old, just the right age for mischief. Kaya must get back to them at once, before they got into danger.

She knew she must leave a gift for the Stick People in return for their help. They became angry with people who didn't treat them respectfully. She found rose hips in the bag she wore on her belt and placed them on the moss. Then she began running back the way she'd come.

SWITCHINGS!

Kaya ran along the riverbank, past
women cleaning salmon and cutting the
fish into thin strips. Auntie was laying
the strips on racks to dry. She raised her hand in
greeting when Kaya rushed by.

But Kaya kept going. She ran up to some girls
setting up a little camp for their buckskin dolls.
They'd made a travois with sticks and pieces of an
old tule mat. A boy pretended to be their horse,
pulling the travois. "Have you seen Speaking Rain
and my brothers?" Kaya asked.

The children shook their heads, and Kaya ran
on, desperate to find them.

The twins had never been like other little boys.

They could understand each other without saying a word out loud. When they were born, the setting sun and the rising moon were both in the sky. Two lights in the sky and two babies who looked alike—they were special children. They could also be twice the trouble if they decided to play tricks.

Kaya ran through some brush and out onto the grassy bank where she'd last seen Speaking Rain with the boys. Speaking Rain crouched by a twisted pine tree, but the twins were nowhere in sight.

"Where are the boys?" Kaya called.

"I don't know," Speaking Rain said. "But I just found the toy I made for them." She held up a little hoop made of grass. "They got tired of my game and ran off. I've been calling them but they don't answer." Her cloudy eyes were wide with alarm. "Maybe they fell in the river!"

Kaya caught her breath. "Did you hear a splash?"

Speaking Rain shook her head. "But where could they be? Maybe a cougar chased them."

Cougars! Cougars sometimes went after small children. Kaya's heart raced, but she tried not to let Speaking Rain feel her alarm. "Come on, let's look for the boys. If they just ran off, they can't be far."

She made herself sound confident, but she was frightened. The boys could be hurt or lost. Oh, why hadn't she thought of them instead of herself?

Kaya looked around. Two trails led away from the riverbank. One turned upstream toward where the women worked. The other turned downstream. Dust-covered leaves hung low over that trail. The little boys probably would have been drawn to that leafy tunnel. "Boys!" Kaya called. "Where are you?"

There was no answer.

"Follow me," Kaya said to Speaking Rain. "I'll look and you listen."

Speaking Rain took hold of Kaya's sleeve and walked right behind her down the trail.

"I see their footprints in the dust," Kaya said. She walked faster. "And here's where they left the trail and went under the bushes. They were crawling. We'll have to crawl, too. Stay close."

The girls got down on their hands and knees and inched forward. Leaves caught in their braids and brushed their cheeks. Kaya kept a lookout for the Stick People hiding in the shadows. Maybe they'd led the boys deeper into the woods.

A little farther on, the prints disappeared. Kaya sat back on her heels. "I've lost their trail. Do you hear anything?"

Speaking Rain lifted her chin and frowned. "I hear the river. There's swift water there. If the boys fell in, they'd be swept away."

Kaya put her hand on Speaking Rain's shoulder. "Let's keep looking," she said. She began to search for prints again.

"I think we should get others to help us," Speaking Rain said. Then she pointed up. "Listen, I hear something up there!"

Kaya got to her feet so that she could see over the bushes. An old spruce tree loomed overhead. A cougar might be crouching in the branches! Or the boys. She'd been so busy following signs on the ground that she'd forgotten the twins could climb trees.

A spruce branch trembled. Two pairs of dark eyes gazed down at her from the green boughs. The boys were clinging to the trunk like raccoons. They were grinning.

Kaya was flooded with relief. She was also angry that the boys had scared her and Speaking Rain.

"Come down right now!" she said.

The little boys crept down out of the tree in a shower of dry needles. When they reached the ground, they started to giggle.

Kaya took their hands and crouched to look into their eyes. "Don't laugh!" she said. "Running off isn't a game. Dangers are everywhere!"

"Yes, dangers are everywhere," a low voice said.

Startled, Kaya and Speaking Rain turned. Someone was coming through the woods behind them.

Hands parted the branches, and Auntie stepped through. Her face was stern. "When you ran by me I sensed trouble, so I followed you," she said. "Now I see I was right. I heard your mother tell you to look after your brothers. But you ran away from your responsibility."

Kaya felt her face redden. She bit her lips. Auntie's words made her ache with shame. "I'm sorry," she whispered.

"You should be sorry," Auntie said in a weary voice. "I must call Whipwoman to teach you a lesson."

As Kaya followed Auntie back to the camp, she kept a strong hold on her feelings so that they wouldn't show, but her eyes stung with unshed tears.

She kept her gaze on her feet when Auntie went to fetch Whipwoman, the respected elder selected to discipline children who misbehaved.

When Whipwoman arrived, she carried a bundle of switches. But it wasn't the switches that Kaya dreaded—it was the bad opinion of the other children. When one child misbehaved, *all* the children were disciplined. They learned that what one of them did affected all the rest.

"Come here, children!" Whipwoman called out. "Come here now!"

One by one, the children old enough to be switched came forward and lined up in front of Whipwoman. She laid her bundle of willow switches on the ground at her feet.

"Lie down on your stomachs and bare your legs," Whipwoman told them. She waited while everyone did as she said.

Kaya lay down, pulled her skirt up to her knees, and pressed her mouth to the back of her hand. She heard the switch hiss through the air and felt it sting her bare legs. She winced, but she didn't cry out or make a sound. Whipwoman moved on to Speaking Rain, then to the next child. On and on she went

*Kaya heard the switch hiss through the air and felt it sting her bare legs.
She winced, but she didn't cry out or make a sound.*

until they'd all been given a switching.

As the children lay there, Whipwoman spoke to them slowly and firmly. "Kaya didn't watch out for her brothers. They ran off into the woods. They could have been injured. Enemies could have carried them away. A magpie that thinks only of itself would have given the boys better care than Kaya did! Nimíipuu always look out for each other. Our lives depend on it. Don't ever forget that, children. Now get up."

When Kaya lifted her head she caught sight of her parents and grandparents looking on. Their sad faces hurt her much more than the stings on her legs.

magpie

Fox Tail got to his knees near Kaya. He grimaced as he rubbed his legs. "Magpie!" he whispered to her. "I'm going to call you Magpie."

"Magpie! Magpie!" echoed the girl next to him.

Speaking Rain inched closer to Kaya and clasped her hand. "Don't mind them," Speaking Rain said. "It's all over now."

But it wasn't over. Kaya thought with alarm, *Magpie! Is Magpie going to be my nickname? Will they never let me forget this?*

"These fish need to be prepared," Kaya's grandmother said to her. "Hold these sticks and give them
to me as I need them."

It was later that day, and Aalah was preparing
a welcome meal for Kaya's family. She knelt on
a tule mat with several salmon in front of her.
She was ready to cut up the salmon and place
wooden skewers in the pieces so that they
could be set by the fire to roast. Other
women had dug deep pits to bake camas
bulbs in. The delicious scent of roasting food
filled the air.

Kaya was glad to be at her grandmother's side.
Her head still buzzed with all the trouble she'd caused.
Her problems had started with her beloved horse.

"I raced Steps High, but she tried to buck me
off," Kaya confessed.

"Hmmm," Aalah muttered. She slid her knife
up the belly of a salmon, cut off its head, took out
its innards, and began to cut the rest into three long
pieces. Her face shone with sweat from the heat of
the fires. Her hands glistened with oil from the rich
salmon.

One by one Kaya handed skewers to Aalah. "But I'm going to train her," Kaya said, thinking out loud. "Someday I'm going to be the very best horsewoman!" When she heard herself boast again, she bit her lip.

"Hmmm," Aalah muttered again. She laced a skewer through a large piece of fish. "I've lived a long time, and I've known many fine horsewomen. First they cared for their families. Then they trained their horses. You must think of others before yourself." She held out her hand for another skewer.

Kaya bowed her head at her grandmother's lecture. She felt a tear run down her nose.

"What's wrong?" Aalah asked. She laid aside a piece of fish and reached for the next one.

"Some children are calling me Magpie. They say I'm no more trustworthy than a thieving bird," Kaya said miserably.

"Nicknames!" Aalah said. "Have I ever told you the awful nickname I got when I was your age?" Her hands never stopped moving as she spoke.

Kaya shook her head. She couldn't imagine her grandmother doing anything to earn an awful nickname.

"Finger Cakes, that's what I was called," Aalah said. "Finger Cakes!"

Kaya couldn't help but smile. Women ground up kouse roots and shaped the mixture into loaves, or little finger cakes, to dry. Everyone liked dried kouse cakes. "That's a funny nickname," Kaya said. "Why did they call you that?"

finger cake

Her grandmother picked up another large salmon. "My mother used to put a few finger cakes into my big brother's shoulder bag," she said. "If he got hungry when he was hunting, he'd chew on the finger cakes. I was jealous that he got extra pieces of my favorite food, so sometimes, when he wasn't looking, I'd steal some of his finger cakes. One day he caught me with my hand in his bag. From then on I was called Finger Cakes."

"Did they call you that for a long time?" Kaya asked.

"Yes, I was Finger Cakes for a long time," Aalah said. "Every time I heard that nickname, I remembered I'd been wrong to steal my brother's food. Every time I heard that nickname, I vowed I'd never again take what wasn't mine. It was a strict teacher, that nickname!"

"But you lost the nickname, didn't you?" Kaya said.

Her grandmother smiled. "Let me tell you something. Sometimes an old friend will call me Finger Cakes just to tease me. After all these years that name still pricks me like a thorn!" She put down her knife and wiped her hands on the grass. "These salmon are ready to roast now."

Kaya was still troubled. "Do you think I can lose my nickname, Aalah?" she asked.

Her grandmother looked closely at Kaya. Her dark eyes seemed to see right into Kaya's heart. "Listen to me," Aalah said. "You're not a little girl any longer. You're growing up. Soon you'll prepare to go on your vision quest to seek your *wyakin*. Work hard to learn your lessons so your nickname won't trouble you. Then your thoughts will be clear when the time comes for your vision quest." She pushed herself up from her knees. "These fish need to be carried to the fire. Everyone is hungry."

Kaya's family gathered beside their tepee for their evening meal. Aalah had laid several tule mats in a row on the grass. The men took their places on one side of the mats. The women set wooden bowls of salmon and baked camas in the center and served the men. Then the women sat down across from them.

Kaya's grandfather led them in giving thanks to *Hun-ya-wat*, the Creator. *Kalutsa* held out his hands over the feast. "Are you paying attention, children?" he asked in his deep voice.

"Aa-heh!" Kaya said with the other children.

"Hun-ya-wat made this earth," Kalutsa said. "He made Nimíipuu and all people. He made all living things on the earth. He made the water and placed the fish in it. He made the sky and placed the birds in it. He created food for all His creatures. We respect and give thanks for His creations." After they all sang a blessing, each one took a sip of water, which sustains all life. Then they all took a tiny bite of salmon, grateful that the fish had given themselves to Nimíipuu for food. After that, Kalutsa motioned for the rest of the food to be passed.

As Kaya ate, she glanced from time to time at the others. She was surrounded by her grandparents, parents, aunts and uncles, and all the children in her family. She gazed at her father with his sharp cheekbones and broad shoulders. She looked at her mother with her shining black hair and her straight brows. Kaya felt how much she loved them all and how much she needed them. She wanted to be worthy of their trust, to be a girl no one would call Magpie ever again.

"It is morning! We are alive! The sun is witness to what we do today!" the camp crier called. He made his way among the tepees to waken everyone and announce the events of that day.

Kaya opened her eyes. Eetsa was already awake. She'd brought a horn bowl of fresh water from the river. Aalah was awake, too. She stood in the doorway of the tepee and faced the east, where the dawn sky glowed pink. With her eyes closed and her chin lifted, Aalah sang a prayer of thanksgiving to Hun-ya-wat, thanking Him for a good night's sleep and the new day. Kaya silently joined Aalah's prayer. Morning prayer songs were rising from all the tepees in the camp.

The prayers over, Kaya stretched and yawned.

Beside her, Speaking Rain rolled onto her back and reached for her folded dress. The twins were sitting on the deerskin blanket they shared. They held out their hands for the root cakes Brown Deer offered them. Brown Deer had arisen before the camp crier passed by, too. Although Kaya hoped to be as hard-working and generous as her older sister, right now Kaya wanted to stay curled up under her soft deerskin as long as possible.

Aalah turned with a smile as if she guessed Kaya's thought. "Come, girls, get up!" she said. "Roll up your bedding. It's time to bathe in the river."

Every single morning of the year, in cold weather as well as warm, all the children went into the river to bathe. The cold water made them strong and healthy. Grandmothers and Whipwoman watched the girls to make sure they got clean.

This morning Kaya delighted in wading into the quiet place at the river bend. A salmon tickled her toes as she walked out on the pebbly bottom to where the water reached her chest. As she splashed, the sun rose over Mount Syringa and flooded light into the green valley.

Rabbit, a girl older than Kaya, ducked

31

underwater and came up next to her. She shook drops from her gleaming hair and gave Kaya a sly smile. "I didn't know magpies could swim," she whispered.

Kaya's cheeks burned. "I can swim, and faster than you!" she said.

"Will you peck if you catch me?" Rabbit laughed. With strong strokes she began to swim for shore.

Kaya swam after her. She could almost touch Rabbit's flashing heels, but she couldn't catch up to her. Kaya waded out of the river with her head bent. "Magpie didn't win that race," Rabbit said with a grin.

That nickname stung like a hornet. *I let myself boast again!* Kaya realized with dismay as she dressed.

Kaya returned to their tepee, where she found her parents talking and laughing quietly together as Eetsa braided Toe-ta's thick black hair. When Eetsa had tied his braids together, Toe-ta beckoned to Kaya. "Let's go work with your horse," he said.

Toe-ta kept his best stallion, Runner, tethered on a long rope near the camp. He put a horsehair rope on Runner's lower jaw and mounted him bareback. He handed Kaya another rope bit and a long rope to carry. Then he lifted her up behind him on the big horse, and they set out toward the herd.

Kaya loved to ride with her father. She leaned against his warm back. The smooth gait of Toe-ta's stallion rocked them gently. "Toe-ta, Steps High tried to buck me off yesterday," she said.

"I thought so," Toe-ta said. "I saw you walking her. If you hadn't had trouble, you'd have been riding."

"I know your horse would never buck you," Kaya said.

Toe-ta was quiet for a little while. "Have I told you about the first time my father put me on a horse?" he said.

"You've never told me that," Kaya said.

"I was a little boy, even younger than your brothers," Toe-ta said. "One day my father put me on the gentle old horse my grandmother rode. He told me to ride around the camp slowly. But after I went around slowly, I wanted to go faster. I kicked the horse as I'd seen my grandmother do. The horse bolted! My father chased us, yelling to me to turn the horse uphill to slow him. I looked for a soft spot and jumped off into the grass instead."

"Were you hurt, Toe-ta?" Kaya asked.

"I was sore all over!" he said. "Do you know

why I told you that story today?"

"Why, Toe-ta?" Kaya asked.

"I want you to know that no one is born know-ing how to ride," he said. "And you have to respect the horse you're riding. It takes a lot of work to learn what we need to know in this life."

Toe-ta swung Runner alongside a group of mares. Steps High was grazing with them.

"Whistle for your horse," he told Kaya. "She knows your whistle."

When Steps High heard Kaya's whistle, she pricked up her ears. As she came forward, Toe-ta tossed a rope around her neck and drew her close.

Each time Kaya saw Steps High, she marveled at her horse's beauty. Steps High was both graceful and strong, the muscles rippling under her skin.

Toe-ta got off his stallion and lifted Kaya down. As he approached Steps High, she tossed her small head and rolled her eyes. Toe-ta put the rope bit in her mouth, then grabbed a handful of mane as he swung onto her back. He held the rope reins firmly as he rode her away from the herd at a trot. Steps High pranced nervously, but she obeyed Toe-ta.

He drew the horse to a halt again by Kaya. "Now it's your turn," he said. "You're a strong rider. If you need me, I'm here to help."

Kaya swung up onto her horse. Toe-ta handed her the reins. But Kaya didn't urge Steps High forward.

"I won't push you too fast or too hard again," she whispered to her horse. "I want you to trust me."

Kaya pressed her knees to her horse's sides. She could feel a shiver run down her horse's back as Steps High began to walk. Steps High pushed against the bit as if she were thinking about running and bucking again, but she stayed at a walk until

Kaya nudged her to trot. Kaya kept her horse gathered in and rode in slow circles until Toe-ta motioned for her to come back to him.

He took her horse's reins in one hand and stroked Steps High's neck. "Tawts," he said to Kaya. "That's just how you must ride her for a long time. Stay slow and stay in control. Work with her a little longer, then come back to camp." Toe-ta turned Runner and rode off.

As Kaya rode her horse in another circle, Fox Tail rode up beside her. He'd been helping some older boys with the horses. His face was dusty and his lips were dry. Herding was hard work in the hot sun. "Do you want to race again?" he asked Kaya.

"Toe-ta said I can't race my horse for a long time," Kaya said.

Fox Tail's grin was a wicked one. "I forgot that magpies don't race!" he cried. He kicked his horse and galloped away from her.

That nickname again! It gave Kaya a sick feeling in her stomach. She clenched her teeth as she circled Steps High back to the herd.

CHAPTER
THREE
—

COURTSHIP
DANCE

 One morning, after many days of
clear skies, dark clouds rolled over
the mountains and rain pelted down.
The tule reeds of the tepee coverings swelled with
water and kept out the rain. The women turned
from preparing food to work they could do inside
the dry, cozy tepees until the storm passed.

Aalah took out the hemp cord and the bear grass
she needed to weave some flat bags. She'd dyed the
bear grass soft shades of red, green, and yellow. She
gave some brown cord to Kaya, then started a bag for
Speaking Rain to work on. Although Speaking Rain
couldn't see, she could make fine cord and could
weave by touch once Aalah set the first rows.

Eetsa and Brown Deer were mending moccasins for the twins, who napped on their deerskins. As he always did, Wing Feather slept with his hand tucked into his baby moccasin, which he cradled under his chin.

For a long time they worked in silence. Kaya liked the quiet tepee. The sound of rain falling on the tule mats soothed her. In fact, she wished she could stay inside their tepee, where no one called her Magpie, and never go out again.

Aalah touched Kaya's weaving to show her where her work was lumpy and uneven. "You're awake, but you're dreaming," Aalah said. "Will you tell me your dream?"

Kaya undid the line of weaving and started it over. She didn't want to admit how much that nickname still troubled her. "I was dreaming about my horse," she said.

"When I was a girl we didn't dream of horses," Aalah said with a smile. "When I was a girl we didn't even have horses. When we traveled we walked on our own two feet, and our strong dogs pulled our loads for us."

"You know about these things," Eetsa said

respectfully. "But dogs couldn't pull the big loads that our horses do. And we couldn't travel as fast on foot as we can on horseback."

"But our scouts could run fast!" Aalah said. "The scouts who lived near the trail to enemy country ran as fast as the wind to warn us of danger." Aalah's fingers flew as she wove the bag. Already she'd finished a plain border and was adding a lovely pattern of triangles.

"It's true the scouts were swift," Eetsa said. "But no man runs as fast as a horse. No man can travel as far on foot as he can on horseback." She began sewing a new sole onto a moccasin with a length of sinew.

"Now the men ride far away, but often they don't come back for a long, long time," Aalah said. "Things were better in the old days."

"I can't imagine our warriors without their horses," Brown Deer said softly. "A warrior is so fierce on horseback! He fights so bravely!"

"Our men were brave warriors long before they ever heard of horses," Aalah said. "And because we have horses, our enemies make more raids on us."

"Aa-heh," Eetsa said. "You're right. But without

his horse my husband wouldn't be such a good hunter. He couldn't bring us so much meat. He always gives meat to the old people, too."

"Horses are so beautiful!" Kaya chimed in. "Especially the spotted ones, like Steps High!" She imagined her horse running with her head held high and her black tail streaming. Was it boasting to call her beautiful?

Aalah reached for Kaya's bag and gently took it from her. When Aalah put the tip of her finger through a hole in a loose row, Kaya realized that she hadn't made the weaving tight enough. She began to unravel her work so that she could make it better.

"Aalah, you've often said we need horses for many things," Brown Deer said.

Aalah sighed deeply. "I've said so and it's true," she said. "The old days are gone. We can't unravel our lives and begin them again, as Kaya is doing with her weaving." She put down her work and placed her hands on her knees. "I want you to listen to me. I'm going to tell you something."

Kaya and Speaking Rain laid down their weaving at once. Eetsa and Brown Deer stopped sewing. When Aalah spoke like that, she wanted their attention.

"I've lived a long time, and I remember many things," Aalah said. "Isn't that so?"

Eetsa and Brown Deer nodded.

"Aa-heh," Kaya and Speaking Rain said.

"One thing I remember is the time of terrible sickness," Aalah said. "Traders told us about strangers with pale, hairy faces who rode from far away to trade at the Big River. With the strangers on horses came a sickness of fevers and blisters, a sickness we'd never known before. My people never saw the strangers with pale faces, but their sickness came to us anyway. Many, many people sickened and died. The most powerful medicine man had no medicine to cure this new sickness."

Aalah was quiet for a while, gazing into space. Then she ran her hands across her cheeks. "You see these pockmarks on my face," she said. "I was one who got the sickness. My own mother died of it—I've told you that, too. These pockmarks remind me how few of us survived. They remind me that not just good things came into our lives with the horses. But the marks also remind me to be strong and help others."

Kaya looked at Aalah's solemn face. She knew

*"With the strangers on horses came a sickness of fevers and blisters,
a sickness we'd never known before," Aalah said.*

Aalah was thinking about the bad times in the past. Kaya was ashamed to be worrying about an unpleasant nickname when so much suffering had come to others. Would difficult times like the sickness come again to Nimíipuu?

"We've talked enough of that," Aalah said. "It's time to go back to work."

Kaya began her weaving again, making each twist of cord as firm and as tight as possible. When she grew up, she wanted to be a wise, strong woman like Aalah.

"The men are getting out the drums again!" Speaking Rain said. "Soon they'll start singing. Listen!"

Kaya listened. From across the camp came the first drumbeats. Every evening, drumming, songs, and laughter filled the air. In the middle of the camp, Toe-ta and some other men were playing the stick game, joking and shouting as they made their guesses. The women watched and chatted with their friends. The children chased each other and played games. Soon there would be dancing, too, until it

was time for the men to light fires along the riverbank and begin their night fishing. Kaya loved being
part of so much excitement.

In their tepee, Kaya watched Brown Deer
dressing herself for the courtship dance. Brown Deer
put on her best dress, decorated with porcupine
quills and elk teeth. She tied on her wide belt and
hung a small woven bag from it. She smoothed the
ankle flaps of her moccasins and tied them neatly.

"Your dress is so beautiful!" Kaya exclaimed.

Speaking Rain folded her arms and grinned up
at her older sister. "Tell us, who do you want to
dance with tonight?"

"I don't know," Brown Deer said with a shrug
and the flicker of a smile.

As Brown Deer hurried to join the others, Kaya
thought her big sister was the prettiest girl in the
whole village.

Kaya and Speaking Rain followed her out of
the tepee. In the light of the rising moon, the twins
were dancing, hopping about and bobbing their
heads like quail. Wing Feather beat two sticks
together. Sparrow turned around and around until
he was dizzy and fell to his knees.

Kaya was too young to join the courtship dance, but the drumbeats and singing made her want to whirl around and around like Sparrow. They made her want to beat the rhythm like Wing Feather. As Kaya listened, she practiced dancing by taking small steps, moving in place. Who could resist the drums!

On one side of the clearing, the older girls began to form a circle. The older boys formed a circle around the girls for the courtship dance. In this dance a boy tried to dance beside the girl he liked best. If a girl let him stay by her side, that meant she liked him best, too. Most families decided who would marry whom, but some paid attention to the choices of the dancers in the courtship dance.

"Brown Deer's dancing near us," Kaya whispered to Speaking Rain.

"Is she looking at any special boy?" Speaking Rain asked.

"She looks at all the boys but one," Kaya said. "She never looks at Cut Cheek."

Cut Cheek was slim and strong. He was a good hunter and a good dancer, too. The scar on his cheek only made him better-looking, Kaya thought. She'd often seen him glance at Brown Deer as he danced, but Brown Deer never returned his gaze.

"When Cut Cheek comes near, Brown Deer looks at her moccasins," Kaya said. "I don't think she likes him at all."

Speaking Rain giggled. "Kaya, you're foolish!" she said. "If Brown Deer can't bring herself to look at Cut Cheek, that means she really likes him."

"But how will he know she likes him if she never looks at him?" Kaya wondered.

"He'll know!" Speaking Rain said.

All the young men and women were in the circle now. When the drumbeats changed, the boys and girls danced slowly forward toward each other. The long fringes on the girls' dresses rippled and swung as the girls moved. The drums seemed to be saying, *Come dance with me! Dance with me!* With exciting music like this, how could the dancers keep their steps so steady and even?

"Where's Cut Cheek dancing?" Speaking Rain asked.

"He's on the other side of the circle," Kaya said. "I don't think he'll be able to get near Brown Deer."

The dancers moved close to each other, then

away, then close again. The next time they were close, a boy eased himself out of his line and placed a stick on a girl's right shoulder. She kept the stick on her shoulder and made room for him by her side. Now they danced as a couple.

The dancers moved toward each other again. As they advanced, Cut Cheek managed to move past the boy next to him. Now he was almost in front of Brown Deer. She held her chin high and looked straight ahead. She made the fringe on her dress snap with each graceful step.

"What's happening now?" Speaking Rain demanded.

"Cut Cheek keeps moving closer to Brown Deer," Kaya said.

Again the dancers moved forward. The boy called Jumps Back moved opposite Brown Deer. He was short, with broad shoulders. Although he often liked to tease the girls, now he looked very serious. When Brown Deer danced close to him, Jumps Back stepped beside her and placed his stick on her shoulder. With a shrug, she knocked the stick off. Jumps Back bent to pick up his stick, and Cut Cheek moved into his place. Now he was opposite Brown Deer.

"Brown Deer just turned down Jumps Back," Kaya told Speaking Rain. "Cut Cheek is right in front of her. But she's looking past him as if she doesn't even know he's there."

"Oh, she knows he's there!" Speaking Rain giggled.

The next time the dancers were close, Cut Cheek left the boys' line. His dark face was gleaming. He stepped next to Brown Deer and placed his stick on her shoulder. Blushing, she took a deep breath as if she were about to dive into deep water. She let his stick stay on her shoulder, and they danced now side by side.

"She chose Cut Cheek!" Kaya said. "She didn't hesitate for a moment!"

The run of salmon up the river was coming to an end. Many, many salmon had given themselves to Nimíipuu. The women had packed the dried salmon into large, woven bags and parfleches made of rawhide. Now they were packing up their belongings as well. Soon the women would roll up the tule mat coverings of the tepees and take down the tepee poles. They would put everything they owned on their horses and the travois and set out. It was time to move higher into the mountains so that the women could pick huckleberries and the men could hunt for *parfleche* elk and deer. Kaya and her family would be part of the group traveling back to Salmon River Country.

Aalah called Kaya to her. She looked worried. "I think I left my knife where we were working yesterday," Aalah said.

"I'll go look carefully," Kaya said.

Kaya already had a rope bit on Steps High. She'd been riding her horse every day, keeping her tightly reined in and held to a trot. Steps High hadn't once tried to buck off Kaya. But Kaya hadn't yet asked Toe-ta if it was safe to run her horse again.

"May I come with you, Kaya?" Speaking Rain asked. Kaya gave Speaking Rain her hand and pulled her sister up onto the horse to sit behind her. Riding bareback, they trotted away from the camp.

At the river, they passed Toe-ta and a few other men fishing for the last of the salmon. As the men speared fish, Fox Tail and some other boys put the salmon into baskets.

Toe-ta stood on the bank with his back to the sun. He had placed a large white stone in the current where the river was shallow. When a fish swam between the white stone and Toe-ta, he could see its outline and spear it.

Downstream, where the river was deeper, Aalah had been cleaning fish on the bank the day before. Kaya reined in Steps High. "I'll start searching a little way down the path and make my way back to you," Kaya told Speaking Rain. "Wait here to mark where I started my search." Speaking Rain slipped off Steps High. As Kaya rode on down the path, she looked for her grandmother's knife.

Steps High was tense and skittish. She shied at a garter snake crossing the path, but Kaya steadied her. When Steps High shied a second time, Kaya reined her in. "What's the matter, girl?" Kaya asked. "What's spooking you?" Steps High snorted and pawed the ground.

Kaya shaded her eyes and looked back to where Speaking Rain had been waiting. Speaking Rain was cautiously making her way through the elderberry

bushes that grew along the riverbank. She couldn't know there was a steep bank on the other side of the bushes. "Stop, Speaking Rain!" Kaya called. She turned Steps High and started back.

Speaking Rain didn't seem to hear Kaya's call. Were Stick People leading her astray? She kept going. "Stop! Don't take another step!" Kaya cried.

Now Speaking Rain heard Kaya's cry. She stopped and turned. As she did, a piece of the bank crumbled beneath her feet. Speaking Rain fell backward. In a shower of stones, she tumbled into the swift river!

RESCUED FROM
THE RIVER

Kaya drove Steps High forward. She jumped her over the bushes and reined her in sharply, her hooves plowing the ground. Speaking Rain was struggling in deep water, trying to swim toward shore. As she thrashed, a branch plunged down in the swift current and hit her. She went under. When she came up again, she was being pulled downstream in the powerful surge of the river.

Fear struck through Kaya like a lightning flash. If Speaking Rain wasn't pulled from the river, she'd drown. If Kaya tried to swim after her, they could both drown. To save Speaking Rain, Kaya's only hope was to run her horse along the bank, try to get

52

ahead of Speaking Rain, and ride into the river to catch her.

Kaya gave her horse her head, then kicked her. Steps High burst forward. In a few strides she was at a full gallop. Kaya leaned low over her neck, clasping her horse with her knees. What if another piece of riverbank gave way? What if her horse bucked? Steps High lengthened out and tore around the next bend, then the next. She seemed as swift as a hawk diving from the sky! Now they were ahead of Speaking Rain, who flailed in the churning river. From here, Kaya had to get her horse into the water and then swim upstream to meet Speaking Rain as she was swept down.

Would Steps High obey Kaya's command to swim? Kaya dug her heels into her horse's sides and again urged her forward. Steps High crossed the beach but paused at the edge of the water. "Come on, girl!" Kaya said, giving her another kick. Then Kaya felt Steps High become one with her again. The horse moved out into the icy current until she was swimming.

Kaya angled her horse upstream. She held tightly to Steps High's mane to keep her balance

against the swirling currents. She'd have to catch
Speaking Rain as soon as she came within reach,
or else Speaking Rain would be swept under the
horse's sharp hooves. In another moment, Speaking
Rain was upon her. Kaya reached and grasped,
caught her arm—she had her! She pulled and
dragged Speaking Rain over her horse's withers.
Holding Speaking Rain tightly, Kaya turned her
horse downstream. She felt Steps High gather
herself.

The horse's strokes evened out as she calmed.
But Speaking Rain was limp against Kaya. Was she
breathing? Kaya headed Steps High toward shore.

In a few more strokes, her horse's hooves
touched bottom. Steps High's head came up, and
she climbed onto the sandy beach. She shook her
head and pranced a step or two as if she knew
she'd done something to be proud of.

Kaya slid off her horse and caught Speaking
Rain as her sister slipped down into her arms.
Speaking Rain lifted her head, moaned, and began
to cough up water. "You're safe, Speaking Rain!"
Kaya said against her drenched head. "You're safe!"

Toe-ta appeared on the bank above them. He

In another moment, Speaking Rain was upon her. Kaya reached
and grasped, caught her arm—she had her!

was followed by the other fishermen and by Fox Tail. Toe-ta leaped down onto the sand. He took Speaking Rain into his arms, bent her forward, and slapped her back with his cupped hand to force more water from her.

Kaya's teeth were chattering. "Speaking Rain, can you get your breath?" she asked.

"Aa-heh," Speaking Rain gasped.

"I heard you shout and I ran," Toe-ta said. "I saw what happened. You did well, Kaya. Your horse did well, too."

"Steps High knew Speaking Rain needed us," Kaya said. "She did everything I asked of her."

"She did what you asked because she trusts you," Toe-ta said. "You've earned her trust, remember that."

Fox Tail crouched on the bank. Was that a look of admiration in his eyes? "You told me you couldn't race," he said. "But you were racing like wildfire, Kaya."

"Kaya wasn't racing to be the fastest," Toe-ta corrected him. "She was racing to save Speaking Rain's life."

Toe-ta's words lifted Kaya's heart. He knew she

hadn't acted for herself, but for Speaking Rain. And Fox Tail had called her Kaya, not Magpie!

Kaya closed her eyes, pressed her face against Steps High's warm, wet neck, and felt the powerful pulse beating there. *"Katsee-yow-yow,* my horse!" she whispered gratefully. Then she held the bridle so that Toe-ta could lift Speaking Rain onto Steps High's back and they could take her back to camp.

The horses needed fresh grass before they could begin the journey higher into the mountains. Kaya rode with Raven, Fox Tail, and some older boys and girls to herd the horses to new pasture. As Kaya rode, she gazed up at a tall peak. She knew the story of how the mountain came to be. An old chief had a vision. His vision told him that men with pale faces would come to steal the shining rocks scattered here. To protect their shining rocks, the people gathered them into a pile and built the mountain over them to hide them. Their treasure was saved because of the old chief's vision.

Kaya thought that if she'd lived in those days, she'd have helped build the mountain over the shining rocks. After all, her name—*Kaya'aton'my'*—meant "she who arranges rocks." Her mother gave her that name because the first thing she saw after Kaya's birth was a woman arranging rocks to heat a sweat lodge.

Will one of us be given a vision someday? Kaya wondered. *Will I?*

She knew that one day soon, like all the other boys and girls, she would go on her vision quest. *Will I be ready when that time comes?* she thought.

When she went into the mountains on her quest, Kaya would seek her wyakin. If her wyakin came to her, she could also receive special powers. Would the hawk give her the ability to see far? Would the canyon wren give her the power to defend her family, the way the wren drives off rattlesnakes? *What creature will my wyakin be?* Kaya wondered. She hoped it would give her powers and a vision to help Nimíipuu, like the old chief in the story.

Fox Tail rode past, his big roan kicking up a cloud of dust. *Fox Tail's too much of a rascal to become a leader of our people,* Kaya thought. But maybe the old chief, whose vision saved the shining mountain, had once been a bothersome boy like Fox Tail.

Kaya reminded herself to think of the work of the day and to do her job well. A frisky young stallion bolted out of the herd and passed behind Kaya and her horse. Immediately, she swung Steps High around, dug in her heels, and galloped after the runaway. Steps High knew her job, too. In a burst of speed, she caught up to the frisky horse and drove him back into the herd again. "Tawts!" Kaya said, and patted Steps High's shoulder. "Tawts, my beautiful horse!"

FOR MY DAUGHTER
LAURA BEELER,
FOR DON READ,
AND FOR MY GRANDDAUGHTER,
MAYA RAIN BEELER BALASSA,
WITH LOVE

Kaya's

ESCAPE!

TAKEN CAPTIVE!

Kaya dug her fists into the sides of her waist and stretched. Her back was sore from bending over to pick huckleberries. Since first light, she and the other girls had moved along the hillside, plucking ripe berries from the bushes and dropping them into the baskets they wore at their waists. Now the sun was high overhead. It was time to sort and dry the berries they'd picked in the cooler hours. Kaya thought dried berries were good, but ripe ones were a feast. When she thought no one was looking, she sneaked a handful for herself.

"Look, Magpie's stealing berries!" Little Fawn cried. "If she eats too many now, we won't have enough when winter comes!" She gave Kaya a teasing grin.

Kaya winced. Not a single day went by without someone calling her by her awful nickname—Magpie. Earlier in the summer, while visiting her father's family in *Wallowa*, she'd gone off to race her horse when she was supposed to be taking care of her little brothers. Whipwoman had told Kaya she was no more responsible than a thieving magpie! When all the children were switched for Kaya's disobedience, they began calling her "Magpie." Each time Kaya heard that nickname, it stung like Whipwoman's switch!

It was now late summer, and Kaya was back in Salmon River Country, where her family had joined her mother's band of *Nimíipuu*. They had traveled upstream and set up camp to pick berries in the higher country. Her father and many of the other men had gone even farther into the mountains to scout the deer and elk trails. It was time for the hunt. Soon the men would bring back as much game as they could so that everyone would have plenty of meat for the winter. With the dried meat, fish, and berries, there would be good provisions for the cold season to come.

Kaya untied the basket from her belt and spread leaves over the berries to keep them from falling out of the basket. She set her basket with those her mother and her big sister, Brown Deer, had filled. All the women and girls had been berry picking. Even the youngest girls wore little baskets—though they were allowed to eat more berries than they saved.

Kaya's grandmother was loading baskets onto her horse. *Kautsa* glanced over her shoulder at Kaya, then nodded at a little girl with her tiny basket. "Remember when you were that young?" she asked Kaya. "Remember how you'd run to give me the first few berries you picked?"

Kaya smiled, glad to be reminded of those happy days. "I remember you always praised me for my berries," she said. "You said I'd be a good picker one day."

"And you are!" Kautsa said. She hung the last bags onto her saddle, then patted her horse. Leading it, she began to walk with the others down to the tepees set in the meadow near the stream.

Kaya walked alongside Kautsa, matching her

strides to her grandmother's long ones. Heat rose
from the stony path and shimmered around her legs.
"The sun's hot, isn't it?" she said.

"*Aa-heh!*" Kautsa agreed. "The day is hot and
our work is hard. But we need to pick berries so we
won't go hungry this winter."

Kaya studied the thick groves of lodgepole pines
that ringed the meadow below. "Could
Speaking Rain and I sleep outside the
tepee tonight?" she asked. "I think we'd
be cooler in the meadow."

"We'll be cool enough inside," Kautsa
said. "I want you two near me. With many of our
men away, we'll be safer if we stay close together.
The boys are keeping the herd close by, too. Look,
there's your horse with the others."

Kaya shaded her eyes. She quickly identified
Steps High by the star on her forehead. Kaya's horse
was grazing at the edge of the herd with some mares
and their foals. Perhaps Steps High sensed Kaya's
approach, for she lifted her head and whinnied.

Kautsa halted her horse. She picked some
large leaves from a thimbleberry plant beside
the trail, then sprinkled a pinch of dried

66

roots on the earth in thanks for what she'd taken. She used the leaves to wipe sweat from Kaya's forehead and then to dry her own face. "Go sit in the shade with Speaking Rain for a little while," she said. "The heat has tired you."

Kaya found Speaking Rain sitting under a pine tree. Speaking Rain was blind, so she'd stayed in the camp with the elderly women and men. She was weaving a beargrass basket that Kautsa had begun for her.

"I brought you some huckleberries, Little Sister," Kaya said. She placed a handful of berries into Speaking Rain's outstretched hands. Since Speaking Rain's parents had died, she'd lived with Kaya's family and been a sister to her.

Kaya sat beside Speaking Rain in the shade of the pine tree. "Our dogs chased two black bears out of the berry bushes this morning," Kaya said.

"Everyone wants these berries," Speaking Rain said. She ate hers one by one, making them last as long as possible. As she munched, she tipped her head toward Kaya. "Why do you sound so sad?"

Kaya knew she couldn't hide anything from

Speaking Rain. Maybe because Speaking Rain couldn't see, she heard everything sharply. "Little Fawn caught me sneaking huckleberries," Kaya admitted with a sigh. "She called me Magpie again."

"I hope that nickname will fade soon," Speaking Rain said. Again she cocked her head, listening. "Isn't that your horse whinnying to you? Go to her. Nicknames don't mean a thing to a horse!"

Gratefully, Kaya squeezed Speaking Rain's hand—Speaking Rain always understood her.

As Kaya walked toward the herd, she whistled her horse to her side. Steps High rubbed her head against Kaya's shoulder. Her horse's muzzle was as soft as the finest buckskin. "Hello, beautiful one!" Kaya whispered against the horse's sleek neck. It always comforted Kaya to stroke her horse.

As Steps High nuzzled her, Kaya glanced back at the clearing where women spread the berries on tule mats to dry in the sun. She saw her two little brothers bouncing on a crooked cedar tree, pretending to ride a horse. Nearby, little girls played with their buckskin dolls. Dogs lolled beside the tepees, their tongues out. In the wide meadow, boys rode herd on the horses. Thin clouds drifted

toward the Bitterroot Mountains in the east. *Stay close to be safe*, Kautsa had reminded her. Kautsa was wise in these things, and Kaya had heard that warning all her life. But right now, this quiet valley seemed the safest place she could imagine.

"Listen!" Kautsa said in a low voice. "The dogs are growling! Wake up!"

Kaya tried to waken in the deep of night. She heard Kautsa's sharp command, but sleep was like a hand pushing her down. Nearby, some dogs growled, then began to bark fiercely. Kaya sat up and rubbed her eyes. What was wrong?

Her mother peeked out the door of the dark tepee, then ducked back inside. "Strangers in our camp!" *Eetsa* said. "Get dressed! Quick! Enemies!"

Enemies! Enemies in their camp! The warning was a jolt of lightning—swiftly Kaya was on her feet. Her heart pounding, she struggled into her dress. Kautsa, Brown Deer, and Speaking Rain were doing the same. They all tugged on their moccasins and crept out of the tepee. Kautsa pushed Speaking Rain and the twin boys ahead of her. Brown Deer picked up one of the little boys. Eetsa picked up the other one. "Follow me!" Eetsa whispered. "Kaya, take Speaking Rain to the woods! We'll hide there!" Crouching, Eetsa ran for the trees, Brown Deer and Kautsa right on her heels.

The moon was rising above the trees bordering the clearing. Kaya could see women, children, and old people hurrying from the tepees for safety in the woods. Some men ran toward the edge of the camp where dark figures ducked between the horses tethered there. Raiders! Enemy raiders! They'd slipped into camp hoping to make off with the best

70

horses, but the dogs had given them away.

Kaya's mouth was dry with alarm. She clasped Speaking Rain's hand tightly. But instead of following Eetsa into the woods, as she'd been told, she went in the direction of the herd. Where was Steps High? Would raiders try to steal her horse?

Kaya saw the woman named Swan Circling head toward the horses, too. A raider was about to cut the rawhide line that tethered her fine horse. Swan Circling had as much courage as any warrior. She stabbed at the raider with her digging stick. She knocked him away from her horse, which reared and whinnied in panic.

digging stick

The raider leaped onto the back of another horse he'd already cut loose. With a fierce cry, he swung the horse around and galloped straight through camp, coming right at Kaya and Speaking Rain!

With a gasp of fear, Kaya tried to run out of his way, pulling Speaking Rain behind her. Too late! Kaya threw herself onto her stomach, dragging Speaking Rain down with her. The raider jumped his horse over them and plunged on.

Kaya struggled to her knees. Now other raiders raced through the camp toward the herd. They lay low on their horses, trying to stampede the herd so no one could ride after them. The horses snorted and screamed with alarm. A few broke away. Was Steps High with them? Kaya whirled around. Nimíipuu men with bows and arrows were running to cut off the raiders.

Arrows hissed by. Kaya clasped Speaking Rain's hand again and ran for the safety of the woods. A horse brushed against her, almost knocking her down. She felt someone seize her hair, then grasp her arm. Speaking Rain's hand was yanked from hers. A raider swung Kaya roughly behind him onto his horse. She sank her teeth into his arm, but he broke her hold with a slap.

Kaya looked back for Speaking Rain. Another raider was dragging her onto his horse. "Speaking Rain!" Kaya cried, but her cry was lost in the tumult. The raiders raced after the herd, which ran full out now. The Nimíipuu men gave chase on foot, but they were quickly outdistanced.

Terrified, Kaya clung to the raider's back. The herd was thundering down the valley, the raiders in

*Arrows hissed by. Kaya clasped Speaking Rain's hand again
and ran for the safety of the woods.*

the rear. The night was filled with boiling dust. Hoofbeats shook the ground and echoed in Kaya's chest. She caught a glimpse of Steps High running with the others. Her horse had been stolen by the enemies. She was their captive, too, and so was Speaking Rain. And it was Kaya's fault!

All that night, and on through the next day and night, the raiders ran the stolen horses eastward. When their mounts tired, they paused only briefly before jumping onto fresh horses and going on. Kaya knew they wanted to get out of Nimíipuu country before they were caught.

Because the raiders didn't rest, Kaya and Speaking Rain couldn't rest, either. The mountains and the valleys below went by in a blur. In her fatigue, Kaya sometimes thought she saw a blue lake in the sky. Sometimes she thought the distant, rolling hills were huge buffalo. And sometimes she did fall asleep, her head bumping the raider's back. He slapped her legs to waken her. She thought, then, about jumping off the running horse, but she knew she'd be injured or killed on the narrow, stony trail. *Maybe it would be better to die than to be a captive*, Kaya thought. But she couldn't abandon Speaking Rain.

When the sun was high overhead, the raiders finally stopped to rest. They left a scout to guard their trail and took the herd to a grassy spot by a little lake where the horses could feed and drink. Kaya saw Steps High standing by the water with the other foam-flecked horses. Their heads were down and their chests heaved from the punishing journey. How she wished she could go to her horse!

When the raiders gathered to share dried meat, Kaya got a better look at them. They were young, bold, and proud of themselves for stealing so many fine horses. She thought they spoke the language of enemies from Buffalo Country. Though Kaya couldn't understand their words, she knew that they boasted of their success. Perhaps they were proud, too, that they had driven the herd all the way through Nimíipuu country to the northern trail through the Bitterroot Mountains.

The raider who'd seized Speaking Rain offered her some of the buffalo meat. When she didn't respond, he waved his hand in front of her eyes, then made a noise of disgust. Kaya knew he was angry that the girl he'd captured for a slave was blind. He pushed her down beside Kaya and stalked back to the circle of men. Kaya held her close.

Speaking Rain leaned against Kaya's shoulder. "Where are we?" she whispered.

"Somewhere on the trail to Buffalo Country," Kaya whispered back. She put some of the food she'd been given into Speaking Rain's hand.

"What will happen to us?" Speaking Rain's voice quavered.

Though Kaya trembled with fatigue, she kept her voice steady. "Don't you remember what happened when enemies from the south stole some of our horses? Our father and the other warriors got ready for a raid. As the drummers beat the drums, all the women sang songs to send off our warriors with courage. Our warriors followed the enemies over the mountains and brought back all our horses! Our warriors will make a raid on these men, too. They'll take you and me back home with them. And they'll take back all of our horses, as well."

"Are you sure?" Speaking Rain murmured.

"Aa-heh!" Kaya whispered. "I'm sure."

But, in her heart, Kaya was far from certain.

Already they'd traveled a long way over the mountains. *Toe-ta* and the other men might not have returned to the berry-picking camp yet. When they did, the raiders might have already left the mountains and hidden themselves securely in the country to the east. What would happen to Kaya and Speaking Rain—and Steps High—then?

Kaya squeezed Speaking Rain's hand. "We have to be strong, Little Sister."

"Aa-heh," Speaking Rain agreed. "We'll be strong."

One of the raiders motioned for the girls to lie down. He tied Kaya's leg to Speaking Rain's with a length of rawhide so they couldn't run away. Lying huddled together, they softly prayed to *Hun-ya-wat*, asking for strength. Kaya was exhausted, but her head buzzed with fears. "I'm afraid to sleep," she whispered to Speaking Rain.

"Me, too," Speaking Rain whispered back. She put her cheek against Kaya's shoulder. "Remember the lullaby that Kautsa used to sing to us?"

Kaya nodded. Then, to her surprise, Speaking Rain began to sing gently, "*Ha no nee, ha no nee.* She's my precious one, my own dear little precious one."

Kaya glanced at the raiders—would they be angry at Speaking Rain's song? The men were lying down to rest. One glanced at Speaking Rain and shrugged as if he had nothing to fear from a lullaby.

Lulled by Speaking Rain's gentle voice, Kaya slept.

CHAPTER TWO

—

SLAVES OF THE ENEMY

The raiders moved the herd eastward over the Buffalo Trail as quickly as they could. As they rode, Kaya caught glimpses of the Lochsa River in the valley, but the trail stayed on the top of the ridge. The going was easier up here than in the wooded gullies filled with windfall trees.

Kaya had been on this trail before. It was an old, old pathway made long before Nimíipuu had horses. In some places it split and braided together again where travelers had walked around fallen trees or boulders. In other places it was only a narrow ledge hugging a cliff. Kaya watched the horses carefully when they came to the dangerous ledges. Surely the raiders were pushing them too fast along this bad part of the trail. A horse that lost its footing would fall down the rocky slope and perhaps be killed.

The gentle old pack horse that belonged to Kautsa often stumbled in fatigue. Kaya kept her eye on the old horse, hoping he could keep up. But on a curving ledge, he slipped on the loose rocks. Kaya held back a cry as the old horse tumbled down the bluff in a shower of stones and lay still at the bottom. Wouldn't the raiders slow the other horses now? But no, they only pushed them faster. Kaya kept her gaze on Steps High and prayed that her horse would keep her footing. *Be strong!* she urged Steps High—and herself. Where were the enemies taking them?

Each night at last light, they camped in open glades where the horses could graze. A raider back-scouted the trail to see if they were followed. Kaya hoped that Toe-ta and other men were coming behind and would overpower the raiders. She thought that young men from Buffalo Country were no match for Nimíipuu men! But when the scout returned and the raiders continued on without rushing, Kaya knew no one was behind them.

At the highest point on the pass, Kaya gazed back at the mountains that loomed between her and her home country. Her courage sank low. She told herself that Hun-ya-wat had made the sky above her and the earth beneath her. *I am in His home no matter where I go,* she thought. Still, fear was a bitter taste in her mouth as they moved farther from her people.

Each night the raiders tied Kaya's leg to Speaking Rain's. At first light, the raiders untied them and sent Kaya to gather heavy loads of wood for the fire. They fed Kaya and Speaking Rain only the scraps from their meals. Kaya felt like the starving dogs that sometimes appeared at camp out of nowhere, cringing and groveling for a bite of food. She vowed that if she ever got back to her people again, she would never chase off those desperate, sad-eyed dogs.

When they passed some hot springs, where steaming water spouted from the rocks, the trail ran down the east side of the mountains. In another day they'd reached the broad river valley below. Kaya remembered passing this way with her family when they went to hunt buffalo on the plains beyond.

Then, this country had seemed full of promise and adventure. Now, it seemed strange and menacing. A wide, swift river flowed north, down the valley. If the raiders crossed the river, they'd be well on their way to their home country. How would she and her sister get home from so far away?

In this valley, the raiders moved the horses at night to avoid being seen. Shortly after first light they came to a small buffalo-hunting camp of their people, hidden in a canyon. The hide-covered tepees were decorated with animals and birds painted in brilliant colors, so different from the brown tule mat tepees of Kaya's people. As the raiders approached the camp, the hunters and the women gathered to greet them.

The raiders rode proudly through the camp, displaying the horses—and the girls—they'd stolen. Though Kaya wouldn't let her feelings show, she was sick to see the raiders praised and honored. She winced when the men looked over the horses and stroked the ones they liked best, Steps High among them. How she hated to have enemy hands on her horse!

All the men and women in the camp were pleased and smiling, except one dirty boy with a sullen face who stared grimly at Kaya. It came to her that the angry-looking boy was a slave, too, and that soon she and Speaking Rain would look as tired and bitter as he.

Kaya stared at her feet when the women came to inspect her and Speaking Rain. The women pinched the girls' arms to feel their muscles, then shook their heads and talked among themselves. They didn't sound pleased.

Kaya and Speaking Rain were dirty and their hair was tangled. They were used to bathing in the cold river and cleansing themselves in the heat of the sweat lodge every single day. Since they'd been captured, they hadn't been able to wash.

sweat lodge

When the women saw Speaking Rain's cloudy eyes, they frowned and spoke angrily to the raiders. Were they saying that a blind slave was nothing more than another belly to feed? Would they decide that Speaking Rain was no use to them and abandon her here, so far from Salmon River Country? But one raider took Speaking Rain's arm and led her to a

83

young mother with a baby. He said something that caused the mother to look more kindly at Speaking Rain. Kaya guessed he'd told the mother that the blind girl wasn't entirely useless—she could sing lullabies and could help tend the baby while the mother worked. Kaya hoped they'd soon realize what a skilled cord maker and weaver Speaking Rain was, too.

One of the older women, with gray hair and a lined face, led Kaya to her tepee. Bold designs of otters were painted on the tepee in bright yellow and red. Kaya thought of the old woman as Otter Woman. She sat Kaya down and gave her buffalo meat to eat. When Kaya had eaten, the woman took Kaya to where other women were cleaning hides. She handed Kaya a sharp-edged rib bone and made a scraping motion. She wanted Kaya to scrape the fat and meat from a hide that was staked to the ground.

Kaya had often helped Kautsa clean hides. She knelt by the buffalo hide and began to scrape at it with the rib bone. Otter Woman watched her work for a little while, then nodded in satisfaction. Kaya scraped even harder, until her shoulders ached and her arms were sore—she vowed to work twice as hard in order to make up for Speaking Rain. Somehow she must protect her sister.

When night came, Otter Woman led Kaya and Speaking Rain into her tepee. She spread hides for them beside her sleeping place and motioned for them to lie down. Taking a thick rawhide thong, she tied it around Kaya's ankle and then around her own. She made the knots tight so Kaya couldn't untie the thong and run away. She didn't bother to tie up Speaking Rain—a blind girl wouldn't try to escape.

Speaking Rain pressed against Kaya's side. "Be strong," Kaya whispered to her.

Otter Woman gave her a sharp pinch that meant, *Hush! Go to sleep!*

Kaya clenched her teeth and vowed she would not cry, not even in the dark. But how could she sleep when her heart was aching so badly? She and Speaking Rain were slaves—they might never see their people again.

At first light, Kaya was sent to gather firewood. She watched the hunters ride away from camp to hunt buffalo in the valley. Later in the day, when the men returned with the buffalo they had killed, they gave the meat and hides to the women. Otter Woman set Kaya to work and led Speaking Rain to sing to the baby.

All day the women worked, cutting up the meat and hanging the strips on poles to dry. They scraped and tanned the hides, wasting nothing. Kaya's arms and back ached from the hard work of scraping. When she grew dizzy from the sun and weary from the work, she told herself to be strong for Speaking Rain.

Black-and-white magpies swooped over the drying meat, stealing bits for themselves. Magpie— Kaya's nickname. She had tried to be more responsible, but then she'd disobeyed Eetsa's order to run for safety in the woods.

That mistake had put her and Speaking Rain into captivity. *Maybe I deserve that nickname, after all,* Kaya thought miserably. She picked up a magpie feather and put it in the bag on her belt, a reminder that she *must* think of others before herself.

From where Kaya worked, she often caught glimpses of Steps High grazing with the other horses. If only she could get to her horse, touch her,

All day the women worked, cutting up the meat and hanging the strips on poles to dry. Kaya's arms and back ached from the hard work of scraping.

stroke her! Kaya watched for a chance to approach the herd, but the boys who tended the horses never seemed to leave them.

One evening, when the sun blazed on the horizon, Kaya saw a horse move away from the herd and come nearer to the camp. The horse was Steps High! The herders didn't seem to notice the lone horse, or maybe the sun blinded them when they looked her way. Kaya ran behind the tepees and into the sagebrush beyond the camp. She stopped there and whistled softly. Her horse raised her head and came closer.

Before Kaya could reach her horse, a man strode up beside her, a rawhide rope in his hand. Angrily, he struck Kaya's legs with the rope and gestured for her to get back to the camp. As she turned to go, she saw him put the rope bridle on Steps High's lower jaw. Confidently, he leaped onto Steps High's back and rode away from the camp.

Kaya watched her beautiful horse galloping swiftly across the plain. *If only I could jump on your back and race away from here!* she thought.

The man kicked Steps High until she was running flat out. Her shadow flew at her heels. Then she began to buck! The man whipped her with his quirt and sawed at the rope bridle in her mouth. He dragged the horse's head around and rode her in a circle.

When he managed to subdue her, he rode her back toward camp and whipped her harder. Blood stained the lather on her neck and shoulders.

Kaya wanted to cry out, *Stop!* But she could do nothing to protect her horse—she was a slave.

When Kaya was sent into the thickets to gather firewood, she sometimes took Speaking Rain along to help carry back the heavy bundles. The slave boy was sent for wood, too. Kaya thought he was about her age, and she wanted to know more about him. But when she came close, he frowned and turned away. Kaya knew he must be ashamed to be doing the work of women. Kaya didn't follow him—these times were her only chance to talk freely with Speaking Rain.

"The hunt will soon be over," Kaya said one

morning. "They have almost as much dried meat as the pack horses can carry."

"Aa-heh," Speaking Rain sighed. "It's getting colder, too. Soon they'll start back to their country."

"If only we could escape before they take us farther away," Kaya said.

"Aa-heh!" Speaking Rain agreed.

"But how can we?" Kaya asked. "We'd have to go when it's dark, and at night I'm tied to Otter Woman."

"Could you cut the thong?" Speaking Rain asked.

"The knife is in her pack, but I can't reach it," Kaya said.

"But I'm not tied up," Speaking Rain said. "I'll find the knife and give it to you."

"Aa-heh!" Kaya thought a moment as she wound a thong around the armful of dry branches that Speaking Rain held.

Speaking Rain was quiet, too. "Even if you cut yourself free, I'd never keep up with you on the run," she said slowly. "You'll have to go without me."

Kaya winced at the thought. "I'd never do that!" she said. She'd gotten her sister into this, and she couldn't leave her here as a slave.

"You *have* to leave me." Speaking Rain's voice was firm. "You must escape so you can bring others back to get me."

Kaya pressed her fingertips to Speaking Rain's lips. "Don't say that! How could I go without you?"

"Because it's our only hope," Speaking Rain said.

Kaya lifted a bundle of wood onto Speaking Rain's back and took the second bundle onto her own. "But even if I escaped, could I get to Salmon River Country before snow falls?" she asked.

Speaking Rain was quiet for a moment, thinking. "Could you take your horse?" she said. "You'd travel much faster on Steps High."

"They're sure to see me if I try that," Kaya said. "I'd have to slip away on foot. But if I go on foot—" Her head was spinning. "I don't know what to do. Help me."

"Think," Speaking Rain said. "If Kautsa were captured, what would she do?"

Kaya blinked. She knew the answer to that. "Kautsa would try to escape."

"Aa-heh," Speaking Rain said. "We must start

hiding some of our food for your journey."

As they trudged back to the camp, Kaya's mind raced with questions. *How can I leave my sister behind? What will happen to Steps High?*

Then a more terrifying thought came to Kaya: *What if I escape, but I'm captured again? What would the enemies from Buffalo Country do to me then?*

When Kaya came back to the camp from scraping hides that day, she saw the skinny slave boy tending a fire. There were burrs caught in his hair, and his only clothing was a ragged breechcloth and worn moccasins.

As she came near him, he motioned for her to stop. He glanced around, then with his hands he threw her the words, *Do you speak sign language?*

Kaya had learned how people talked with gestures when they couldn't speak each other's language. She answered with her hands, *I speak sign language.*

What tribe are you? he signed.

She pointed to herself, then swept her hand from her ear down across her chin. *I am Nimíipuu,*

her hands said. *What tribe are you?*

I am Salish, he signed. Then he ducked his head because others came near.

Kaya went on to the Otter tepee, but her thoughts were on the boy. Her people had many friends among the Salish. Nimíipuu often fished and traded with the Salish. Some had even married Salish men and women. Perhaps she and this boy could find a way to help each other.

The next time she had a chance, she picked up some sticks and took them to where the boy was building a fire. Placing the sticks by his feet, she crouched beside him. Would he frown and turn away again?

Instead, he met her gaze—maybe he, too, had been thinking they might help each other. She threw him the words, *What are you called?*

I am called Two Hawks, he signed.

She signed to him, *I am called Kaya.* "Kaya," she said out loud.

He narrowed his eyes and said slowly, "Kaya."

She nodded. Then she had an idea. Perhaps she and Two Hawks could escape together. Two would have a better chance to make it back to the Buffalo Trail and over the mountains than one traveling alone. Would he come with her?

And could she trust this boy? She wished she could know him better before she risked telling him her plan—he might betray her to the enemies in the hope of being rewarded with more food.

Kaya watched for a chance. It came when she and Two Hawks were sent to bring cooking water from the river.

When Kaya was sure no one could see them in the reeds by the river, she signed, *How long have you been a slave?*

I've been a slave for a long time, he answered. *I was captured in a raid on our village. I don't know where my family is, or even if anyone is alive.*

Kaya glanced over her shoulder. They were still alone, but it wouldn't be long before others came here for water. This could be the only chance she'd have to tell him her plan. She'd have to take the risk. *Pay attention to me!* she signed. *I'm going to go to Nimíipuu country. Soon. Come with me to my family!*

His dark eyes bored into her. Then he threw her the words, *I want to go to Nimíipuu country with you.*

Though his solemn expression gave away nothing, she realized he understood! *We will need hides. We will need food,* she signed.

He shook his head. *No! Let's go now!*

Kaya frowned. *This foolish boy!* she thought. If he acted recklessly, he'd put them both in danger. Didn't he know they'd have to wait for a dark night when they couldn't be seen? Didn't he realize they must plan ahead if they were to make it back safely? *Be patient!* she signed. *I'll give you a signal.*

Now! he repeated. Then he pointed to the horse herd not far downstream.

Kaya looked. Men were separating a few horses

from the herd. Other men were tying bundles of buffalo hides onto the backs of the horses. She saw that Steps High was one of the horses carrying a load of hides. *What are they doing with those horses?* she signed.

I understand their words a little, he signed. *They're going to trade those horses and hides to another hunting party. Then they'll leave for Buffalo Country. Soon! We must run away now!*

Kaya's mind was whirling—Steps High was going to be traded away! Even now the men were riding off with the loaded horses. Steps High tossed her head and whinnied. She trailed behind the others as if she knew she was being taken far away from Kaya.

Grief was a knife in Kaya's chest as she watched her beloved horse disappear over the rise. Two Hawks was right—they must escape soon or be taken much, much farther from home country.

Kaya bit her lip. How could she bear to leave her sister, and lose her horse as well?

ESCAPE!

Toward last light, the clouds turned red and the west wind blew more and more strongly. Kaya smelled the scent of rain in the wind. She heard small birds sing the high, whistling notes that meant a storm was on the way. By dark it would be raining hard, and everyone would stay inside the tepees with the door flaps closed. The storm would give her and Two Hawks a chance to escape.

When she saw lightning spike down from the clouds, she went to find him. He was banking the fires with ashes. She caught his eye and signaled to him, *Go! Tonight! Meet at the big tree!*

Soon rain lashed the tepees and thunder shook

the earth. The dogs huddled down with their heads buried in their tails. Everyone, except for a lone guard, gathered inside. Otter Woman tied Kaya's leg to hers and settled down under several hides to sleep out the storm.

Kaya waited until she was certain everyone slept soundly. Then she whispered in Speaking Rain's ear, "The knife—in the pack beside the door."

Kaya felt Speaking Rain slowly inching herself away from their sleeping place. If she made any sounds, the wail of the storm covered them. After what seemed a long time, Kaya felt Speaking Rain's hand on hers, then the knife in her palm. Gently, Kaya began to work the knife against the rawhide thong—there, she'd cut it! She forced herself to lie still a while longer to be sure Otter Woman hadn't felt anything.

At last, Kaya eased herself away. To deceive Otter Woman if she woke, Speaking Rain took Kaya's place beside her.

Quickly, quietly, Kaya dressed, slid the knife into her bag, and folded up a sleeping hide. She put the little bag of food they'd saved into her bundle, too. Then her courage almost failed her—how could she leave her sister? She clasped Speaking Rain's hand. Speaking Rain squeezed back. Their touch was a vow that they'd be together again. Kaya dragged herself on her stomach under the edge of the tepee until she was outside in the howling storm.

The camp was shrouded in darkness and the rain blew sideways. Kaya didn't see the guard—maybe he was checking on the horses. She crept, keeping low to the ground, until she left the tepees behind. Then she began to run as she had never run before. She sped, wet sagebrush stinging her legs, until she made out the big cottonwood towering over the woods. Was Two Hawks there? Had he been able to escape, too?

As Kaya skidded down the slope toward the big tree, she slipped. She was on her hands and knees when she heard Two Hawks call softly from the bushes, "Kaya?" Never had her name been more welcome to her!

She didn't see the boy until he was right in front of her. In a flash of lightning, she saw that he carried a bundle and wore leggings he must have stolen from a raider. He beckoned for Kaya to follow, then

In a flash of lightning, she saw Two Hawks.

started running across the open plain.

They ran westward into the wind. They had to cover as much ground as they could. As soon as it was light, the raiders would discover that their captives had run off. They'd follow swiftly on horseback. Kaya and Two Hawks must be well away and hidden by then.

All night they ran through lashing rain, but before first light the storm had passed over. Behind them the gray sky shimmered like an abalone shell. They ran along a rocky outcropping until they found a shallow opening beneath an overhang. Two Hawks dragged tumbleweeds over their tracks to cover their trail. Then they spread a hide under the rocky shelf, lay down on it, and covered themselves with the other hide. Two Hawks pulled a tumbleweed into the opening to shield them. Kaya thought she was too frightened to sleep, but in only a moment she fell into a black slumber.

A hand pressed over her mouth woke her. Who held her down? A raider? Then she realized it was Two Hawks signaling her not to speak or move. She heard distant hoofbeats, then the sound of horses running not far from where they lay. Scouts had followed them! Scarcely breathing, she pressed herself against the earth. The hoofbeats became fainter and disappeared. Kaya and Two Hawks had hidden themselves well. But would the scouts find them on their return? The boy must have been thinking the same thing. *Stay still!* he signaled to her.

All day they lay under the ledge. Slowly the light faded and night returned. The enemy scouts hadn't come back. Perhaps they'd given up their search, but there was no way to know. Kaya and the boy would have to be on the lookout every moment so they could see without being seen.

At last Two Hawks signaled to her, *Let's have a look around.* They crept out of their hiding place like prairie dogs out of a burrow. They ate some of their dried meat and sipped rainwater from a hollow in a stone. Then they made their way to the top of a low ridge and paused there to get their bearings. The moon seemed to float up out of the dark lake of waving prairie grasses. The stars were low and bright.

Kaya had been told many stories about the stars to help her find her way. She gazed up at the vast star-map shining above them. She saw the group of stars called the Seven Duck Sisters. But she concentrated on the star that never moves, the North Star, called Elder Brother. With Elder Brother as a guide, she calculated the way west.

Follow me! she signaled to Two Hawks. He shook his head. Again she motioned for him to follow her, but he stayed put. *Does he think I can't read the stars?* Kaya thought. She stamped impatiently and started walking. Before she'd gone more than a few steps, he came after her. Oh, she hoped she wouldn't lead them astray. If she made a mistake in her directions, they wouldn't be able to find the Buffalo Trail.

All night they walked into the wind, which was rising and getting colder. They were near the foothills now, but they would never be able to discover the Buffalo Trail in the dark. They would have to chance moving by day if they were to find it. But first they must rest for a while. When the morning star appeared, Kaya signed to Two Hawks, *We need a lean-to for shelter.*

Enemy scouts might still be looking for them, so Kaya chose a spot hidden deep in a thicket. With the knife, she cut several branches from a pine and leaned them together to make a frame. Then she cut an armful of thick, short branches.

Help me, she signed to Two Hawks.

His lips turned down and his eyes were slits. *Building a shelter is the work of women,* he signed. *I won't do the work of women anymore!*

Don't you want to get warm? Kaya signed. *Come on, help me.*

You work, Two Hawks signed. *I'll keep a lookout.* He turned his back on her.

Kaya wove branches into the frame until the shelter was completed. She crawled inside, with Two Hawks right behind her. There was room enough for them to sit upright and eat the last few bites of their food. Kaya chewed slowly. Her belly ached with hunger and her legs shook with fatigue. As they wrapped up in their hides, her mind was filled with worries. Would they manage to find the trail again? Could they cross the mountains before snow blocked the pass? In spite of her exhaustion, sleep was a long time coming.

Kaya woke to full sun and the sound of geese.

When she crawled out of the lean-to, the last grass-hoppers of the season sprang up around her. Two Hawks stood grimly gazing up at the flock of geese flying south. Did he know their flight meant snow could be on the way?

Hunger made Kaya dizzy—surely Two Hawks was hungry, too. She pointed to the dark mass of the foothills ahead. She knew there would be fish in the streams running through the hills. *Let's get some fish*, she signed. *Follow me!*

Two Hawks glowered at her. *Men lead and women follow. You follow me!*

Kaya huffed in exasperation. But she decided not to fight with him—maybe he wouldn't be so disagreeable after they got something to eat.

Soon they were deep in the foothills. Kaya kept looking back, but she saw no signs of enemy scouts. Perhaps they were already on their way to their own country in the east. Before her, the Bitterroot Mountains seemed to reach up to the sky. Snow already lay on the highest ridges. Kaya clutched her hide around her shoulders and shivered. She and Two Hawks didn't have much time. But she was so tired and hungry that her legs wobbled. She needed food and water, and she needed rest. *We must stop here*, she signed.

Two Hawks frowned. *We must go on!*

I can't go on, she signed.

He looked at her hard, his jaw set. *We have to go on!* he signed. He walked off as if he didn't care whether she followed or not.

If this skinny boy can keep going, then so can I! Kaya thought. She caught up with him, but they made slow progress. The woods were full of windfall trees they had to climb over. Twigs tore at Kaya's face and arms, and often she stumbled and fell. Then she heard the sound of a stream. Was this the stream that led to the Buffalo Trail? *We'll rest here and fish tomorrow,* she signed.

Two Hawks turned to her with a sullen expression. *Don't tell me what to do. My father is a warrior. Someday I will be a warrior, too.*

Right now you're only a boy! she signed. *And I know better than you.*

You're not the leader, he signed. *I am! I say we go on!*

Anger flared in Kaya's chest. It had been her idea to escape. If it hadn't been for her, he'd still be a captive. She was the one who had gotten them this far. She knew they'd never make it home if they didn't guard their strength carefully. *I say we build a shelter and rest!* she signed.

Two Hawks screwed up his face in a scowl. *I am not your slave! I am no one's slave anymore! I do as I choose!* He turned on his heel and started running alongside the stream. In a moment he'd broken through some bushes and disappeared.

Kaya was so upset that her heart was beating like a drum. How could this boy be so foolish! Should she let him go on alone, or try to catch up with him again? She knew they'd be safer if they stayed together, whether he thought so or not—and she didn't want to face the night alone. So, against her will, she started plodding wearily upstream.

Kaya ducked under branches and climbed over rocks. When she smashed her head against a cedar limb, she went to her knees in pain. *Let him go on if he wants*, she thought. *I need to rest.* Crawling on her hands and knees, she started to move under the cedar tree to sleep.

Her hand touched something warm and furry. What was it? She pushed back the branches and looked. It was the body of a fawn that an animal had killed. She knew that cougars hunted elk and deer in these woods. This was a fresh kill—the cougar that had made the kill must be nearby. Surely it would come back for its meal. But if the cougar came upon a running boy, it might think that he was more prey and go after him.

Kaya's first thought was to get away from the kill and hide—let Two Hawks look after himself! Then she thought of the magpie feather in her bag. She'd kept that feather to remind herself that she must think of others before herself. She got to her feet and hurried upstream.

Around the bend she saw Two Hawks ahead of her on the pale, sandy shore. He was crouching at the edge of the stream, drinking from his cupped hands. When she heard her coming, he glanced her way. And as he did, she saw the flash of a cougar leaping down from an overhanging limb!

ON THE BUFFALO TRAIL

"Look out!" Kaya cried. Two Hawks spun onto his side, and the cougar landed on the sand beside him. Kaya ran splashing up the stream, shouting and flapping her deer hide at the cougar. It clawed and bit at Two Hawks's arms and shoulders. Kaya lunged forward and pounded her fist into the cougar's nose. With both hands, she grabbed handfuls of sand and threw them into the cat's eyes.

Blinking and snarling, the cougar released Two Hawks and began to back away. It was a thin, young cat with a lot of scars. Showing its teeth, it turned tail and retreated into the woods.

Two Hawks yanked off his deer hide. Kaya

motioned for him to let her see the wounds on his arms. She washed away the blood and exposed the scratches, which were not deep. The deer hide he wore—and Kaya's quick action—had saved him from deeper slashes.

Kaya knew how to stop the bleeding. Although it was almost last light now, she found the plant called *wapalwaapal*, good medicine for his wounds. She silently offered a prayer of thanks as she made a poultice of the leaves and packed it onto the cuts.

wapalwaapal

Then she sat back on her heels and drew a deep breath. *We must look out for each other,* she signed. *You and I are not enemies.*

No, we are not enemies, Two Hawks signed.

We have to stay together, she added. *We have to help each other.*

He nodded, his eyes downcast. *You did a good thing for me. How do you say "good" in your language?*

"*Tawts!*" she said at once.

After a moment, Two Hawks repeated, "Tawts. Tawts, Kaya."

When light came again, Kaya and Two Hawks made their way up the stream, looking for a good

110

place to fish. Kaya's breath clouded at her lips. During the night, a skin of ice had formed along the shore. How much longer would snow hold off?

Here the stream widened into a basin before tumbling farther down. This was a good place to catch trout or mountain whitefish.

Kaya untied a piece of fringe from her skirt to use as a sniggle. She lay on her belly by the pool and dangled the fringe in the water. Fish would think the sniggle was food and bite into it. If she was quick, she could flip the fish onto the bank.

Two Hawks tugged a piece of fringe from the side of his leggings and lay down near her. He dangled the fringe in the water and waited. Almost at once, a fish bit the fringe. Expertly, he flipped a large trout onto the stones.

Soon Kaya felt a tug on her sniggle. With a flick of her wrist, she flipped another trout out of the stream and onto the bank. Good—they had enough for a meal.

I'll build a fire, Two Hawks signed.

Kaya watched him choose a sharp stick for a fire drill. He put the point of the drill into a hole in a dry branch. Then he rubbed the stick between his palms until tiny sparks fell onto dried moss. Soon a little flame burned, which he carefully fanned into a fire.

Kaya silently thanked the trout for giving themselves to her and the boy for food. Then she cleaned the fish and placed them on sticks by the fire to cook. When the fish were done, she and Two Hawks sat by the fire and ate them. She licked every bit of oil from her fingers. Never had anything tasted more delicious than this meal they'd made together.

As Two Hawks made a fire bundle to save the coals of their fire, a fine, cold rain began to fall. *Hurry!* Kaya signed. They had to find the Buffalo Trail before it was hidden by ice and snow.

As Kaya and Two Hawks made their way uphill, the cold rain turned into sleet. Kaya pulled her deer hide over her head, but the sleet made it hard to see. She thought they'd been following the stream that would lead to the Buffalo Trail, but nothing here looked familiar.

After a time, the stream they followed was nothing more than a small creek racing down the mountainside. Bighorn sheep leaped across ledges above them. Slipping on icy stones, Kaya and Two Hawks struggled upward. At last they reached the top. Two Hawks gave her a hand, and she climbed up onto a trail that ran along the ridge.

The trail split around fallen trees—a path made by people on foot. Hoofprints were everywhere along it, too. *It's the Buffalo Trail!* she signed to Two Hawks. Her heart lifted—then she felt a stab of loss again. *If only Speaking Rain were with us!* she thought.

Up here the wind was bitterly cold. Kaya and Two Hawks put their heads down and started along the trail. Kaya saw horse droppings and the remains of fires, but the marks weren't fresh ones. With winter coming, travelers had already left the mountains for shelter in the warmer valleys. But Kaya knew enemies used this trail, too. *Keep a lookout!* she signed. How terrible if enemies should catch them now, with home country only a few sleeps away!

Wet and shivering, the two of them worked together to build a small lean-to against a rocky outcropping far off the trail. Because there was no water up here on the ridge, they scooped handfuls of sleet to suck.

If I had a bow and arrow, I could get us food, Two Hawks signed.

But there's hardly any game up this high, Kaya answered. *We'd still have nothing to eat.*

Then she saw that some pines were marked where people had stripped back the bark to get at the soft underlayer. The underlayer was food for both men and horses when they had nothing else to eat.

Here is food, Kaya signed. She began stripping back the bark with her knife.

As Kaya and the boy ate, wolves began to howl to each other across the ridges. Kaya and Two Hawks huddled together for warmth like puppies.

At first light, ice crystals glittered on frozen branches that rattled in the wind. Kaya and Two Hawks lined their moccasins with moss to keep their toes from freezing. Their fingers were blue and their teeth chattered when they took to the trail again, but during the night the sleet had stopped.

Even though she was cold, this old, worn trail comforted Kaya. She felt the presence of the people who had passed this way before her.

After walking a long time, they came to a large cairn, a pile of stones that marked a special place. People had built many cairns along the Buffalo Trail. The cairns marked sacred places where spirits were very strong. Two Hawks went on down the trail to scout their way, but Kaya stopped by the old cairn.

As she stood there, she thought she heard the voices of spirits. Were they reminding her that her name meant "she who arranges rocks"? Were they telling her to build another cairn at this sacred place?

She couldn't lift big stones, so she collected small ones and piled them up until she'd made a mound. She wanted to offer something of her own, too. She opened her bag and looked inside. There was the magpie feather she'd kept. "Magpie," her nickname. She tucked the feather under the top stone of the mound.

All day, and all the next day, they climbed higher and higher. Kaya and Two Hawks looked around as they walked, often glancing up at the birds and clouds for signs of the weather. Suddenly, Two Hawks pointed to a large tree far off the trail. There, high in the tree, was a platform of branches. A bundle was tied onto the platform. Had hunters left food here for their return journey?

Two Hawks climbed up the tree to see. He came down with a rawhide bag slung over his shoulder. The rawhide was from the top part of a tepee, darkened from smoke that made it waterproof. *This is a Salish bundle*, he signed. *My people hunt on this side of the mountain. My people hid this food here!*

Eagerly, they opened the bag. Inside were dried camas cakes and pemmican, a mixture of dried meat, grease, and dried berries. They sat under the tree to eat the tasty, nourishing pemmican. This unexpected find would give them the strength to push on.

They were hurrying up along the trail when Two Hawks signaled for Kaya to halt. *Look,* he signed. *Do you know that country?*

Kaya looked where he pointed. In the far, far distance she could see what seemed to be a stretch of prairie. Was that the prairie where her people sometimes dug camas bulbs? If it was, they were closer to home country than she'd thought. *Soon we will be with my people!* she signed.

Come on! Two Hawks answered. *Let's get a better look!*

Kaya's heart was light as they scrambled up off the trail to a place where they could see more clearly. From up here, the prairie looked like a brown blanket laid over the land. Two Hawks was even more eager than she to see it. He climbed a tall pine until he was almost to the top, leaned out, and shaded his eyes.

With a sharp crack, the branch he stood on snapped under his weight! Crying out with surprise, he pitched backward and fell. He crashed down through the branches. With a thud he hit the rocky ground and tumbled down the hill on the far side. He cried out again, this time in pain.

Kaya rushed down to him. Clutching his ankle, he lay on his side. She crouched and saw a lump on his ankle. When she touched it, he gasped.

She handed him a stick to use as a cane. He seized the stick and tried to rise, but when he put weight on his injured leg, he collapsed in pain. He tried again, only to fall a second time. His face was wet with sweat from his struggle. *My ankle is broken*, he signed.

Kaya bit her lip. She knew she wasn't strong enough to carry Two Hawks more than a little way. Maybe he could crawl a little way, too. But if he couldn't, how would they get out of the mountains?

She hugged herself. What should they do now? The cold wind whipped about them, and last light was coming soon. They needed a shelter and a fire.

Kaya collected dry twigs and sticks and handed Two Hawks the fire bundle he'd made. Grimacing in pain, he unwrapped the coals in the fire bundle and set about building a fire. As he worked, she gathered branches and built a lean-to shelter. How she wished for many, many hides to make the shelter windtight! They had the Salish food, but Two Hawks was in too much pain to eat. His teeth chattered and his whole body shook. His eyes were wide with fright.

How could Kaya help him? She lay down against his back and put her arms around him to keep him as warm as possible. Still, he trembled violently, though he would not cry.

Then Kaya thought of the lullaby that Speaking Rain had sung. Kaya put her lips close to the boy's ear. *"Ha no nee,"* she sang very softly. *"Ha no nee."* When at last he did sleep, he groaned over and over.

Somehow, Kaya slept, too. She opened her eyes to a white world. Snow was falling thickly. Glittering flakes filled the air and drove into the opening of the lean-to. Snow covered the ground and weighed down the branches of the trees.

Two Hawks tried again to rise, only to collapse onto his side. Kaya knew she couldn't carry him on the steep and icy trail. She'd have to leave him here, hurry on, and try to reach her people. If he stayed in the lean-to with some food, perhaps he wouldn't freeze before she returned with help.

She crawled out of the lean-to and looked up toward the ridge. Drifts and blowing snow were all she could see. By now, snow would have covered the Buffalo Trail as well.

As she stood in the whirling white, she saw a woman standing under a pine tree on the slope. The woman was tall and strong, like the woman named Swan Circling. She wore an elk hide over

her shoulders, and snow glistened in her braids.
Light surrounded her, like the sun shining on ice.
While Kaya watched, the woman turned and strode
up toward the ridge, looking back over her shoulder
from time to time.

Kaya clutched her hide around herself and
followed. Upward she climbed, wet snow falling
onto her shoulders from pine branches when she
brushed against them. Snow fell onto her head and
into her eyes. She wiped her eyes, and when she
looked again, the woman was gone. In her place, a
wolf stood gazing at Kaya with yellow eyes. She saw
the black tips of its raised ears and its thick, yellow-
gray coat. It watched her intently as she climbed up
to the ridge.

When Kaya reached the top, the wolf trotted
slowly down the slope on the other side. It paused
now and then and looked back at her, as if waiting
for her to come along. Was the wolf a *wyakin?* Kaya
hurried after it, and then, with a bound, the wolf
leaped down into the trees and disappeared.

"Wait for me!" Kaya whispered. With the wolf
gone, the woods seemed much lonelier.

As she searched the hillside for the wolf, she

When Kaya looked again, the woman was gone.
In her place, a wolf stood gazing at her with yellow eyes.

121

saw something moving. She ducked out of sight behind a tree and peeked around through the veil of snow. Farther down the hillside, she made out a horse and a rider wrapped in a buffalo hide. Enemy? Friend? The rider led a pack horse and rode a large bay stallion. Could it be Runner, her father's horse? Could Toe-ta be here in the mountains?

Kaya went slipping and skidding down the hill, snow flying up around her feet. "Toe-ta!" she cried as she went.

"Kaya!" he called back, and turned the horses uphill to meet her.

Then he was leaning over, lifting her up, putting her onto his horse in front of him. He wrapped her in the warm buffalo robe he wore and held her close. "Daughter, you're alive!" he said. "And Speaking Rain? Is she alive, too?"

Kaya put her face against Toe-ta's chest. It was like a dream to be in his strong arms again.

"Speaking Rain's alive, but she's a slave of our enemies," she said. "I escaped with a Salish boy, but he broke his ankle. He's over that hill!" She pointed.

Toe-ta took fur-lined moccasins from his pack and put them on Kaya's cold feet. He pulled out another buffalo robe, wrapped it around Kaya's shoulders, and set her behind him on Runner. Leading the pack horse, they started back over the ridge to get Two Hawks.

Kaya clung tightly to Toe-ta's back. "How did you find me?" she asked.

"We searched and searched but found nothing," Toe-ta said in his deep voice. "Then two sleeps ago, a scout came to our hunting camp on the Lochsa. He'd come down from the Buffalo Trail to the river because snow was coming. He told us he'd seen a new cairn at a sacred place along the trail. The cairn was made of small stones—ones someone with small hands might choose. Hands like yours, Daughter.

"The scout said a magpie feather was stuck into the little cairn. I thought of your nickname—Magpie. I left our hunting camp and came up here to search for you. But if you hadn't seen me and come running, I wouldn't have found you in this snow. Were you watching the trail?"

"I didn't know where the trail was—" Kaya began, but then she stopped herself. She wouldn't speak of the spirit woman who led her away from the lean-to. She wouldn't speak of the wolf who had brought her in sight of the Buffalo Trail and Toe-ta, either. If the wolf was a wyakin, she would not tell anyone until the proper time came.

So much had happened to Kaya—how could she tell all of it? Where would she start? "Toe-ta, the raiders traded away my horse," she said.

"She's a good horse," he said slowly. "Perhaps you'll see her someday."

"And Two Hawks—can we help him get back to his people?" she asked.

"We'll help the boy join his people when the snow melts and it's time to dig roots again," Toe-ta assured her.

Kaya pressed her face to Toe-ta's back. She closed her eyes tightly and forced herself to say what she had to admit. "It's my fault Speaking Rain's a slave," she whispered. "I thought of my horse before I thought of Speaking Rain's safety. But I made a vow I'd bring her back to us—somehow."

Toe-ta reached back and pulled the buffalo robe closer about Kaya. "We'll do all we can to find Speaking Rain, but you must not blame yourself that you were taken captive," he said. "You were taken far from home, and you've endured much. But,

Daughter, you are alive and well! Let us give thanks to Hun-ya-wat that you're with us again!"

FOR MY SON, MARK,
HIS WIFE, SUE,
AND THEIR BOYS, SAM AND MAX,
WITH LOVE

Kaya's
HERO

RUNAWAY HORSE!

Kaya knelt on a mat in the winter lodge and leaned over the baby named Light On The Water, who lay in her *tee-kas.* *"Tawts may-we!"* Kaya crooned to her. "Are you unhappy this morning?"

Light On The Water gazed steadily into Kaya's eyes, but her mouth trembled and turned down as if she was about to cry.

Kaya stroked the plump, warm cheek. "Are you wet? Is that what you're telling me?" she asked. She loosened the lacing of the buckskin that wrapped the baby and pulled it away from her feet and legs. The soft cattail fluff that cushioned the baby's bottom was soaked. Kaya pulled it out, dried the baby, and placed fresh fluff underneath her. She squeezed one of the baby's little toes and kissed her forehead. Light On The Water smiled now. *"Tawts!"* Kaya said as she laced up the covering again.

Running Alone, Kaya's young aunt, put her hand on Kaya's shoulder. "Won't you make the lacing just a little tighter?" she asked. "We're going to ride out to gather wood for the fires, and I want my baby very safe."

Kaya tightened the lacing, then carried the baby out of the lodge. The day was chilly, and Light On The Water's breath was a small cloud at her lips. When Running Alone had mounted her horse, Kaya handed her the baby. Running Alone slipped the carrying strap of the *tee-kas* over her saddle horn and gazed down at her smiling daughter. "She likes your gentle touch," she told Kaya.

"She's so easy to care for," Kaya said. "Not like my little brothers. Look, they think I can't see them hiding behind that tree." She pointed at the two sets of dark eyes gleaming through the branches of a pine. "Boys, let's go riding!" she called to the twins, and they came running, clutching robes of spotted fawn skin around their shoulders. Like all *Nimíipuu* children, they loved to be on horseback.

Kaya helped one twin climb up behind her older sister, Brown Deer. Then Kaya mounted a chestnut mare and lifted up the other twin. As she waited for the other women and children to mount, she glanced up toward the north. The foothills of the distant mountains were already white-robed with snow, but here in Salmon River Country the earth was still brown and bare. Each winter, Kaya's band came to these sheltering hills to make their winter village. They put up their lodges near the banks of the stream and stayed until spring, when it was time to move up to the prairie to dig nourishing roots and bulbs for food.

Kaya pulled her elk robe more tightly around her shoulders. Even dressed warmly in fur-lined moccasins, leggings, and her robe, Kaya shivered in the chill of winter. But she remembered the heat of late summer, when enemies from Buffalo Country made a raid on her people to steal horses. Kaya's horse, Steps High, was stolen with other Nimíipuu horses. And in the raid Kaya and her sister, Speaking Rain, were captured as slaves and taken far away to the enemy camp. There they met a

131

Salish boy, Two Hawks, who was also held as a slave. Kaya and Two Hawks had managed to escape and cross the mountains back to her people. But Speaking Rain, who was blind, had insisted that she couldn't keep up—that Kaya must leave her behind.

Kaya shivered again. She remembered, too, how cold—and hungry!—she and Two Hawks had been as they made their way over the Buffalo Trail. Now she and the boy were safe again, fed by the meat and warmed by the hides of animals that had given themselves to her people. But Two Hawks had broken his ankle on the trail, and it was slow to heal. He sat alone and homesick all day.

Kaya felt as if she had two aches in her chest. One ache was a sharp-edged gratitude that she was with her family again. But the other was a stab of grief that Speaking Rain was still a captive. Kaya had promised that they would be together again, but where was her sister now? If Kaya could find her, how could she save her? And would she ever see her beautiful, beloved horse again?

Soon Kaya was riding single file with the others. After a time, they came to a bowl-shaped canyon where trees grew thickly. The children ran to play, and the women fanned out along the creek to gather wood. A girl named Little Fawn and some boys were climbing aspen saplings and swinging to and fro on them.

"Magpie, fly into the trees with us!" Little Fawn called to Kaya.

Magpie! Kaya winced. She tried to ignore that awful nickname the children had given her when they were all switched for her offense.

"Not now!" she called back. "I'm going to look for more fluff for the baby."

She glanced toward Light On The Water and Running Alone, who was tethering her horse to a tree. The baby, lulled by the rocking ride, napped in her tee-kas on the saddle horn. Taking a twined bag, Kaya started for the stream after the other women.

Suddenly, a sharp crack echoed across the canyon. Kaya whirled around—the branch Little Fawn was pulling on had broken off. Little Fawn jumped to the ground. The branch slashed down like a spear and struck the rump of Running Alone's horse. The startled horse reared up in alarm and broke her tether. Wild-eyed, the panicked horse began to bolt down the canyon, the baby in the

133

tee-kas still hanging on the saddle!

"Stop! Stop!" Running Alone cried out. She ran after the galloping horse.

Kaya ran, too. The fleeing horse was already halfway down the canyon and heading for the narrow opening and open country beyond. The tee-kas bumped against the horse's shoulder with each plunging step. Would the baby be tossed off? Light On The Water could be hurt badly—or killed!

Near the canyon opening, the young woman named Swan Circling came rushing from the woods. Dropping her robe behind her, she ran swiftly to cut off the horse's escape. She reached the opening of the canyon first and spun around to face the galloping horse, which was thundering straight at her. Taking a stand, she spread her arms wide, like an eagle in flight.

Would the horse run her down? Swan Circling stood her ground. Right in front of her, the runaway skidded to a halt. The horse snorted and tossed her head, flinging lather onto both Swan Circling and the baby.

Swan Circling seized the horse's reins. She held the horse firmly in place as Running Alone came

Swan Circling spun around to face the galloping horse,
which was thundering straight at her.

135

rushing to get her baby.

Running Alone lifted the tee-kas from the saddle horn and clutched it to her chest. "My little one!" she cried, kissing her baby's face over and over. "You saved my baby, Swan Circling! *Katsee-yow-yow!* I can never thank you enough!"

Kaya came running right behind her aunt. She reached to take hold of the reins, too, and stroked the horse's neck and shoulder to calm her.

"I saw you step in front of my horse, but how did you get her to halt?" Running Alone asked. "She could have run right past you—or right over you!"

"I didn't think of that," Swan Circling said. "I wanted her to stop, and she did. Is your baby all right?"

Light On The Water was grinning. She thought the bouncing, runaway ride was a game.

Swan Circling glanced at Kaya, who was still stroking the horse's lathered neck. "You seem to have a way with horses," she said approvingly. "She's quieting down. Will you lead her back now?"

Kaya held the reins of the uneasy horse securely as she and Swan Circling returned to the others. As they walked, she studied Swan Circling's calm face.

Kaya had been curious about Swan Circling ever since she'd married Claw Necklace and joined the band. And now Kaya remembered that the woman who appeared to her when she was lost on the Buffalo Trail had looked like Swan Circling. Had that vision been a sign that they would be friends? Kaya hoped so. She wished she could become as strong as this brave young woman who hadn't even flinched when a horse charged straight at her!

Later that day, Kaya sat with other girls and women at one end of a lodge that several families shared. Many layers of tule mats and hides covered the lodge. Parfleches and piles of hide blankets were stacked along the bottom to keep out drafts. The women unfolded the hides they'd tanned in the summer and set about making moccasins and clothes and carrying cases. They took out the hemp cord they'd twisted and wove baskets and bags. They made their clothes beautiful with fringe and beads and quill decorations. Kaya loved working with the others in the warm winter lodge.

Kaya watched Brown Deer stringing a necklace of beads made from shells. From time to time, Brown Deer ran her fingers lovingly across the beads. The necklace was for a man—and Kaya guessed her sister was making it for Cut Cheek. The two had danced together last summer, and soon they'd see each other again when he came with other neighboring villagers for the winter gatherings. Each day now, Brown Deer combed her hair and dressed it with fragrant oil so it would grow long and silky.

Kaya's mother, *Eetsa*, was finishing a large twined storage bag, one of the many, many gifts they would give to family and friends when they came to visit.

Kautsa, Kaya's grandmother, was weaving a small hat. Kaya watched her grandmother's expert work closely—because the hat was for her. Kaya would wear it in the spring when she went to dig roots with the other girls and women. She loved the red zigzags that Kautsa worked into the design.

Kaya put aside the basket she was weaving and picked up her sister's worn buckskin doll. Speaking Rain had carried her doll everywhere she went. With her sister gone, Kaya kept the doll close to her. As she adjusted the doll's dress, she discovered a tear in her back, a bit of deer-hair stuffing poking out. She decided to mend it and have it ready for Speaking Rain when she was with them again.

Kaya wanted to care for the doll because she feared she hadn't taken good care of Speaking Rain. When the enemies had made their raid in the night last summer, Eetsa had told Kaya to take Speaking Rain to hide in the woods. But Kaya went first to look for her horse—and enemies seized her and her sister and carried them off. How Kaya regretted that she hadn't done as her mother told her! *If I were as strong as Swan Circling,* Kaya thought, *I'd find a way to get my sister back.*

"Kautsa, may I ask you a question?" Kaya asked quietly.

"*Aa-heh,* you may ask me anything," Kautsa said. A slight smile crinkled the corners of her eyes. "Ask— then I'll decide if I want to answer you."

"You're teasing," Brown Deer said, laughing. "You always answer us!"

"It's true," Kautsa said. "I've always answered

your questions—so far! What do you want to know?"

Kaya threaded her bone needle with a bit of
sinew and began stitching the tear in the buckskin
doll. "I want to ask about Swan Circling. What
makes her so—different?"

"Different?" Kautsa said. "You must be asking
me how Swan Circling came to be a warrior woman.
Now, there's a story!"

"Can you tell us?" Brown Deer asked eagerly.

Kautsa nodded. Her fingers were busy as she
twined the brown hemp with the yellow beargrass.
"Swan Circling came to live with us when she and

Claw Necklace married, three winters ago. We all saw right away that she was a strong girl, eager to help. Then . . ." Kautsa paused and held the hat she was weaving above Kaya's head to check the size. The many strands of cord trailing from the hat tickled Kaya's nose.

"Then?" Kaya prompted her grandmother.

"Then?" Brown Deer echoed. "What happened then, Kautsa?"

Kautsa put the hat back into her lap and began to work on it again. "Then Swan Circling went with her husband on a hunting trip to Buffalo Country. While they slept one night, enemies attacked them!"

"To steal horses, as they did with us?" Kaya asked.

"Not to steal horses," Kautsa said. "They came to fight—or to show their courage just by touching our warriors! Our men rushed from the tepees to defend themselves. Claw Necklace hurried into the skirmish. But in his eagerness to fight, he left behind his bow and arrows."

"He didn't have any weapons?" Kaya asked.

"Aa-heh, he was in great danger!" Kautsa said.

141

"Instead of running for cover with the other women, Swan Circling picked up his weapons and ran after him into the fight. Arrows flew around her. One even singed her arm, but it didn't pierce her flesh. She gave her husband the bow and arrows so he could fight well, and then she tended our wounded men. She was never wounded by arrows, though a few tore her dress."

"Did Swan Circling tell you this?" Kaya asked.

"She would never speak of her bravery," Kautsa said. "It was Claw Necklace who told us what had happened. After our men won the fight, they gave Swan Circling an eagle feather for her bravery—a very high honor, as you know."

"I know she goes to battles," Brown Deer said. "She brings fresh horses to the riders whose horses have been hurt."

"So she does," Kautsa said. "Swan Circling has brought many things to us. You were with her when she saved Running Alone's baby, weren't you, Kaya?"

"Aa-heh, Kautsa," Kaya said. "I saw it all."

"Then you know she's fearless," Kautsa said. "I believe she wouldn't hesitate to fight a grizzly bear! There's only one sad thing—"

Brown Deer stopped stringing beads and looked up. "What sad thing?" Brown Deer asked.

"As you know, Swan Circling doesn't have any children. That's sad, don't you think?" Kautsa asked.

"It would be very sad not to have any children," Brown Deer said slowly, as if she were imagining how she'd feel if she were Swan Circling.

"But she and her husband are young," Eetsa broke in. "There's still plenty of time for them to have children."

"Aa-heh," Kautsa agreed. "There's time for children. And they'll be strong, like her, I'm sure of that." Then she tapped Kaya's hand. "I'm glad you mended your sister's doll, Granddaughter."

Eetsa rose to her knees and peered into the cooking basket. "We need some water so we can cook our meal," she announced.

Right away Kaya got to her feet to go fetch the water. She caught up with Little Fawn on the trail to the stream. Like Kaya, Little Fawn carried a large water basket, but she was limping. "Did you hurt yourself when the branch broke?" Kaya asked. "Maybe you climbed too high."

Little Fawn winced at each step, but she shook her head. "It's nothing. I've jumped out of trees much higher than that."

Other women and girls were drawing water at the stream. Kaya saw Swan Circling a little way downstream, leading a spotted mare. As the mare drank, Swan Circling dampened a bundle of leaves and tied it onto the mare's back. Kaya went downstream to her side. She'd been eager to see Swan Circling again, but now that she stood beside her, she didn't know what to say. She stroked the mare's flank. "This is a pretty one," she said. "Has she got sores on her back?"

"Aa-heh," Swan Circling said. "The men saw her rolling in a patch of sage to heal herself. They asked me to make a poultice of the sage for her."

"The spots on her rump remind me of my horse, Steps—" Kaya stopped, afraid to go on for fear her voice would break.

Swan Circling glanced at her with concern in her eyes. "You miss your horse, don't you?" she said. "I just saw the boy who escaped with you."

Kaya leaned out and dipped her water basket into the stream. "Two Hawks can't put weight on his broken ankle yet," she said. "He has to be patient."

"You're right," Swan Circling said. "It takes time for bone to heal. But he looks lonesome and grumpy."

"That's because he doesn't like to be patient!" Kaya said.

Swan Circling laughed. "That's the kind of boy he is! It's good you were with him when you escaped. You're a dependable girl, I can see that. You two were very strong to run away and find your way back. It's too bad he's unhappy here with us."

Kaya's cheeks burned with pleasure at this praise from the woman she admired so much. To keep Swan Circling from seeing that she was blushing, Kaya turned her head.

Little Fawn was standing on the shore a little way upstream, a basket of water in her arms. When Kaya looked her way, Little Fawn lifted her chin and narrowed her eyes. "Magpie flew back to her nest!" she said, and limped away. Was she jealous of the praise Kaya had been given?

"Magpie?" Swan Circling said. "Is that your nickname, Kaya?" She patted the mare's rump and took her lead rope.

"They call me that sometimes," Kaya said.

Swan Circling gave Kaya a searching look. "Some nicknames dig into us like bear claws," she said. "As you grow older, they don't hurt so much. Will you remember that, Kaya?"

"Aa-heh," Kaya said. "I'll remember."

"Tawts!" Swan Circling said with approval. She started to lead the mare back to the men who tended the horses.

Kaya bit her lip as she watched Swan Circling walking back to the herd. Swan Circling had offered her good advice about her nickname. But, of course, she didn't know that Kaya had gotten it last summer because she'd gone off to race her horse instead of taking care of her brothers. Whipwoman had scolded Kaya, saying she must learn to think of others before she thought of herself. If Swan Circling knew that, she'd certainly regret calling Kaya strong—or dependable. And if she knew it was Kaya's fault that she and Speaking Rain had been taken captive, would Swan Circling have any respect for her at all?

CHAPTER TWO

LESSONS FROM A BASKET

The next day Kaya went to find Two Hawks, who was sitting outside one of the lodges. Sometimes he sat there all day without moving, an antelope hide wrapped tightly around him. "I know you can't walk yet, but I bet you can ride," Kaya said to him.

Two Hawks frowned—he understood only a few words of her language.

Kaya used her hands to speak to him. *Do you want to ride with me?*

"*Wah-tu!*" he said. He'd learned the word for "no" right away. He shrugged, his lips turned down. With his hands he signed, *Leave me alone!*

But Kaya wasn't going to leave him alone. She'd

been thinking about what Swan Circling had said—
Two Hawks was unhappy. Kaya's father had
promised they would help Two Hawks get back to
his people in the spring, but that time was a long
way off. Since Two Hawks had been here, he hadn't
smiled once. Kaya couldn't help him get home any
faster, but she could be a better friend to him.

She signed to him, *You can't just sit there. I'm
going to get a horse for you.*

"*Wah-tu!*" he said again and shook his head.

But the word "no" was a challenge to Kaya. She
went to get the chestnut horse she rode and another
gentle mare. She put light rope bits on them and led
them back to where Two Hawks sat, his chin on his
knees. "Two Hawks!" she called to him. She threw
him the words, *Let's go! Let's ride!*

He shook his head angrily. *I can't ride,* he signed.
My ankle is broken. He pointed to the splint that was
bound to his ankle.

You can do it! she signed. *I'll help you,* she added,
though she wasn't sure how she could get him onto
the horse.

Two Hawks grimaced as if he was determined
to prove her wrong. He pushed to one foot,

supporting himself with a crutch made from a cottonwood branch. Kaya led the gentle mare close to him. Two Hawks looked at Kaya darkly, as if to say, "What now?"

She thought a moment. Then she signed to him, *Put your knee in my hands. I can lift you onto the horse.*

Two Hawks looked at the horse, then back at her. He shook his head. Did this stubborn boy think she wasn't strong enough to lift him? She clasped her hands and held them by his injured leg. After a moment, he gingerly placed his knee in her grip and grabbed the horse's mane with both hands. "Now!" Kaya said. She lifted, he threw his good leg over the horse's back, and he was mounted.

Kaya studied him. He wasn't grimacing with pain. In fact, he looked pleased. She climbed onto her horse and beckoned for him to come with her. She'd thought of something Two Hawks could do while his leg healed. She threw him the words, *We have to find an elderberry stick so you can make a flute.*

Overnight it had grown colder. A sharp wind whined around the lodge where Kaya and other

children were dressing themselves after their
morning swim. But the lodge was warmed by five
fires lined up down the center, smoke rising through
the long opening at the top. Eetsa and the other
women were already cooking a morning meal
because there was much work to do that day.

Kaya knew that soon friends and family would
come from other villages nearby for the new year
celebration, when the short winter days begin to
grow longer again. People would share their news
and give each other gifts. They'd feast and tell
stories and honor *Hun-ya-wat,* who made the
seasons and held them in balance.

Today the women were putting up another
lodge, one large enough to hold everyone for the
feasts. When Kaya joined them, she saw Swan
Circling helping to raise one of the long lodge poles
and set it onto the frame of tepee poles. Kaya
thought the framework looked like the backbone and
ribs of a skeleton of a huge horse. After the women
completed the frame, they would cover it with tule
mats and hides. Kaya helped other girls carry the
rolled-up mats and place them near the builders.
She kept Swan Circling in sight, hoping to have a

chance to talk with her again.

With the lodge finished, Kaya followed Swan Circling to another lodge where women were preparing more food so that there would be enough for the visitors. Eetsa and Running Alone were making pemmican, a mixture of dried meat and berries. With a stone pestle, they were pounding dried deer meat in one of the large mortars. When one of them got tired using the heavy stone pestle, they traded places. Kaya thought the steady *thump, thump, thump* sounded like a heartbeat.

Swan Circling joined the women, and Kaya went to peek at Light On The Water, who was snug in her tee-kas.

"Would you give my baby a piece of this dried meat?" Running Alone asked Kaya. "She's getting a new tooth, and she needs something to chew on." She turned back to breaking strips of the meat and putting the pieces into the mortar to be ground fine.

Kaya broke off a bit of the meat and held it to Light On The Water's lips. But the baby pressed her lips shut tightly, her eyes merry as if she and Kaya were playing a game. "Isn't she precious!" Kaya

Kaya kept Swan Circling in sight,
hoping to have a chance to talk with her again.

exclaimed. Then she glanced at Swan Circling. Kautsa had said it was sad that she had no children yet. Did she mind that Kaya was making a fuss over the baby?

Swan Circling was using the large pestle. Her strong arms gleamed with sweat from the hard work. "When I saw you girls in the stream this morning, I thought of the time when I was your age," she said when Kaya caught her eye. "Do you like to swim?"

"Aa-heh!" Kaya said.

"So do I," Swan Circling said. "I come from a place where the Snake River joins the Big River. My friends and I swam every chance we got. My mother called us the Fish Girls. Someday I'll show you my favorite places to dive from the cliffs, Kaya."

"You're always thinking of the future, aren't you?" Eetsa said to Swan Circling. "Many times I've heard you say 'someday this' or 'someday that.'"

"It's true," Swan Circling said. She smiled at Eetsa, who was her good friend, and passed her the pestle. Then she wiped her face with the back of her hand. "Do you often think of what's to come, Kaya?"

Kaya was thinking that no one had ever asked her as many questions about herself as Swan Circling did. Kaya liked that. "I think of seeing my horse again," Kaya said. "Mostly I think of getting my little sister back. But I don't know how I can do that."

"When a way opens, you'll be ready," Swan Circling said with confidence. "I saw you riding with Two Hawks yesterday. I don't know how you persuaded him to get on a horse, but you did! He looked as if he was in a much better mood. You have a strong will, Kaya, and I'm glad you think of the needs of others."

Kaya gently rocked the baby in the tee-kas. Lulled by the motion and the voices of the women, Light On The Water was falling asleep. Oh, how Kaya wanted to be the girl Swan Circling believed her to be. And how she feared she wasn't!

"Pay attention, I have something to tell you," Kautsa said to Kaya and the other girls and women who were gathered around making baskets. On these long winter evenings, when the wind howled like a pack of wolves, they stayed close to the glowing fires in the warm lodge. Kautsa never missed a chance to teach the children with stories or legends. She was a wonderful storyteller and acted out the different parts with her hands and her low, musical voice.

Kautsa held up a basket made of cedar bark. "Here's a basket traded to me by one of our friends to the west," she said. "She told a story to go with the basket, a story about how Cedar Tree taught them basket making," she continued. "Listen, and I'll tell it to you."

Kaya sighed with pleasure. She glanced over her shoulder at Swan Circling, who was twining a basket as she listened with the others. Swan Circling caught Kaya's glance and nodded, as if to say, *Yes, I love to listen to stories, too.*

"It was so, my children, that a long time ago all the animals, plants, trees, and creatures could walk and talk the way that people do," Kautsa began. "In those long-ago days, Gray Squirrel was a girl, like all of you. But she was a little slow in her thoughts, and she was clumsy, too. Day after day she sat all alone under a cedar tree. Cedar Tree began to feel sorry for Gray Squirrel and decided to help her. He couldn't allow her to grow up without learning what a girl needs to know.

"Wise old Cedar Tree sent Gray Squirrel to pick beargrass, dry it, and put it into bundles. Then he told her where to find dyes and how to cut and dry his own roots to make cedar strips. When she had all the materials she needed to make a basket, he taught her how to weave it. She was so proud of her work! But Cedar Tree told her to dip her basket into the stream. Was it woven tightly enough to hold water? When water ran out of her basket, Gray Squirrel hung her head and cried.

"'Don't cry, little girl!' Cedar Tree said." Kautsa made her voice strong and low, the voice of a wise old tree. "He told her she'd have to practice and practice in order to make a basket successfully. Then he sent her out to look for designs to weave into her basket.

"Gray Squirrel went looking. Rattlesnake gave Gray Squirrel the zigzag design on his back. Mountain gave her the design of his peaks and valleys. Grouse gave her the design of his track marks. Stream gave her the design of his waves. To find all these designs, Gray Squirrel had studied the world so closely that now she was much, much wiser.

"Gray Squirrel wove a beautiful basket with all of the designs she'd been given. And when she dipped it into the Big River, her basket didn't leak! Now she was very proud of herself—and Cedar Tree was proud, too. But he told her that she should set down her basket in the woods and leave it there. She must give her basket back to the earth to show that she was thankful for what was given to her.

"Gray Squirrel didn't like that one bit! But Cedar Tree insisted that if she didn't give away the basket, she would never be a good weaver. And she had to make five little baskets and give away those, too! She must learn to work for others, not just for herself.

"Coyote was coming up the Big River at that time," Kautsa continued, finishing the story. "He saw Gray Squirrel's fine basket, and he was impressed with it. He told her that soon people would come into that part of the world. Already people were so close that Coyote could hear their footsteps. He said that from that day forward, the women of that land would be well known for their cedar baskets. And it's so, isn't it?" Kautsa spread her strong, gnarled hands on her knees.

One little girl gazed up at Kautsa longingly. "Tell us another story?" she asked.

Kautsa smiled. "Instead, why don't you make a little twined basket like the one Kaya is working on? I'll start it for you, and she'll help you if you get into trouble. Won't you, Granddaughter?"

"Aa-heh, Kautsa," Kaya said. She would do anything that her grandmother asked of her. But she hoped Swan Circling had heard how quickly she agreed to Kautsa's request—she wanted her friend to think well of her. It seemed that no matter what Kaya was doing, she had Swan Circling on her mind.

The next morning as Kaya stepped out of the stream where the girls had taken their morning swim, she saw Swan Circling beckoning to her. The frigid air made Kaya feel like running and jumping with energy. She pulled her elk robe around her and hurried to meet Swan Circling.

"Tawts may-we!" Kaya said.

"Aa-heh, tawts may-we, Kaya," Swan Circling said. "That story your grandmother told last night set me thinking. I have something I want to show you. Would you like to work with me today?"

"Aa-heh!" Kaya said. "If Kautsa says I may, I'll work with you."

"Run and ask her then," Swan Circling said. "I'll be in the lodge."

After Kautsa said that Kaya could work with Swan Circling, Kaya joined her again. Swan Circling was kneeling on a mat in the crowded lodge. Kaya knelt at her side and watched her untie the flaps of a large parfleche painted with triangle designs in red, blue, green, and yellow. "Your grandmother's story reminded me of a basket I made when I was a little girl—my very first one," Swan Circling said.

"My first was awfully lopsided," Kaya said, "but I gave it to Kautsa anyway."

Swan Circling lifted out her special ceremonial dress and moccasins from the parfleche and set them aside. Then she took out a little brown twined basket and handed it to Kaya. "You can see that my first basket's lopsided, too."

Kaya smiled at the lumpy little basket. She liked to imagine Swan Circling as a girl with small hands and big ideas—a girl just like Kaya. She was happy to be sitting at her friend's side. "Didn't you give your first basket to your grandmother?" she asked.

Swan Circling nodded. "Aa-heh, I did. After she died, it was given back to me. I'm glad. This basket taught me many lessons."

Kaya turned it over. With her fingertip she traced the weaving. "Was one of the lessons to make your twining tighter?"

Swan Circling smiled. "Aa-heh, to pull the cord tighter was one thing I learned. But that wasn't all— I learned about patience, too. I was a very bold, headstrong little girl. I thought that there was nothing I couldn't do!"

"But you can do everything, can't you?" Kaya asked.

Now Swan Circling laughed. "Of course I can't!" She put her warm hand on Kaya's knee. "You see, I'd been watching my grandmother weave her baskets, and I was sure I knew how. I decided I was going to make a beautiful one just like hers. I got my basket started, but I made mistake after mistake. Finally, I had this pitiful little thing to show her."

"What did she say about it?" Kaya asked.

"She thanked me and said I'd made a start. But I expected more praise than that," Swan Circling

160

admitted. "I remember I was pouting. I asked her why she hadn't corrected my mistakes, as if the lumps in my basket were her fault! Then she told me, 'Everyone has to have her own experience. Everyone has to learn her own lessons.' Little by little I understood that to make a mistake is not a bad thing. But I should be wise enough not to make the same mistake again—and again."

Kaya understood that Swan Circling wasn't speaking now of basket making—she was speaking of life.

This was a chance for Kaya to tell Swan Circling about how she'd gotten her nickname and why the enemies were able to capture her and Speaking Rain—and about her guilt for escaping without her sister. She could tell Swan Circling the truth. "I've made mistakes, too," Kaya began. "I—"

Swan Circling waited for her to go on.

But then Kaya lost her nerve. What if she told Swan Circling the truth, but her friend lost respect for her? If she did, she wouldn't seek out Kaya anymore. No, Kaya couldn't risk losing Swan Circling's friendship.

"I left holes in a basket I was making," Kaya

said in a determined voice. "But my grandmother showed me right away so I could do a better job." She handed back the clumsy little basket.

Swan Circling repacked it with the other things and tied the parfleche. "Is something troubling you?" she asked Kaya. "There's a crease right here." She put her fingertip between Kaya's eyebrows.

Kaya didn't meet Swan Circling's gaze. "No, nothing's troubling me," she said.

Still Swan Circling waited. After a moment, she put the parfleche back on the stack against the lodge wall. "Maybe we've done enough talking," she said. "Come, let's pack up the pemmican and put it into storage."

CHAPTER
THREE
—

A SICK BABY

During the night a light snow fell. Kaya
was sweeping it away from the outside
of the lodge when she heard a soft
sound that gently rose and fell—the sound of a flute.
She cocked her head. Someone was playing sweet,
winding notes that sounded both happy and sad at
the same time.

The melody made Kaya think of a warm spring
breeze blowing in the depth of winter. Had Two
Hawks finished the little flute she'd helped him
begin? Was he playing it? When she'd swept the
ground bare with the piece of sagebrush, she hurried
to find him.

She found Two Hawks in the lodge near the

door. He was sitting with an older boy named Runs Home, who held a flute to his lips. The sweet music Kaya had heard was the older boy's skilled playing. Kaya knew Runs Home liked to serenade girls on long summer evenings.

When Two Hawks saw Kaya, he raised his flute to his lips and blew. A squeak! He blew again. Another shrill squeak and then a squawk!

Runs Home frowned. He took the flute from Two Hawks and compared it to his. He showed Two Hawks that the slit he'd made in the top was too small and the holes in the side were too large.

Two Hawks seized his flute and shoved it out of sight under a parfleche. He folded his arms over his chest and gave Kaya a fierce look of anger and disappointment.

Since Two Hawks had been with her people, he'd put on some weight and he looked much healthier, but at that moment he reminded her of the skinny, bitter boy she'd first seen in the enemy camp.

"Can you help him find another elderberry stick?" Runs Home asked her. "He can learn to make a good flute if he'll let me work with him."

Kaya threw Two Hawks the words, *Come with me. We'll find another stick.*

Two Hawks turned his head. Kaya thought that if his ankle was healed and he could run away from them, he would.

You can't make something perfect the first time you try, she signed to Two Hawks. *You have to practice! I'm going to get horses for us so we can find another stick for you.*

"Will he go with you?" Runs Home asked her.

"He did before," she said firmly. "He will again. I'm sure of it."

Listen to me, Runs Home signed to Two Hawks. *I'll teach you some things.*

Two Hawks looked closely at Runs Home, then at Kaya. He set his jaw and shrugged. Then he got to his feet and hobbled outside right at Kaya's heels, as if he was relieved that she and Runs Home hadn't let him quit on his first try.

Kaya and Brown Deer were helping Kautsa take wrapped camas cakes from a storage pit when a crier came riding through the village. "Friends are arriving! Get ready for them!" he called out. They all stopped what they were doing and gathered to welcome their visitors.

A northeast wind, the coldest one, blew fine flakes of snow. Kaya shaded her eyes as she watched the horizon. Soon she saw a dark line of horses and riders come over the snow-covered rise and descend to the village.

What could be better in this cold season than the warmth of greeting friends and family! Everyone hugged and smiled and talked and handed around gifts. Men, women, and children crowded inside with their belongings until all the lodges were pleasantly full.

Kaya caught sight of Cut Cheek standing with *Toe-ta* and *Pi-lah-ka*. He'd come with the others from a winter village nearby. She'd forgotten how handsome Cut Cheek was, with his broad forehead, flashing eyes, and high cheekbones, a scar on one of them.

Would Brown Deer hurry to greet him, as others were doing? He was looking around the gathering. Kaya searched the crowd, too—where was her older sister?

Then Kaya saw her. Brown Deer was standing

modestly by the doorway of their lodge. Her cheeks were burning, as if she knew Cut Cheek was looking her way. Then she raised her eyes to his. Something passed between them like a shiver of heat lightning. Kaya smiled to herself and thought, *Someday soon Cut Cheek will wear the necklace Brown Deer is making!*

Kaya's aunt from a nearby village greeted her with a strong hug and a kiss. "Scouts told us about your capture and escape," she said. "We're so glad you're well!"

"Did your scouts have any news of my sister?" Kaya asked.

The smile left her aunt's face. "No one has any news of her," she said. "Of course, no one can cross the Buffalo Trail now. Our enemies must have taken her back to their country with them."

Biting her lip, Kaya turned away.

Swan Circling touched Kaya's arm. "Will you help me carry these baskets of food?" she asked Kaya gently. "We have so much to do for the gathering tonight."

When night came on, Kaya and the others dressed in their best clothes and entered the ceremonial lodge for the new year gathering. This was the shortest day of the year—and the darkest. The clouds had cleared, and stars shone in the sky, where the new moon, thin as a fish bone, had risen. Four big tepees had been put together to make this lodge, but soon the large space was crowded with people of all ages.

Several men held a drum made of hide. The fires in the center of the lodge cast their light on the walls, and the air smelled sweetly of cedar boughs and tule mats.

When everyone was in the lodge, To Soar Like An Eagle raised his hand to get attention. He wore a feathered headdress and a painted hide shirt decorated with porcupine quills. He was a very respected old chief with white eyebrows and a low, powerful voice that came from deep in his chest. Kaya watched his lined face as he spoke.

"Hun-ya-wat has made this night longer than all the others," To Soar Like An Eagle said. "In this darkest time, let us reflect on the days that have gone before and on the days that lie ahead. It is time to renew life."

The drummers began, filling the night with drumbeats that echoed back from the surrounding hills. After the drumming, men and women began to speak of births and deaths and of the gifts Hun-ya-wat had given them in the past year. They told of good deeds and acts of bravery. They gave thanks for successful hunts and for ample fish and roots and berries. Together they prayed that all might keep their minds and hearts pure so there would be enough food in the year to come.

Kaya listened closely to the prayer songs. She looked at her parents and grandparents standing near her. Firelight played over their solemn faces. Brown Deer, too, was sober and thoughtful. Even the twins, such lively little boys, seemed to be listening closely to the singing.

Two Hawks, who couldn't understand the words, gazed steadily at the others as though he understood everything from their serious expressions.

Kaya could see Swan Circling standing with her young husband, Claw Necklace. Her dark eyes reflected the firelight, but her thoughts seemed far away, as if she was thinking of the future again.

Kaya considered her own life over the past year.

She had much to be thankful for, but she had many regrets, too. Her good and bad feelings mingled like the streams of smoke rising from the fires. Her eyes smarted with them.

When Kaya glanced again at Swan Circling, she realized what was troubling her most tonight—she hadn't yet told her friend how she got her nickname or how her disobedience had gotten her and Speaking Rain captured. She hadn't been brave enough. But until she did, Swan Circling wouldn't really know her.

Kaya closed her eyes. *Hun-ya-wat, make me honest and strong in character,* she prayed silently. *Help me face life with an honorable, truthful, and strong will.*

When the prayers came to an end, it was time for the midnight feast. Women brought out steaming salmon broth followed by bowls of mashed roots and berries. As Kaya watched the preparations, she felt a quiet, calm resolve in her heart. Her prayer had given her courage. She would tell Swan Circling everything— and as soon as possible.

Kaya watched for a chance to speak with
Swan Circling, but with all the visitors crowded into
the lodges, they were never together. After several
days, the visitors left for their own villages. Now,
surely, Kaya could take Swan Circling aside and talk
with her.

One morning Kaya was piling wood beside the
cooking fires when Running Alone hurried over.
"Would you look after my baby for a little while?"
Running Alone asked Kaya. "I'm troubled about her.
I want to find Bear Blanket and ask her for help."

Kaya was worried as she followed Running
Alone through the lodge to her sleeping place. Bear
Blanket was a powerful medicine woman who had
cured many, many sick people. Light On The Water
must be sick, or Running Alone wouldn't be looking
for the medicine woman's help.

Light On The Water lay in a hide swing hung
from the lodge poles. Kaya leaned over her.
The baby's face was flushed, and each time
she drew a breath she coughed. Tiny beads
of sweat covered her forehead and cheeks.
Her eyes were open, but she didn't gaze up
at Kaya. She didn't seem to see anything at all.

171

When Running Alone hurried off, Kaya placed her finger in the baby's hot little hand. Light On The Water didn't tug at it, as she usually did. "Are you sick, little one?" Kaya whispered. "There's help for you. You won't be sick for long."

Soon Bear Blanket came through the door of the lodge. She was an old, gray-haired woman, but her back was as straight as an arrow. Kaya knew that Bear Blanket always kept her mind and body clean so she would be ready to help those who needed her. Her animal spirit helper was a grizzly bear. Long ago she had received medicine power—the power to heal—from this *wyakin.*

Bear Blanket carried a medicine bundle in one hand. Swan Circling followed right behind her.

Running Alone motioned for Kaya to stand aside so that Bear Blanket could see the baby. The old woman studied the baby's face and bent over to listen to her coughing. Then she spread her hands over the baby's head and began to sing one of her medicine songs.

As she sang, she passed her hands up and down over Light On The Water's body. Kaya saw the baby's eyelids tremble and shut, then open

The old woman studied the baby's face
and bent over to listen to her coughing.

again when she coughed harder.

Bear Blanket drew Swan Circling aside and spoke to her, then went back to her singing.

Swan Circling frowned. "She wants me to bring her the inner bark of a special tree to boil for a healing drink," she said to Running Alone. "I'm going to get my horse and go after it now."

"But it's very cold," Running Alone said. "The northeast wind is blowing again. Will you be all right?"

"I can't wait," Swan Circling said. "Your baby needs the medicine now."

Running Alone put her hand on Swan Circling's arm. "Then hurry!" she urged her. "Kaya will round up your horse for you while you get your blankets and your knife."

Kaya threw a deerskin over her shoulders and grabbed a rope bridle. Her breath was a white plume at her lips as she ran out to the herd grazing near the village. She found Swan Circling's white-faced horse, placed the bridle on her lower jaw, and rode her back to the lodges.

Swan Circling was wearing otter-skin leggings and mittens and had her elk robe around her. She

held her beautiful saddle of wood and painted rawhide. Kaya reined in the horse and slipped off. She put on the saddle and reached under the horse's belly for the cinch. Already Swan Circling was hanging her bags from the saddle horn.

"Cinch it snugly," Swan Circling told her. "I'm going to ride as fast as possible. Bear Blanket said the baby is very sick." She tested the saddle cinch with her weight, then swung up. "Good work, Kaya. I'll be back before last light. Watch for me." She urged her horse forward and, in a few strides, was running full out across the frozen ground.

"I'll watch for you!" Kaya called after her. But the wind snatched away her words.

All day Kaya stayed with Running Alone and her baby. Bear Blanket sang her medicine songs, but the baby only coughed harder and harder. Her little face was red, and her eyes screwed shut with her effort to breathe. Kaya watched her anxiously—did the baby have the terrible sickness of blisters that the men with pale faces had brought to the land? Kaya was afraid to ask.

As the light began to fade, Kaya went to watch for Swan Circling's return. At dusk there were no colors in the valley. The river was a shining black curve, like a snake, and the trees were black slashes against the white snow. Under dark clouds, a hawk rode the wind in slow, wide turns.

Where is Swan Circling? Kaya thought. *Why doesn't she come back?*

Then she saw a horse appear in the trees at the far end of the valley. Kaya ran up the hillside a little way to get a better look. The horse had a white face—Swan Circling's horse. Kaya caught her breath in relief. But as the horse came closer, out of the trees, Kaya saw that it

176

was limping as though it was hurt—and that it had no rider.

C H A P T E R
F O U R

GIFTS FROM SWAN CIRCLING

Kaya watched as Claw Necklace, Toe-ta, and two other men saddled their horses and rode off to search for Swan Circling. Kaya couldn't believe that anything bad could have happened to her friend—she was so young, so strong. Maybe she'd fallen off her horse, and it had run away from her. Surely she was coming home on foot and the men would soon meet up with her. In the meantime, here was her bag—still hanging on the saddle horn.

Kaya ran with the bag to find Bear Blanket. The medicine woman was with Running Alone and her baby, who lay gasping in the baby swing. Bear Blanket opened the bag and took out a handful of bark. "This is the good medicine I asked for," she said.

"Tawts!" Running Alone exclaimed. "I knew Swan Circling wouldn't fail us."

Kaya dug her fingernails into her palms as she gazed down at the baby's red face and dry lips. Would blisters soon break out on her cheeks? Her people had never seen the men with pale faces, but their sicknesses had killed many Nimíipuu. "Tell me," she asked fearfully, "does the baby have the bad sickness that kills?"

"Not that," Bear Blanket said quickly. "She has a weakness in her chest."

Kaya unclenched her fists. "Will the medicine help her, then?"

"I'll make a healing drink with it," Bear Blanket said. "Soon she'll breathe more easily. Go rest, Kaya. There's nothing you can do now."

Kaya was warm under a blanket of woven strips of rabbit fur, but she couldn't sleep. Her thoughts were with Swan Circling, who was somewhere in the darkness and the cold wind. Perhaps she'd built herself a lean-to for shelter, as Kaya had done when she escaped from the enemies. Or maybe, any moment now, Swan Circling would come walking into the lodge with Claw Necklace. She had to be all right!

Kaya slept fitfully. Before first light she awoke to a cold draft on her cheek. She pushed up onto her elbow. A few people were stirring in the lodge, and someone had pulled back the covering of the doorway. Had Swan Circling returned? Kaya crawled from underneath her blanket. She saw Eetsa leaving the lodge, a torch in her hand. Kaya pulled her elk hide robe around her shoulders, followed Eetsa to the door, and peeked out.

The moon had already set, and the sky was turning gray. In the space between the lodges, Eetsa joined a group of men and women. Kaya saw Kautsa, Pi-lah-ka, and other elders wrapped in their robes. Toe-ta was speaking to them. And now she made out Claw Necklace walking toward the lodges. He carried something. Kaya blinked. Then she realized it was Swan Circling that Claw Necklace held in his arms.

Kaya couldn't get her breath. No!—Swan Circling would be all right! She would be! Kaya pulled her robe over her head and hid her face in it.

In a moment she felt firm hands on her shoulders. She lifted her chin and looked up into Kautsa's face. In the gray early light, her grandmother looked very old and very tired. "Our men found her body beside the stream," Kautsa said quietly. "It seems her horse broke through thin ice and stumbled, and she was thrown off. Her head struck a boulder, and the blow killed her." She opened her arms and took Kaya into her warm embrace.

Through her tears, Kaya heard Kautsa's gentle voice at her ear. "She was full of light and love," Kautsa said. "It's hard to let her go, but we must help her spirit journey on."

Kaya walked in a daze after Swan Circling's death. She felt as if a jagged hole had been torn in her heart. Mixed in with the pain of her friend's death was another pain—one of regret. Oh, why hadn't she quickly called up the courage to tell Swan Circling everything? Now it was too late.

Everyone in the village grieved and mourned for Swan Circling. They comforted each other with gentle words and tried to console Claw Necklace, too. Runners took the bad news to neighboring villages. Though it was the heart of winter, one runner volunteered to travel all the way to the Big River to tell Swan Circling's family.

None of Swan Circling's family lived close enough to help with the burial, so the women in her husband's family took charge of all the preparations. They got to work right away. The best hide workers took out fresh white deer hides, clean and unused, to make a new dress and moccasins to clothe the body. Other women prepared food to serve the whole community after the burial ceremony. Some stayed with the body, never leaving it alone, even for a moment.

Kaya stayed close to Running Alone and her baby. The medicine had helped Light On The Water. She wasn't coughing so hard now, and she gazed up at Kaya's face when Kaya rocked the sling and sang to her. Light On The Water didn't need encouragement to sleep, though—she was still weak and listless.

Even when the baby slept, Kaya kept singing the lullaby, "She's the precious one, my own dear little precious one." She was sure Swan Circling was listening. Until her body was buried, her spirit would stay close by.

Kaya was gently rocking the sleeping baby when she thought she heard a canyon wren singing somewhere near the lodge. Kaya cocked her head. Was Swan Circling sending a message through a bird? Kaya went outside to look for it.

Wrapped in his antelope hide, Two Hawks was standing near the lodge. He still used a stick for a crutch, but he could put more weight on his leg now. He saw Kaya and limped over to meet her. When he was in front of her, he put the little flute he'd been working on to his lips. His cheeks puffed out as he played *tee, tee*— the sweet, descending notes she'd mistaken for birdsong.

"That's a pretty sound," Kaya said. "May I look at your flute?"

He handed it over. His face was solemn, but his dark eyes were lively—she saw that he was proud of what he'd made.

The little flute had a good feel in her hands. It was well and carefully made, and Two Hawks had smoothed the wood to a gloss. "Tawts!" she said. "Good work, Two Hawks."

"Runs Home helped me," he said. "He's my friend now."

"I see he's helping you with words, too," she said. "And you've made a good flute. Now you have to learn to play it."

"I can play!" he insisted. He brought the flute to his lips and blew, his eyes narrowed in concentration. *Tee, tee, tew,* he played. This time he was able to add a third note to the song.

Two Hawks's success lifted Kaya's sad heart a little. His leg was healing, and he was a happier boy now. And it seemed that Light On The Water would get well. These were things to be thankful for in this dark time. Surely Swan Circling's spirit would find comfort in these things, too.

Before first light on the third morning after Swan Circling's death, Toe-ta and other men went to the burial place on a rise above the stream to dig a grave. When they sent word that the grave was ready, everyone gathered in the faint light for the ceremony.

Swan Circling's body and some of her things

had been wrapped in clean hides and fresh mats and placed on a horse-drawn travois. Fighting her tears, Kaya followed with the others as the body was taken to the burial place—which faced the east, where the sky would soon brighten.

A medicine man with strong spirit powers led the way. He was a short man with a broad chest and shoulders, and he wore a fur headdress set with mountain sheep horns. At the graveside, he praised Swan Circling's strength, her unwavering courage, and her willingness to help her people. He spoke of everyone's sorrow to lose such a good woman. Then he urged her spirit to travel on.

As the first streak of dawn stained the pale sky, the men placed the body in the shallow grave and covered it with another mat. First the women, then the men stepped one by one to the grave and dropped in a handful of earth. When it was Kaya's turn, she vowed silently, *All my life I'll think of you! I'll strive to be like you, I promise!*

But Swan Circling's spirit wouldn't be able to rest until all of her belongings had been given away or burned. Because Eetsa had been a close friend of

Swan Circling, she took charge of the give-away.

In the lodge, Eetsa placed all of Swan Circling's belongings on a mat. After all the people had eaten the meal the women had prepared, they gathered around the mat. One by one, Toe-ta called them to step forward. With a few words, he gave Running Alone the mortar and pestle. Little Fawn received the digging stick, and Kautsa a large parfleche. To Brown Deer he gave a pair of deerskin moccasins. He gave other women and girls Swan Circling's baskets, necklaces, shells, and hides until there was nothing left on the mat by his feet but Swan Circling's saddle.

Then Toe-ta motioned for Kaya to come forward. She kept her gaze on her moccasins as her father spoke to her. "Claw Necklace told me his wife admired your care for horses and your love of them," he said gently. "He's certain she would want you to have her saddle."

"Katsee-yow-yow," Kaya murmured.

Then Toe-ta rubbed his lips with his thumb. He thought a moment. "She also wanted you to have something much more important than a saddle," he said.

In his deep voice Toe-ta told how Swan Circling had recently come to him and Eetsa and asked to speak with them. "She told us she had a dark dream, a dream of her death," he said. "She wasn't frightened, but she said that if she should die, she wanted Kaya to have her name. As you know, her name was hers to give as she chose. She was fond of you, Kaya, and she spoke of your special friendship. She believed you would carry her name well. We accepted her gift to you with gratitude."

Now a very old woman lifted her head to speak. It was her job to remember how everyone was related to each other. "What Kaya's father says is true," she said firmly. "I was there when Kaya's parents accepted the name. I say this is so."

Kaya hugged the beautiful saddle of painted wood and hide that Toe-ta had handed her. But as she turned and walked back to her place, her mind couldn't take in the second gift that Swan Circling had given. Her name! That was the greatest gift anyone could give. Kaya's thoughts rushed back and forth between gratitude and doubt. How honored she was to have been given her friend's name! But could she truly be worthy of it? And

*"She also wanted you to have something
much more important than a saddle," he said.*

would Swan Circling have given it if she'd known Kaya's failures? If only Swan Circling were here, for it seemed to Kaya that her friend was the one person who could quiet these racing doubts and fears. But Kaya was alone with her torn feelings.

It wasn't until that night that Kaya could talk with her mother. Eetsa had heated stones in the fire and was putting them into a water basket to boil deer meat. She stirred the hot stones rapidly to keep them from scorching the basket. Kaya crouched by her side.

"Eetsa, I'm troubled about my namesake," Kaya said, careful not to say the name of the dead out loud.

Eetsa lifted out the cooled stones with a forked stick and put in more hot ones. "What troubles you, Daughter?" she asked.

"I don't think she'd have given me her name if she'd known the mistakes I've made," Kaya admitted. "I never told her about my nickname or how I got myself and Speaking Rain taken captive."

When Eetsa glanced at her, Kaya saw her mother's eyes soften. "But there's nothing to be troubled about," Eetsa said. "She knew about your nickname, but she said it didn't matter to her. And she said it took great strength to leave your sister behind and that you were wise to do so."

"She said that to you?" Kaya asked.

"Aa-heh," Eetsa assured her. "She often spoke about you. She told me she had confidence that you would grow to be trustworthy and strong. And she said you have a generous heart, Daughter—which you do. It's not time for you to use her name yet, but when that time comes, you'll know. Is anything else troubling you?"

Kaya pressed her lips together and shook her head. Her heart was full—she was afraid that if she spoke, she'd burst into tears of both gratitude and relief.

The next morning, Kaya sat with her little brothers on her rabbit-fur blanket. The twins lay on their stomachs with their chins in their hands. They were watching as she shaped and tied long pine needles to make three little horses.

"Is one of those horses for me?" Wing Feather asked.

"If my brother gets a toy, so do I!" Sparrow demanded. "Don't I, Kaya?"

"Yes, one of these horses is for you," she said, tapping Wing Feather on his nose. "And one's for you," she told Sparrow and tugged his braid.

Kaya put the finishing touches on the little horses and handed one to each boy. "Here they are," she said. "Now you can have races."

"Katsee-yow-yow!" the twins said at the same time. They seized their toys and scampered with them to the pile of hides where other children were playing.

Kaya cut a small piece of hide and tied it with a bit of fringe onto the third little horse's back—there, now this one had a saddle. Then she wrapped herself in her elk robe and left the lodge without telling anyone where she was going. Since she'd wakened, she'd known what she must do.

The trail to the burial place led around the sides of low hills. Bare trees cast blue shadows on the thin covering of snow. Coyotes hunting rabbits had left tracks in the snow, and she saw the wing print of a hawk that had swooped down for a kill.

On the east-facing side of the hill, she turned off the trail. There were many graves here, marked with rocks. Mourners had left small gifts on some of them. Kaya went to the place Swan Circling was buried and put the little horse made of pine needles on her grave.

"I've been thinking about things," Kaya said softly to her friend. "I want you to know I'm going to live up to your expectations—and that I'm grateful for your trust. And your name. But I hope to get my sister back before I use it, and maybe my horse, too. I want to deserve what you've given me. I want our people to think well of me when they call me by your name."

Kaya looked back at her village. In the cold, only dogs moved between the lodges. Everything was quiet, but soon family and friends would return for the Winter Spirit Dances, and the village would be crowded again. She stood a moment more, squinting into the morning light that flooded the long, broad valley, and then she started home.

FOR MY DAUGHTER KRIS,
HER HUSBAND, PAUL, AND THEIR
SONS, WILL AND PETER,
WITH LOVE

Kaya
AND LONE DOG

A STARVING DOG

As Kaya helped her mother and grandmother set up the tepee poles and cover
them with tule mats, she heard the *honk!
honk! honk!* of geese flying high overhead. She stopped
work, shaded her eyes, and gazed up into the deep
blue sky. Flocks of geese, swans, herons, and cranes
were flying northward from their wintering grounds
in the south. As she listened to the noisy chorus of
their cries, she heard other sounds, too. The warm
spring wind gusted across the rolling hills, rustling
the greening prairie grasses. Larks and swallows
called softly while they built their nests. Her bothersome little brothers laughed and squealed as they
scampered about with the other children. She heard

197

her grandfather sigh with pleasure when he tilted up his face to the warm sun that eased the aches in his bones. Everything Kaya heard joined in the song of new life returning to the land.

After the long, cold winter, Kaya and her family had left the sheltered canyons of Salmon River Country and journeyed upland to dig fresh kouse roots, the delicious, nourishing food her people needed. This spring they'd come to the beautiful Palouse Prairie, where they'd met *Nimíipuu* and other peoples with whom they shared these root fields. There would be many reunions with friends, and much trading, dancing, games, and horse racing, too. But Kaya's family had chosen to come here for another reason—they'd promised to help Two Hawks, the boy who had escaped with Kaya from enemies while in Buffalo Country. He needed to get back to his own people, the *Salish*. Salish often came to the Palouse Prairie to dig roots and trade. A trader might take Two Hawks to his home. Kaya looked around for Two Hawks. He was herding horses with some other boys. She thought he looked happy, but she knew he badly missed his family.

Her grandmother touched Kaya's arm. Kaya started. She'd let her attention wander.

"Why are you watching the boys when you should be working?" *Kautsa* asked. Her usually gentle voice was stern. "And you're frowning. What have I taught you about making yourself ready to dig roots?"

"You've told me not to have bad thoughts that might make the roots hide themselves," Kaya said. "And I must stay away from sad thoughts, too, so the roots won't make us sick when we eat them."

"*Aa-heh*," Kautsa said. "You must have a pure heart to do your work well and be worthy of your namesake."

Kaya knew her grandmother was right, but she'd found that staying away from bad or sad thoughts was very, very difficult. Her younger sister, Speaking Rain, was still a captive of enemies from Buffalo Country. Kaya's horse had been captured, too, and then traded away. And each time Kaya thought of Swan Circling's death, she had to fight to keep her heart from aching. Swan Circling had been a respected warrior woman, and she had wanted Kaya to have her name, the greatest gift a person could give. Kaya hoped that one day she'd feel ready to use it. Sometimes, just for a moment, Kaya wished she could be a carefree child again, like her twin brothers, who were happily trying to sneak up on green racers and catch the little snakes with their bare hands.

"Will the root digging begin soon?" Kaya asked.

"Very soon!" Kautsa said with a smile. "Two women elders went to check the fields today. They came back with good news. The roots are waiting for us. The roots are singing!"

Kaya felt a shiver down her back. *Hun-ya-wat*, the Creator, sent both animals and plants so that Nimíipuu might have food to live. But if anyone treated these gifts disrespectfully, then the fish, the deer, the berries, or the roots might not give themselves to The People. Kaya prayed that nothing she had said or done—or thought— would cause her people to go hungry.

Kautsa put her strong arm around Kaya's shoulder. "I see that something troubles you,

Granddaughter." Now she spoke gently, as if she understood Kaya's troubled thoughts.

"I still have a lot of sadness in me," Kaya admitted. "Do you think I should keep away from the digging?"

"Only you know your own heart," Kautsa said.

"I want to work with you and the others!" Kaya blurted. "I want to do my part, like my namesake always did."

"Of course you do!" Kautsa said. She squeezed Kaya to her, then held her at arm's length to look at her. "But you've told me your heart is troubled. For now, let others work with the food until your dark thoughts leave you and the time of mourning is over in your heart. You can join us when your thoughts are clear again."

"Aa-heh," Kaya said with a sigh. She knew her grandmother's advice was wise, but the realization that she wouldn't be working with the other girls and women made her feel even lonelier.

Kautsa glanced at the sun, high overhead. "We need firewood so I can get our meal started," she said.

"I'll get some," Kaya said at once. She was glad

to walk across the greening field to the stream, which was rushing with the runoff of melted snow. As she went, she saw horses rolling on their backs to shed their thick winter coats. When she bent to pick up driftwood, she saw the first early blooms of yellowbells. Soon her thoughts were lighter, but still she felt uneasy, as if she were being watched. Were the Stick People peeking at her? Was a bear prowling nearby, hungry after its long winter sleep? She stood and looked around.

Kaya's father had taught her that even the smallest of signs carry big messages. He'd taught her to look for the tip of a deer's antler, or the tremble of a branch after an elk has passed. So Kaya let her gaze move slowly across the scrub brush, searching for any little sign of what might be hidden there. In a moment, she saw the amber glint of two eyes watching her through the leaves. Those eyes reminded her of something—what? Then she remembered the yellow eyes of the wolf that had led her through the snowstorm toward her father when she was stranded on the Buffalo Trail. But a wolf wouldn't come so close to where people camped. She crouched. Now she made out a pale muzzle and a black nose, the head of a large dog.

Drawn by the dog's searching gaze, Kaya inched closer. The dog moved slowly out of the bushes toward her, the tip of its tail wagging slightly. She could see scars on its back and shoulders. She could also see its ribs showing plainly, though its belly was swollen with pups soon to be born. It wasn't one of their camp dogs, which she knew well. Perhaps it had come here with another band. But why had it strayed off alone?

Gazing up at Kaya with sad eyes, the dog whined low in its throat.

"Are you asking for food?" Kaya said. "I don't have any for you, but your people will feed you. Go back to them. Go!" When she raised her hand, the dog cowered as though afraid Kaya would strike. "Go!" Kaya repeated.

The dog gazed at Kaya for a long moment, perhaps hoping she'd change her mind. Then it slipped away into the bushes, quickly vanishing from sight.

As soon as the dog disappeared, Kaya had the

sinking feeling that she'd just done a terrible thing.
She remembered that when she and her sister were
slaves, fed only on scraps, she'd vowed never again
to chase off the starving dogs that sometimes
appeared at the camp. This hungry dog had asked
for her help, but she'd chased it away. Kaya whistled
to call the dog back to her side. But it was too late—
the lone dog was gone.

On the day chosen for root digging to begin,
the lead diggers rose before first light and went to
the sweat lodge to cleanse and purify
themselves. Kaya's older sister,
Brown Deer, was one of the lead
diggers this year. Kaya watched as
Brown Deer dressed herself in her best

sweat lodge

moccasins and her white deerskin dress decorated
with elks' teeth and shell beads. Kautsa set Brown
Deer's work hat on her head. By the time the lead
diggers reached the root fields, the eastern sky
bloomed pink as a prairie rose. Soon Kaya heard the
women begin to sing the sacred song of thanks for
the gift of new food—the root harvest would be a

good one! Kaya knew it was right for her to stay away from the digging, but how she longed to wear her own new work hat and to dig with the other women and girls.

As Kaya prepared a morning meal for the twins, she gazed out over the rolling hills, hoping to see the hungry dog she'd chased off. Every day she'd looked for that lone dog, but she hadn't seen it again. How terrible if it had starved to death!

"Little Daughter, I've been looking for you!" *Toe-ta's* deep voice came from behind her. She turned and saw her father gazing kindly at her, as if he understood that she was sad. "I've been thinking that we need to train another horse to pull a travois," he said to her.

"I worked with my namesake when she taught a horse to pull one," Kaya said, always careful not to say the name of the dead aloud.

"*Tawts!*" Toe-ta said. "I can use your help. I think the old gray horse your grandmother used to ride would be a good one to work with. Come with me and we'll put a training harness on it. Bring the twins with you—they can help, too."

Toe-ta tied the gray horse to a bent shrub.

While the boys waited impatiently, Kaya and her father looped a rawhide rope around the horse's neck. Long rawhide lines attached to the rope led back to a dried buffalo hide that rested on the ground a few feet behind the horse's hind legs. When the training harness was secure, Toe-ta gestured for Kaya to climb onto the hide to add weight to the drag. The hide was back far enough so that if the horse kicked, its legs wouldn't reach Kaya.

Kaya crawled onto the buffalo hide, sat, and held onto the lines with both hands. Then Toe-ta led the horse forward by the halter, speaking all the while in a low, reassuring voice. But the gray shied and dodged and started to kick at the unaccustomed burden it pulled. Kaya laughed as the buffalo hide bumped and skidded over the smooth ground—this horse wouldn't toss her off! The twins laughed, too—they wanted to ride on that swaying rawhide.

After a short time, the horse quieted down and walked steadily as Toe-ta led it around the ring of tepees. At last he drew the horse to a halt and motioned for Kaya to stand up and take the lead-rope from him. "You boys get on now," he told the twins, and they eagerly jumped onto the hide as

Kaya took hold of the halter.

Toe-ta watched as Kaya led the gentle horse away from the tepees, the little boys grinning as they hung tightly to the rawhide lines. When Toe-ta was satisfied that the work was going well, he nodded. "In a few days, when the horse is accustomed to the feel of the drag, we'll add travois poles to the harness," he said. "Go slowly, Kaya. Walk around the village a few more times, then put the horse back with the herd."

Kaya knew her father had asked her to help train the horse because she couldn't dig roots with the other women and girls. And her father had been wise—her heart was lighter now. Like Swan Circling, Kaya loved to work with the horses. When the training session was over and she took the harness off the gray, she noticed that one of its rear hooves seemed worn and sore. She resolved to make a rawhide shoe to fill with medicine for that sore hoof—another lesson her namesake had taught her.

As Kaya walked back to the village from where the horses grazed, she heard a dog growling nearby.

Her father had been wise—her heart was lighter now.
Like Swan Circling, Kaya loved to work with the horses.

208

The growl was low and challenging. Kaya went through the brush to see what had alarmed the dog.

On the far side of the hill, she came upon Snow Paws, the big black leader of the village dog pack. His hackles were up, his ears were pricked forward, and his teeth were bared. When he saw Kaya approaching, he snarled more fiercely at something backed up against a rocky outcropping. It wouldn't be a skunk—Snow Paws was much too smart for that. What did he have there?

Kaya parted the bushes. There, beside the rocks, was Lone Dog, the one she'd been searching for. Lone Dog's teeth were bared, and she was growling, too, facing off against the big male. With a glance, Kaya saw that Lone Dog's bones showed even more sharply. Hunger must have given her courage, for tough old Snow Paws could drive off any dog that approached. Even now he was beginning to bark, and soon he'd charge at Lone Dog and bite her.

This time Kaya wouldn't lose her chance to help the starving dog. She stepped between the two dogs and shook a stick at the barking Snow Paws. "Leave her alone!" she ordered him. "Get away from her! Go on now, get away!"

Growling, Snow Paws backed up a few steps. Maybe he thought Kaya had given him the wrong command. But when she shook the stick again, he reluctantly turned tail and stalked off, looking back over his shoulder.

When Snow Paws had gone, Kaya crouched, holding out her hand for Lone Dog to sniff. But the dog kept near the rocks, where she'd been digging out a den. She gazed warily at Kaya, as if Kaya might take up the attack where the black dog had left it.

"Here, come here," Kaya crooned. "I won't chase you away again." She reached into the bag on her belt and took out the pieces of dried salmon she carried for a quick meal. She held out the fish to Lone Dog. "Here's a little food for you. Come on, eat it."

Still Lone Dog hesitated, although the scent of fish made her tremble. Her yellow eyes gazed intently into Kaya's.

Kaya placed the fish on the ground and stepped back. "Please, don't be afraid of me. Take the food," she said.

This time Lone Dog didn't need urging.

She sprang forward, snapped up the fish, and gulped it down as she bolted away.

Kaya watched Lone Dog round the outcropping and disappear. "I'll bring you more food," she whispered. "You asked me for help and I'll give it. I promise."

Later that day, Kaya sat beside her grandmother as they worked. Kaya held a circle of thick elk hide on her lap. She was lacing a rawhide drawstring through holes she'd punched along the edge of the hide. When she pulled the drawstring tight, she'd have a round moccasin that would fit over the gray horse's hoof and hold a poultice to heal the sore place.

Kautsa was peeling the skins off roots so they could be dried in the sun. She handed Kaya a cleaned root to munch on. Fresh roots were welcome after a season of dried food.

"I have something I want to tell you about a dog," Kaya said.

"You always have stories to tell me," Kautsa said with a smile. With her small stone knife, she peeled off the dark root skins. The pile of pale, clean roots on the tule mat in front of her was growing quickly. "Is this story about a dog fight?"

Kaya looked closely at her grandmother, who always seemed to know so much. "How did you know about the fight?"

"I have ears!" Kautsa said with a laugh. "What happened, Granddaughter?"

"A lone dog came to our village for food," Kaya said. "The dog's starving, and she's going to have pups soon. I felt sorry for her. Snow Paws tried to chase her away—that's the barking you heard. But I made him stop."

Kautsa nodded, thinking. "Snow Paws has been the leader of our pack for a long time," she reminded Kaya. "He's a wise dog, and a strong-hearted one. You remember how he got his name, don't you? When he was hardly more than a pup, a hunter took him along to hunt elk. It was winter, and an avalanche crashed down a cliff and buried the man! Snow Paws dug and dug through the snow until he uncovered the hunter. He saved the man's life. A dog like that is one to be trusted. He must have a reason for trying to chase

212

off this lone dog you speak of."

"Snow Paws might think Lone Dog would take his food," Kaya suggested.

"We give our dogs enough to eat," Kautsa said. "If they're hungry, they know how to hunt for more to fill their bellies."

"But Snow Paws chases off every strange dog, doesn't he?" Kaya asked.

"He lets strange dogs join our pack if they accept him as the leader," Kautsa corrected her. "But he chases off dogs that might be dangerous for some reason. Snow Paws senses these things. Perhaps the lone dog is sick, and might make our dogs sick as well."

"Her eyes are bright and her fur's not falling out," Kaya said. "She doesn't look sick—she looks hungry."

"You told me your story to ask what I think about it, didn't you?" Kautsa said. "I think Snow Paws knows more about this lone dog than you do, Granddaughter, that's what I think."

Kaya bit her lip. Her grandmother was wise in all things. But Kaya had given her promise to Lone Dog. As Kaya did so often, she tried to think what Swan Circling would do if she were here. Kaya decided that if Lone Dog wasn't a menace, Swan Circling certainly wouldn't let her starve.

NEWBORN PUPPIES

The next morning Kaya went to the stream as the first rays of sun struck through the blanket of mist hanging over the water. Sandpipers were stepping along the shoreline, and a raccoon searched for crawfish in the shallows. Kaya dipped in her water basket, then drank from her cupped hand. It was a quiet morning, though she could hear the voices of the boys taking their morning swim downstream.

As Kaya drank, she saw Lone Dog appear on a rise a little distance away, then look around warily as she trotted to the stream to drink. Kaya set down her water basket and waited until Lone Dog had drunk her fill. "*Tawts may-we!*" Kaya greeted the dog softly. "Look, here's food for you. I didn't forget." She held out the bone she'd brought with her on the chance she would see the dog.

Lone Dog's ears pricked up and she stood with her head lifted, sniffing all the scents traveling over the water and land. Kaya knew Lone Dog smelled the bone, but she didn't come to take it from Kaya's hand as Kaya had hoped. It wouldn't be easy to earn this dog's trust.

Kaya called again, but this time Lone Dog began to back away. "Don't go," Kaya said. "You need this food."

When Lone Dog hesitated, Kaya put down the bone by the stream. She picked up her water basket and started walking, as if she didn't have a thought for the dog. When she glanced over her shoulder, she saw Lone Dog seize the bone and lope off into the brush with it. In a moment the dog had disappeared.

"Did I just see you feeding a coyote?" Raven called to Kaya. Several other boys laughed. They were running back to the village from their swim, water dripping from their bare arms and their hair.

They were full of the energy that the fresh, cold water had given them.

"You know that wasn't a coyote," Kaya said crossly. She walked faster. She wasn't in any mood to be teased by these bothersome boys, who swarmed around her like a cloud of gnats.

One of the boys was Fox Tail, who had challenged her to race when they were at *Wallowa*. He gave her a sly grin. "You say it's not a coyote, but it acts like one," he insisted. "Coyotes travel alone, but dogs stay with their pack."

"And it should be guarding the camp," Raven added. "Our dogs are supposed to protect us. That's their job. You shouldn't reward a lazy dog with a bone!"

"My people would chase off a dog that didn't do its work," Two Hawks added. He was one of the gang now.

Kaya gave Two Hawks an angry glance—it wasn't fair that he would criticize her after all they'd been through together. "When that dog gets used to us, she'll join our pack," she said. "You'll see."

"We'll see her get fat on our food, then go her own way!" Raven insisted.

"Aa-heh! Now I know why Kaya likes that dog!"
Fox Tail cried. "She likes it because it thinks only of
itself—just like a magpie! Isn't that right, Magpie?"
He swung around and walked backward, so he
could see Kaya's burning face as he taunted her.

It took all of Kaya's self-control to keep herself
from giving Fox Tail a swat—or letting a tear slide
from her eye. Would she never outgrow that awful
nickname she'd gotten when she failed to take care
of the twins? Would the others never forget that it
was her fault they'd all been switched? Fiercely, she
bit the inside of her lip so that she wouldn't let her
anger, or her disappointment, show.

"No one can tame a coyote—or a wolf!" Fox Tail
said. "Some girls can't tame a dog, either!" With
that, the laughing boys bounded off.

You're all skunks! Kaya thought. Fighting to be
calm—and to have good thoughts—she trudged
back to the camp.

Each day when all the women and girls went
to dig roots, Kaya put the harness on the gray horse
and trained it to pull the buffalo-hide drag. Its sore

218

hoof was healing well, and soon she was able to add lightweight poles to the harness. The gentle horse began to learn to pull those, too. As Kaya worked with the horse, her mind was on Lone Dog. Would she ever come to trust Kaya?

Kaya looked for Lone Dog every time she went to the stream. She waited on the shore as long as she could, but Lone Dog didn't appear. Where was she? Perhaps Lone Dog had already moved on, as the boys had said she would. The thought that Lone Dog might leave made Kaya sad. With her sister in captivity, Kaya often felt alone—like the dog. She realized she wanted the dog to become her friend.

One morning, as Kaya gazed at the empty shoreline, a thought came to her—perhaps Lone Dog was working on the den she'd begun on the hillside. After Kaya took the water basket she had filled to her tepee, she went looking for that place again.

Kaya was almost upon the den before she saw it. Lone Dog had hollowed out a deep circle beneath a rocky overhang. When Kaya crouched, she made out Lone Dog's yellow eyes gazing over the top of the nest, her face barely visible through the long grass.

"Tawts may-we," Kaya said gently. "I thought

"What a good mother you are . . . Here, you must be hungry, too."

I might find you here." She slowly went closer, hoping not to scare off the dog. Lone Dog watched her come. She wasn't wary, or nervous.

Kaya got down on her stomach and looked into the nest where Lone Dog lay. There, snuggled up next to one another against their mother's side, were four little newborn puppies. They were nursing, their paws pushing at their mother's belly. With their stubby legs and big bellies, they looked to Kaya more like ground squirrels than like dogs.

Panting heavily, Lone Dog gazed up steadily into Kaya's eyes. She seemed calm and sure of herself now that she'd given birth to her pups.

"What a good mother you are!" Kaya whispered to her. She watched the puppies nurse a little longer, then placed the food she'd brought at the edge of the nest. "Here, you must be hungry, too."

Lone Dog sniffed the meaty bone, then shifted herself and got to her feet so she could eat. When she stood, the puppies lost their hold on her and squealed as they tumbled onto their sides. Their eyes weren't open yet, but they found one another by the warmth of their bodies and crept close together to fall fast asleep.

Lying beside the nest, Lone Dog began to gnaw on the bone. Suddenly, her ears pricked up and she began to growl.

Kaya looked around. She didn't see anything. "It's all right," she said soothingly. "Your pups are safe."

But now Lone Dog was on her feet, her hackles raised along her back and her tail lifted straight up. She growled again, then lunged partway up the hillside, barking ferociously.

Kaya jumped up, too. Was a cougar after the helpless pups?

Instead of a cat, Kaya saw Snow Paws stalking along the top of the hill. Maybe he was only investigating the new scents, but sometimes male dogs went after newborn pups. He must not harm Lone Dog or her little ones! "Get away! Get!" Kaya commanded him. Lone Dog continued to bark violently to keep him at bay.

Snow Paws bared his teeth, as if he were about to charge Lone Dog. Then he changed his mind. He snarled and began backing off. He didn't want a fight with this fiercely protective mother—or with Kaya, who had seized a thick stick and was shaking it at him.

Even after Snow Paws disappeared, Lone Dog continued to bark. Only when she was satisfied that the intruder was gone did she return to her nest. The puppies had slept peacefully through all the commotion. Gnawing the bone, Lone Dog lay down beside them again.

"Aa-heh, you know how to take care of your pups," Kaya murmured to her. "I'll come visit you again soon."

"These willow branches must be carried down to the streamside," Kautsa said to Kaya and Brown Deer. "We need to build a larger sweat lodge." She handed the girls bundles of willows and took one on her own back. They walked downhill to the bank of the stream, where Kaya's mother was hollowing out a shallow pit in the gravel.

Each day, in winter as well as summer, Kaya and the other girls and women bathed in a sweat lodge. The men and boys did the same. Sweat baths relaxed them and made them clean and healthy in both body and spirit.

Kautsa set to work bending willow branches to

form a dome over the pit. Brown Deer and Kaya followed her lead, placing the branches so that they followed the four directions. The girls often helped to build a lodge like this one—they put up sweat lodges everywhere they stayed.

"Why are you gazing at the hills instead of doing your work, Daughter?" *Eetsa* asked Kaya. "Here, hold these willows so I can tie them together."

"I was thinking about Lone Dog," Kaya admitted to her mother. "I found the den she made in the hillside."

"It's too bad that dog doesn't come to live with us," Eetsa said. "She could help guard our camp."

"That's what the boys told me," Kaya said. "They teased me about Lone Dog. They said she thinks only of herself—like a magpie. Like *me*, they meant. They won't let me forget that nickname." Swan Circling had promised that the nickname wouldn't matter so much when Kaya got older—but that day seemed a long time coming.

Kautsa stood upright to rub her sore back with both hands. "Don't you remember the story of how dogs, wolves, and coyotes came to be as they are, Granddaughter?"

"I *think* I remember," Kaya said.

"It's an old, old story," Kautsa went on, weaving and tying willows into the framework again. "Four brothers were roaming the hills together. They were looking everywhere for food, because they were very hungry. When they spotted tepees in a valley, and smelled meat cooking, one of the brothers went down for a closer look. People gave him some meat to eat, and he went running back to the other three brothers and told them what had happened. 'If we go live with people, they'll feed us!' he said. 'We won't go hungry anymore.'

"But the other three brothers didn't agree with him. Two of them said, 'If people feed you, they'll expect you to work hard for them in return. We'd rather go off together and hunt for our own food.' The other brother said, 'I don't need people at all, and I don't need companions, either. I'll go hunt by myself.'

"So the first brother became a dog, and chose to eat our food and do our work," Kautsa continued. "The brother who went off to live all by himself became a coyote. And the two brothers who chose to stay together and hunt

coyote

225

as a team became wolves. Remember, Nimíipuu are like wolves. We're strong as individuals, but we always work together. That's how it should be."

"It's not natural for a dog to live all alone," Brown Deer chimed in.

"She's not all alone anymore," Kaya said. "She's had her pups, four of them, like the story. But they'll grow up to be dogs, not coyotes or wolves."

"Daughter, don't be too sure of that," Eetsa warned. She began laying rye grass thickly over the frame to create a covering.

"What do you mean?" Kaya asked.

"I mean I've had a glimpse of that dog," Eetsa said. "She looks to me as if she's got some wolf blood in her. That would be bad, you know. A dog obeys its master, but no man can be master to a wolf. If there's wolf blood in that dog, she might challenge her master. You said you thought Lone Dog had been beaten—maybe that's why."

"Aa-heh," Brown Deer agreed. "She might have bitten a child, or snapped at a baby. She could be dangerous." She laid more armloads of rye grass onto the framework.

226

"I think you should keep away from Lone Dog," Kautsa said firmly. "I think you should stay with the dogs we're sure we can trust."

Kaya felt a stab of dismay in her chest. "There's something I must ask you," she said in a low voice.

"Aa-heh, ask me anything," Kautsa replied. "I'll answer you as I think best."

"I hope you'll allow me to go on feeding Lone Dog," Kaya said carefully. "I gave her my promise that I would help her. Shouldn't I keep my word to a dog, as well as to a person?"

Kautsa picked up several fir boughs and laid them on the floor of the new sweat lodge. She didn't speak as she spread out the sweet-smelling boughs, and Kaya knew her grandmother was considering how best to answer. She held her breath.

Finally Kautsa straightened up and put her hands on her hips. "I think I understand you, Granddaughter. You want to be someone who always keeps her word, and that is right. You may go on feeding Lone Dog, as you promised you would. But I want you to be very, very careful for any sign that she might bite. Take my warning seriously, Granddaughter."

"I will," Kaya said quickly. She felt the ache in her chest ease.

"Tawts!" Kautsa's stern face softened and her dark eyes sparkled. "Now I'd like you to start piling up stones to use in our sweat lodge. Your mother named you for the first thing she saw after you were born—a woman arranging the stones for a sweat lodge like this one. That's your job today, Kaya'aton'my'. Do it well."

MORE WARNINGS

Every day now, more and more people arrived at the digging fields of the Palouse Prairie. This was a very good place for digging kouse. It was also a very good marketplace for traders. Friends from the north traded skins of bear, beaver, and mink from the mountains where they lived. Friends from the west traded their special cedar bark baskets. In return, Kaya's people traded deer and elk skins and the delicious dried salmon that everyone wanted. And every day Kaya kept a lookout for the arrival of Salish traders—she hoped they'd take Two Hawks back to his family. But, as others arrived, there was no sign of anyone from his country. Weren't they going to come to the Palouse this year?

Kaya visited Lone Dog and her pups every day. Often, as she approached the nest, she found Lone Dog sitting beside it, gazing in her direction. The dog seemed to be waiting for Kaya now. And sometimes it seemed to her that Lone Dog smiled as she ran the back of her hand along the dog's muzzle. "You know I want to be your friend, don't you?" Kaya asked quietly. And Lone Dog wagged her tail as if to say, *Aa-heh, I want to be your friend, too.*

One morning when Kaya was coming back from visiting Lone Dog and her pups, she heard the crier calling out that a new trader had arrived. He had come from far away, where the Big River flows into the sea. Quickly Kaya's grandfather dressed in his best hide shirt and leggings, wrapped his deerskin robe over his shoulder, and went to meet the man. Her grandfather was a shrewd

The Big River meets the sea. trader. He took with him camas cakes, buffalo hides, and bundles of tules, things that people from the coast would be sure to want.

All day Kaya looked forward to *Pi-lah-ka's* return. Her grandfather would have many stories

230

to tell, and he might have heard something about Speaking Rain. Slaves were sometimes traded to other tribes—could her sister have been traded to people from the west?

Pi-lah-ka didn't ride back for a long time. When he did, there were big packs tied onto his pack horses.

Two Hawks was helping Kaya's father coil up hemp rope for trading. Toe-ta and Two Hawks hurried with Kaya and the others to crowd around Pi-lah-ka. Toe-ta motioned for everyone to be seated. Then Pi-lah-ka opened up a pack and showed them what he'd gotten in trade with the man from the coast. First, he handed around a few special beads he'd gotten in exchange for a fine buffalo hide.

Kaya held one of the precious beads in her palm. It gleamed a deep blue, as if she held a piece of the evening sky. Oh, it was beautiful!

Kautsa held up another blue bead to the light. But instead of smiling, she frowned. "These beads are a lovely color," she said slowly. "But I think our bone and shell beads are best for our clothes. I like the old ways."

231

"For you, old is always better," Pi-lah-ka teased in his deep voice.

"Old ways are safe ways," Kautsa said stubbornly.

Pi-lah-ka took a very small pouch from his bundle and placed it in her lap. "Then here's something that will please you," he said.

Kautsa opened the pouch and lifted out a strand of glistening dentalium shells. As she held up the valuable shells for everyone to admire, her face lit up like sun shining after a storm. "You did well!" she said to Pi-lah-ka.

Brown Deer's face was alight, too. "Some of those shells would be beautiful on a dress!" she exclaimed.

"Aa-heh, on a dress for a young woman who hopes to marry soon!" Kautsa added with a smile. "These shells are just the decorations we need."

"The trader told of many beautiful new things," Pi-lah-ka insisted. "He told of cloth dyed the brightest red he'd ever seen."

Kautsa's eyes grew wide. "Where did he see bright red cloth?" she demanded.

232

"The trader said men in huge boats—men with pale, hairy faces—had such cloth," Pi-lah-ka admitted.

Kautsa folded her arms over her chest and drew herself up tall. "Listen to me. I want to tell you something," she said in her most serious voice.

Toe-ta gestured for everyone to pay attention. Kaya and Brown Deer put down the beads. The twins stopped whispering to Two Hawks and turned toward their grandmother to hear what she had to say.

When Kautsa had everyone's attention, she began to speak. "One night not long ago, I had a vision. In my vision, I was holding a piece of bright red cloth. Then, as I held it, the red cloth vanished, and my hand was red with blood!" She turned to her husband. "My vision is a warning—harm will come to us from the men with pale faces."

Kaya shivered. Her grandmother had told them her visions before. They were given to her so she could help protect The People.

Pi-lah-ka and Toe-ta nodded solemnly. They always respected Kautsa's visions.

But out of the corner of her eye, Kaya saw Two Hawks turn to look at the arrival of more new traders riding by with their many pack horses. After a moment, he jumped to his feet.

"Sit, Two Hawks," Toe-ta said sternly to him. "Pay attention to your elders."

Two Hawks sat again. Kaya could see that he was trying to be respectful, but he was almost too excited to hold still.

"Tell us," Pi-lah-ka said. "What's troubling you?"

"I think those traders are Salish," Two Hawks said. "They're hauling hide tepee covers like my people use, and I think I recognize that big black horse. Maybe those men know what's happened to my family. Can't we follow them?"

Toe-ta stood up right away. "Get your horse," he told Two Hawks. "Kaya, come with me on my horse. Let's see if these men are Salish." He put his hand on Two Hawks' shoulder. "If they are, we'll trade this boy to them for a worn-out moccasin. That would be an even trade, wouldn't it?"

Two Hawks grinned at Toe-ta's joke. Then his glance caught Kaya's, and his smile dimmed. She saw that he was very happy—and also a little sad. Of course, he wanted to get back to his home again. But now he felt at home with her people, too.

The traders were setting up their camp on the eastern edge of the clusters of tepees. Toe-ta signaled a greeting to them as they rode up. But Two Hawks reined in his horse and circled around behind Toe-ta as if he were feeling shy.

A young trader stepped forward, shading his eyes against the setting sun. Toe-ta threw him the words, *This boy is Salish. Do you know him?*

The trader squinted up at Two Hawks and beckoned for him to ride closer. After a moment, the trader shook his head—it had been a long time since Two Hawks was taken captive, and the man didn't recognize the boy.

But Two Hawks recognized him! He slipped off his horse and ran to the young man. Two Hawks threw his arms around the man's waist and pushed his forehead against his broad shoulder. Then they were both laughing and talking at the same time.

When Kaya and her father joined them, Two Hawks turned to them excitedly. "This is my uncle— my mother's brother!" he cried. "He says my parents are alive and well. My sisters are well, too. He'll take me home with him!"

"Tawts!" Toe-ta said. "Two Hawks, ask your

uncle to share a meal with us. We have much to talk over with him."

Eetsa prepared a meal of kouse mush, berries, and deer meat. Afterward, the men talked. Because Two Hawks spoke both Nimíipuu and the Salish language of his people, he acted as interpreter. Sometimes they used sign language, too.

Kaya closely followed what they said. Two Hawks told of his time as a slave of enemies from Buffalo Country, and of his and Kaya's escape, and how Toe-ta had found them on the Buffalo Trail. Young Uncle told of everything that had happened to Two Hawks's family while he was gone from them. Toe-ta made plans to join some Salish men to hunt buffalo in their country to the east, and they agreed to meet again the next day to trade with each other.

Then Toe-ta asked about Speaking Rain. Had Young Uncle seen or heard of his little daughter, a blind girl? She'd been a captive, too, but she might have escaped, or been traded. Was there any news of her?

Young Uncle frowned sadly. *I have not heard of the girl you describe*, he said with his hands.

Kaya clasped her hands tightly to keep from crying. But now Two Hawks turned to look her in the eye. "You helped me and brought me to my family," he said to her. "I give my word that I'll try to find your sister and bring her to you."

Kaya blinked back her unshed tears. Two Hawks was her friend after all. "*Katsee-yow-yow*," she said to him gratefully.

Then Two Hawks and Young Uncle spoke together for a little while. Two Hawks turned to Toe-ta. "My uncle gives you his pledge, too," he said. "When it's time for salmon fishing at Celilo Falls, some of my people will join your people there. Maybe we'll have news of your daughter then."

Toe-ta nodded. He threw Young Uncle the words, *Thank you for your help.*

Kaya glanced at her mother. Eetsa sat with her head bowed, her lips pressed tightly together. Kaya saw the sadness in her father's face, too. She understood that to lose a child was a terrible thing. And to lose a sister was terrible as well.

Two Hawks leaned toward Kaya. "I asked my uncle about your horse with the star on her forehead," he said. "He hasn't seen your horse, but we'll be on the lookout."

"Katsee-yow-yow," Kaya murmured a second time. Then she got to her feet and moved away from the others.

All the bad news she'd heard tore at her heart, and soon Two Hawks would be leaving, too. Where could she find comfort? She knelt beside her sleeping place and slipped Speaking Rain's buckskin doll out of her pack. As she clutched the doll to her chest, she thought of Lone Dog. She remembered how Lone Dog had licked Kaya's hands when she'd visited her that morning. So Kaya tucked the doll away again, put some scraps of food into her bag, and headed toward the hillside where Lone Dog had her den.

As Kaya came near the den, she called softly, "Here I am, girl, I'm back again." She saw Lone Dog's gold eyes watching her, then the pale tip of her wagging tail. Kaya knelt and parted the grass in front of the nest. The puppies were sleeping in a heap by their mother's side. Lone Dog lifted her head, pricked her ears, and gazed long and hard into Kaya's eyes.

"Are you telling me you know I'm sad?" Kaya asked the dog softly. She placed the food into the nest, and Lone Dog ate without getting to her feet, as if she didn't want to disturb her sleeping pups.

After Lone Dog had eaten, Kaya leaned closer and stroked the dog's ears and the soft fur under her jaw. She sank her fingers into the thick coat on her back and scratched. "You always let me touch you now," she said to Lone Dog. "Would you let me touch your puppies? You know I won't hurt them. I'm their friend, too."

Moving slowly, Kaya gently stroked the largest pup's warm head with her fingertip. Would Lone Dog growl her away? Panting lightly, Lone Dog looked on calmly.

Then, as Kaya watched, the pup's eyelids parted for the first time. His milky-blue eyes seemed to be looking right at Kaya, but she knew he was too young to see her yet.

That unseeing gaze reminded Kaya of her blind sister's, and she remembered the lullaby she and Speaking Rain loved so well. "*Ha no nee, ha no nee,*" she sang softly to the puppy. "Here's my precious one, my own, dear little precious one."

As Kaya sang, the other puppies began to stir and whimper, crawling against their mother, wanting more milk. Kaya watched the peaceful scene, the ache in her heart easing. She'd been right to come here.

Crack! A stick broke. Then the long grass bent down and rose again.

Kaya sat up quickly. The twins! She could see the tops of their dark heads in the grass. They were sneaking up the hill, playing hunters with their small bows and arrows.

"Boys!" she hissed. "Stay away! This dog might think you'll hurt her puppies and—"

Wing Feather jumped to his feet. "Puppies!" he cried.

Sparrow sprang upright, too. "Can we see them?" he asked.

Before Kaya could stop them, the boys ran up the slope and fell to their knees beside her. "Keep back!" she said. "Lone Dog doesn't know you!" She held out her arm to keep the boys away from the nest, and they settled down on their heels, gazing wide-eyed at the pups.

"She always protects her puppies," Kaya told

"Ha no nee, ha no nee," Kaya sang softly to the puppy.

the boys. "I'm not sure she'll trust you." If they came too close, would the dog threaten them with a growl, or lunge at them, as she had at Snow Paws?

But Lone Dog didn't seem at all worried by the little boys. Her gaze took them in, then returned to Kaya. Brown Deer had said Lone Dog might have bitten a child or nipped at a baby. *Surely Brown Deer is wrong*, Kaya thought. *Lone Dog knows the twins are no danger to her pups.*

Sparrow was inching closer to the nest. He reached out toward one of the pups, but Kaya caught his hand in hers. "You mustn't touch them," she said firmly.

"Why not?" Wing Feather asked. "Dogs like to be petted."

Kaya thought for a moment. Lone Dog wasn't like the other dogs. Kaya had come to trust Lone Dog, but others thought she might be dangerous, and Kaya couldn't prove that they were wrong. Her grandmother had warned her to be cautious around the dog—and Kaya must take good care of her little brothers, no matter what.

"Listen to me. I want to tell you something," she said to the twins. She hoped her voice sounded like her grandmother's when she commanded attention.

The twins looked up at her right away.

"Lone Dog trusts me," Kaya said. "That's why she lets you two near her puppies. But I'm not sure what she'd do if I weren't with you. To be safe, you mustn't come here by yourselves. Do you hear my warning?" She looked right into their eyes.

After a moment, the little boys nodded.

"Tawts!" she said to them. "Don't forget what I told you. Now come with me. We need to get back to camp."

DANGER FOR THE PUPS

Each morning when Kaya awoke, she thought first of Lone Dog. She dressed and left the tepee even before her grandmother began to sing her morning prayers. Kaya loved spending time with the puppies before the work of the day began.

"Tawts-may-we, Lone Dog!" Kaya called softly as she approached the den in the early mist. "It's me again!" Every day a surprise awaited her as the puppies grew and changed.

After the pups had opened their eyes, they learned to use their stubby legs to creep about. Once they could walk around their den, they began sniffing it, too—and sniffing each other. Then their

244

baby teeth began to show, and chewing on one
another's ears and paws became their pastime. And
soon after they began to chew, their hearing
developed. Now, as Kaya approached them, the
puppies turned toward her voice. The largest pup,
which she called *Tatlo* because he still made
her think of a ground squirrel, peeked
over the side of the nest.

"Are you glad to see me?" Kaya
asked Lone Dog, who lay among her
puppies. Lone Dog's tail wagged as Kaya patted her
and then stroked Tatlo's soft little ears.

As Kaya stroked the three other pups, Lone Dog
jumped out of the nest and took the bone Kaya had
brought her. She carried it off a short way and lay
down to chew on it. She was leaving her puppies
more and more often, though she still stayed nearby
to protect them.

Of course, the puppies didn't like their mother
leaving them, even for a little while. They yipped
and pawed the sides of the nest, trying to call her
back to them. Enjoying her bone, Lone Dog ignored
their whimpers and cries.

"Hush, hush," Kaya crooned to them. "Your

mother needs a rest. She'll come to you soon enough."

With his paws on the edge of the nest, Tatlo watched Lone Dog contentedly munch the bone. The pup impatiently scratched harder and harder, wanting to follow her. Then he got his hind feet going, too, and managed to creep higher. For a moment he teetered on the edge of the nest, then thrust himself over and tumbled out. His high-pitched yelp brought Lone Dog to his side. She licked her startled pup to calm him.

Tatlo's wail excited the other pups to more frantic yipping. Kaya knew that very soon they'd learn how to follow their brother out of the nest. "How will you take care of the pups when they can roam about?" Kaya mused aloud.

Lone Dog's yellow eyes gazed into hers. She seemed to be saying, *I'll teach them to come back to this safe place if there's trouble.*

Kaya scratched Lone Dog behind her ears. "But what if a coyote trails them?" she asked. "What if a bear finds your den?"

Lone Dog nudged Tatlo back into the nest, then jumped in after him. The pups swarmed over their mother as she lay down again to nurse them. She rested on her side, her eyes still on Kaya. She seemed to be saying, *They'll obey me. Wait, you'll see.*

"I'd like to wait," Kaya said. "But I have to join the others now. I'll come back as soon as I can."

Kaya ran all the way to the stream, where the women and girls were splashing in the icy water before taking their morning sweat bath. Beside the sweat lodge, a fire burned on the pile of stones, heating them red-hot. Eetsa was pushing some glowing stones into the lodge to warm it while the others swam. Kaya undressed and joined them.

When everyone had crowded into the dimly lit lodge, Eetsa pulled a deerskin over the doorway. Then she sprinkled cold water onto the heated stones. They sizzled and popped, sending up a cloud of steam. The women and girls joined in a song of thanks and praise to Grandfather Sweat Lodge for helping them and guarding them against illness. Hugging her knees, Kaya sat beside her grandmother.

"I was looking for you, Granddaughter," Kautsa said. "Where were you?" She rubbed her shoulders

and arms with the soft tips of the fir branches that
covered the floor.

"I went to see the puppies again," Kaya said.
Already she felt sweat running off her face and down
her back.

"How is the lone dog behaving now?" Kaya's
grandmother asked, handing her a handful of the
sweet-smelling fir to scrub herself.

"She likes me to visit her," Kaya murmured.
Although her grandmother had given her permission
to feed Lone Dog, Kaya knew she didn't really trust
the dog. "Her pups are getting big and fat."

"Tawts," Kautsa said. "Soon she'll start to wean them. Then they'll join our dog pack—if the lone dog lets them."

Kaya leaned closer to her grandmother. "Sometimes Lone Dog seems to be talking to me with her eyes," she whispered. "Do you believe me?"

"Aa-heh!" Kautsa said right away. "I believe you. Animals talk to us in many, many ways."

"But I mean she really *speaks* to me, too," Kaya whispered even more softly.

Kautsa sat with her head bent, silently breathing in the cleansing steam. After a time, she said, "I'm thinking about my mother. When she was a girl, she received a wolf spirit, and after that she could talk with wolves. One day, when she was very old, a wolf trotted along the trail where she was picking berries. The wolf was sad because her puppies had died. My mother was very sorry for the wolf. She asked the wolf if she could help her. The wolf told her that she was leaving the mountains, and refused help. But then she gave my mother the gift of her wolf power. That power made my mother even stronger."

"The wolf spoke to her?" Kaya asked. "Like Lone Dog speaks to me?"

249

"All creatures have wisdom to share with us," Kautsa said. "Soon you'll prepare for your vision quest, and I hope you'll receive a *wyakin* of your own. If you do, you must always listen closely to what it tells you."

"Aa-heh!" Kaya said. With all her heart, she hoped to be ready for her vision quest. Would she receive wolf power, as her great-grandmother had? As Kaya tried to imagine that, Eetsa pulled aside the deerskin covering the door and signaled everyone to leave the steamy lodge and plunge into the stream again.

"You're too old to quarrel like this!" Kaya said to the twins. "Listen to me and do as I say!" She held Wing Feather by one hand and Sparrow by the other. The little boys had been wrestling playfully on the hillside when their game suddenly became too rough.

Sparrow tried to pull his hand from her grasp.

Wing Feather scowled. "We lost most of our arrows," he said. "If you make us some more, I promise we won't fight over them."

"Aa-heh," Kaya said. "If you sit there quietly, I'll make more arrows for you." She sighed as she cut some straight twigs from an elderberry bush. Her little brothers were full of energy and full of tricks. Eetsa told Kaya to take care of them even more often now that she couldn't dig roots with the other girls and women.

But the twins didn't pay enough attention to Kaya's warnings. Kaya wished she could teach the boys to obey her as easily as Lone Dog had taught her pups. Usually it took the dog no more than a soft growl or a shake to bring her troublesome pups in line again.

Like the twins, the pups romped and wrestled and tugged and chased one another all day. But sometimes Lone Dog gave a special growl that meant, *Take cover!* Then they tumbled back into the den, where they were safe from bobcats, or an eagle hovering overhead. *She's taught her pups well,* Kaya thought as she finished cutting notches in the arrows.

"Here, boys," Kaya said. "I've made two arrows for each of you. You can go hunting again."

Wing Feather had fallen asleep on the soft grass, his hand tucked into his baby moccasin, which he always kept with him. He rolled onto his back and rubbed his eyes with it. "Katsee-yow-yow!" he said, reaching for the little arrows.

Kaya looked around for Sparrow. He'd been lying on his stomach by his brother, but now he was nowhere to be seen.

"Is that bothersome boy hiding from me again?" Kaya asked Wing Feather. "I have to find him. Do you know which way he might have gone?"

Wing Feather's lower lip stuck out. "He should have waited for me. I told him we couldn't visit the puppies without you, but he—"

Puppies! Kaya's pulse sped. She imagined Sparrow sneaking up on Lone Dog's den, determined to touch the pups. She didn't believe that Lone Dog would hurt the boy, but she couldn't be certain. She knew only that she had to get to her brother as fast as she could. "Come on!" she said. She grabbed Wing Feather's hand and started running.

Kaya and her little brother rushed down the path alongside the stream. Then they turned and ran up the long, steep hillside. Lone Dog's den was on the far side of the hill, hidden from view by underbrush.

Kaya paused on the crest of the hill to look for

Sparrow. In a moment, she saw him coming around the base of the hill below her. He was running as silently as a shadow, as he'd been taught. He was going to get to the den before she could. Would Lone Dog chase him away with a nip?

Kaya could barely make out the entrance of the den. Something dark moved there, but it didn't look like a dog. Then Kaya realized that a bear was digging at the opening of the den, trying to get at the hidden puppies! And, running uphill, Sparrow wouldn't be able to see the bear until he'd reached the clearing!

"Stay here!" Kaya commanded Wing Feather, and she took off racing for the den as fast as she could. But it was like running in a bad dream—her feet felt as if they were weighted with stones. She didn't shout for Sparrow to stay back because she didn't want to startle the bear—if it turned on her little brother, it could kill him with a single swipe of its sharp claws!

Then the bear heard Sparrow coming. It swung around and lumbered away from the den, its huge head swaying, its jaws wide. Just at that moment,

Sparrow burst into the clearing. He saw the bear and skidded to a halt. Then he scrambled toward the den as if he wanted to crawl into it with the puppies. But there was no way for him to hide from the bear, which was heading right for him!

A SAD PARTING

A pale streak flew by Kaya and plunged down the hill toward the den—it was Lone Dog! She was barking ferociously with alarm, her teeth bared and her hackles raised. With a long leap, she hurled herself down at the bear. She snapped viciously at its heels and lunged at its flanks. The bear rose onto its hind legs, swatting at Lone Dog, trying to grab her with its claws. There was blood on Lone Dog's back and shoulders, but she kept up her fierce attack. She was determined to protect her pups—and Sparrow—even if it meant her life.

Kaya ran into the clearing. She yelled as loudly as she could, waving her arms over her head.

The bear looked her way. It went down on all fours again and backed off a little, confused by the noise. Then it chose not to fight. As it turned away, Lone Dog continued to bite at its heels, moving it along until it had disappeared into the thick underbrush and was gone. Still barking, Lone Dog dashed back to the den and her puppies.

Kaya ran to Sparrow. Hugging himself, he crouched against the hillside. He was crying. Kaya threw her arms around her little brother and held him close.

Wing Feather came leaping down the slope. "I saw it all!" he called out as he came. "Lone Dog fought just like a wolf! She saved her puppies, and she saved Sparrow, too!"

"Aa-heh, you're safe now!" Kaya tipped up Sparrow's chin so she could look him in the eye. "But if it hadn't been for Lone Dog, you wouldn't have had a chance against that bear. You owe your life to a very brave dog."

A few days later, Kaya piled some deerskins onto a travois and hitched it to the gray horse.

"You owe your life to a very brave dog," Kaya told Sparrow.

The gentle gray's hoof was healed, and she accepted the travois as if she'd always pulled one—Kaya's training had been good. As Kaya rode out to the dog den on the hillside, she considered her plan. Lone Dog had weaned her pups, and Kaya knew they were at an age when they should get accustomed to other dogs and to people, too. She thought that if she took the pups to the village with her, maybe she could lure Lone Dog to follow. She hoped Lone Dog would live by their tepee and be her special dog now.

The pups were prancing about in front of the den. Tatlo had a small bone in his mouth, and the other three pups were chasing after him, trying to get it. When his little sister managed to pry it away, Tatlo rolled her onto her back and buried his face in her neck, growling. She pawed at Tatlo's face. They seemed to be fighting, but their tails were wagging.

Lone Dog lay on the hillside above the den, her head resting on her paws. With the help of a poultice of *wapalwaapal* that Kaya had made, her wounds were healing well. When Kaya slid off the horse, Lone Dog got to her feet and stretched. Then she came to lean affectionately against Kaya's legs. Kaya

258

scratched her back just above her tail. "Your pups are growing fast, aren't they?" Kaya said to her friend. "Now they can become part of our dog pack."

Lone Dog looked toward her pups wrestling for the bone, then back at Kaya. Would this solitary dog allow her pups to live among people?

"And I hope you'll come to live with me, too," Kaya said softly.

Lone Dog looked away. After a moment, she went back to the hillside and lay down again. She seemed to be thinking over what Kaya had said.

Kaya rounded up the puppies and put them into the makeshift nest on the travois. They curled up together, as if pleased to be going on a ride. Kaya mounted the horse and called, "Come, Lone Dog! Come!" Hoping that Lone Dog would follow, she began to ride slowly toward the path that led to the village. When she glanced over her shoulder, Lone Dog was trotting down the hillside to follow them.

But Kaya's worries were far from over. Everyone trusted Lone Dog since she'd saved Sparrow, but Kaya wasn't sure what Snow Paws would do when he saw Lone Dog approach the village. Would he still think she was a danger? In an all-out fight, he could injure or kill her. As Kaya rode toward the tepees, she watched warily for the big black dog.

Soon Snow Paws came barking loudly to confront Lone Dog. He took a stand near the tepees and set himself to defend the village.

Kautsa was making finger cakes with some other women. "Snow Paws, go!" she commanded the dog. "Go!" she repeated even more loudly. "Lone Dog belongs here now!"

Snow Paws stopped barking, but he approached Lone Dog slowly on stiff legs. Lone Dog stood perfectly still, her ears slightly back—she was in his territory now. He sniffed her, then allowed her to sniff him in return. When he walked back to the other dogs, Kaya knew he had accepted Lone Dog as one of the pack. Oh, she hoped Lone Dog would stay with her here in the village!

Kautsa was stringing dried roots and dried kouse cakes on hemp cord so they could be carried easily when it was time to travel again. Kaya worked at her grandmother's side, cutting the cord into even lengths and handing the pieces to her as she needed them.

The season for digging roots here was coming
to an end. Soon everyone would leave the
Palouse Prairie and journey to the meadows
to dig camas there. Kaya knew the camas
plants were already in bloom, their deep
blue flowers making the meadows look like
vast, shimmering lakes. And soon it would
be time for the spring salmon runs, too.
Kaya loved to travel, but now she worried
that Lone Dog might not follow her when they
broke camp, although her pups had joined the
dog pack.

camas plant

Lone Dog didn't seem to be at ease around
people or the other dogs. When Kaya was in the
camp, Lone Dog stayed near her side. But when
Kaya left the camp for wood or water, Lone Dog
ran off by herself into the hills, sometimes staying
away all night.

"Is something troubling you, Granddaughter?"
Kautsa asked. She held out her hand for another
piece of cord.

"Aa-heh," Kaya admitted. "Do you remember I
told you that Lone Dog sometimes speaks to me?"

"What does Lone Dog tell you these days?" Kautsa asked.

"I think she's saying that she's going to leave us," Kaya said. "She's not meant to be a village dog."

Kautsa nodded. "It's true that she's different from our other dogs. Perhaps it's her nature to live alone."

"But I don't want her to leave me!" Kaya burst out. "I want her to be my dog always!"

Kautsa thought for a while. Then she picked up the ball of hemp cord and held it out to Kaya. "You could tie this rope around her neck so she couldn't run off. Have you thought of doing that?"

Kaya frowned in concentration. She tried to think what Swan Circling would do. "If I tied up Lone Dog, she'd be the same as a captive, wouldn't she?" she asked miserably. "The enemies from Buffalo Country tied me up every night. The rope kept me from running away, but I was desperate to escape. Lone Dog would feel the same way. I couldn't do that to her. I couldn't!"

Her grandmother put her warm hand on Kaya's shoulder. "Listen to me. I have something to tell you."

Kaya looked up at her grandmother, who was gazing at her with love and concern. "I know it will be hard for you to let Lone Dog go her own way," Kautsa said thoughtfully. "But, as you said yourself, someone who has been a captive understands the powerful need to be free. Can you respect what's best for her?"

Kaya bit her lip. She didn't want to imagine her life without Lone Dog in it.

On the morning the women began to pack up all their belongings for the journey to the camas meadows, Kaya went looking for Lone Dog. She hadn't seen the dog since the men had rounded up the horses the day before and brought them to camp to be loaded for the trip. Kaya looked all around the camp, calling her name. Where was she? Was she up there on the ridge? Kaya ran up to the top, then over the hill to the abandoned den on the far side. She saw the striped face of a badger that had taken over the empty den. But Lone Dog was nowhere to be seen.

Kaya remembered that sometimes

Lone Dog had been gone for longer than this. But by the time the women had rolled up all the tule mats and stashed the tepee poles to be used the next year, Lone Dog was still missing.

Raven came by, leading some pack horses. "I hear your dog's run off," he said, but he didn't sound pleased about it.

"She isn't *my* dog," Kaya said, as firmly as she could. "She belongs to herself. Anyway, she might follow us later." But in her heart, Kaya knew that Lone Dog had gone on her way—alone—as she needed to be.

Don't cry! Kaya told herself. *Keep good thoughts!* But her throat was tight with tears.

As Kaya was helping the twins climb onto a travois, she felt a tug at the hem of her dress. It was Tatlo, pulling at her skirt and begging to play.

When Kaya ignored him, he began to sniff the bundles piled up near the horses. She heard him give his puppy growl, then saw him drag something from one of the bundles. With another growl, he started shaking what he'd found—it was Speaking Rain's doll!

"Tatlo, that's not a toy for you!" Kaya cried.

"Bring that to me!" She knew if she chased him, he'd run away from her with the precious doll. So she sat on the ground to encourage him to come closer. He paused, his head cocked. Then he trotted to her and dropped the doll into her lap, his whole body wiggling as if he knew he'd done something good.

"Tawts, Tatlo!" Kaya said. She pushed the doll behind her and lifted the pup onto her lap. "Are you telling me you're going to help me find my sister someday?" she asked him.

Tatlo put his paws on her shoulders and looked at her with his amber eyes. Then he nipped at her braids and licked her cheek and her chin. Kaya couldn't help but laugh as the rough little tongue tickled her face.

"Jump down, now," Kaya told him. But instead of jumping down, Tatlo turned around and around until he'd curled up in her lap. As soon as he laid his head on Kaya's legs, he was asleep.

Kaya gently stroked the sleeping puppy. His muzzle was pale, like Lone Dog's, and his big paws meant he'd grow to be large, like her. "I think your mother sent you to be my dog now," Kaya whispered to him. "We have a long, long way to travel, and I'll be very glad to have you with me."

TO MY STEPDAUGHTER BETSY,
WITH LOVE

Kaya

SHOWS THE WAY

THE SOUND
OF THE FALLS

Long before Kaya could see the waterfalls on the river ahead, she began to hear their voices. She and her family were riding over hot, dry plains, so the murmur of running water was a sweet promise. But as they rode closer to the river, that murmur grew into a powerful song, like many men drumming. When the riders crested the last hill and looked down at the shining river, Kaya saw the falls plunging over black cliffs. Even at this distance the falls roared like thunder. The earth seemed to tremble.

Kaya's little brother Wing Feather was seated behind Kaya on the chestnut horse. He held her tightly around the waist. "Is that a monster roaring?" he asked in a small voice.

Kaya patted his leg. "That's the sound of the falls you hear," she said. "Remember when we stayed here last summer? Remember how you and Sparrow played all day with your cousins, and there were games and races every night? And remember how many salmon gave themselves to all the fishermen?"

Wing Feather only hugged her more tightly, one hand tucked into his baby moccasin. Kaya knew he was trying to be strong, but the roar of Celilo Falls frightened many children.

"The water sounds angry!" Sparrow said. He was riding behind Kaya's older sister, Brown Deer.

"But the river's our friend, and you'll soon get used to its roar," Brown Deer said. Her voice was calm, but her cheeks were flushed with excitement. Kaya knew her sister was eager to meet family and friends here at the falls. Brown Deer would also meet Cut Cheek again, whom she hoped to marry.

Kaya's father, who rode ahead, signaled for everyone to halt before beginning the steep descent from the bluffs into the valley. He and other men and women dismounted and began checking the heavy packs to make sure they were tied tightly and wouldn't slip and injure a horse or rider.

Kaya dismounted and gazed down at the vast river valley. Stony islands clustered in the river, white water sweeping around them. Kaya saw large horse herds grazing on the flatlands. Many fishing platforms of sticks lashed together had been built out over the water. Hundreds of tepees and lodges lined both shores as far upstream and downstream as she could see. The villages were those of many different peoples—some who lived on the river all year and others who visited from the plains, the mountains, and the ocean to fish and trade. Kaya's band, and many other bands of *Nimíipuu*, were

273

joining them for the yearly return of salmon up the Big River.

Kaya shaded her eyes and peered at the mist that rose like thick smoke from the waterfalls. She saw bright rainbows arching low over the falls, and her heart lifted. Rainbows were good signs. She hoped to meet up with her friend Two Hawks here at the falls. He'd said that when they met again, he might have good news of Kaya's sister, Speaking Rain. When she and Two Hawks had escaped from their enemies, they'd had to leave Speaking Rain behind.

But Kaya knew that Two Hawks might be bringing bad news instead. He might have learned that Speaking Rain had been abandoned by their captors—or injured, or lost. For how could a blind girl get along without someone to care for her?

As if Tatlo sensed Kaya's troubled thoughts, the pup bounded up to her, his pink tongue hanging out. He was growing fast, and his legs were getting long. Kaya bent and put her face against his soft ear. "You'll help me find my sister, won't you?" she whispered to him. He licked her hand, his tail wagging in circles, as if he were saying, *I'll try.*

274

Kaya's grandmother climbed off her horse and began adjusting the travois on a pack horse. When *Kautsa* saw the twins' worried frowns, her lined face softened. *"Aa-heh,* the falls are hissing and raging, boys," she said, "but that's because they're so steep and so wide. Don't you remember how Coyote made them for us?" She turned to Kaya. "Would you comfort your brothers with that story while I fix this travois?"

"Aa-heh," Kaya said quickly. Each day she reminded herself to do her very best. She wanted to be trustworthy like her friend Swan Circling, the warrior woman who'd given Kaya her name to use when she was older.

Wing Feather and Sparrow slid off the horses. "Tell about Coyote!" Sparrow begged her.

"Tell about his tricks!" Wing Feather added. Everyone loved stories about Coyote, who was always playing tricks and teaching lessons at the same time.

Kaya sat with the twins on a travois, and Tatlo, panting, lay down in the shade at their feet. "One day Coyote was coming up the river," she began. "And in those long-ago days the river was calm, because the River People had dammed it up—they wanted to

275

keep all the salmon for themselves. Coyote was hot and tired, like we are, and he decided to swim in the cool water. He swam around until he saw five beautiful river girls on the shore. He saw a chance to play a trick on the River People, so he turned himself into a baby and came floating over the water toward the girls."

"I remember what Coyote did then!" Wing Feather cried. "He bawled like a baby—*Wah! Wah!*—to get the girls' attention!"

"Aa-heh," Kaya said. "He cried, and the girls quickly swam out to pull him from the water. 'What a precious baby!' they said. But the youngest sister wasn't fooled. 'Watch out!' she said. 'That's no baby. That's Coyote!' The baby put out his lower lip as if he was about to cry again. 'Don't tease him,' the other girls said. 'Let's take him home with us.'

"The girls fed the baby and took care of him, and he grew fast. One day he spilled a cup of water. 'Get me more water!' he demanded. The youngest sister, who still didn't trust the baby, said, 'Let's make him get water himself.' So the baby began to crawl toward the river. When he was out of sight, he jumped up and ran. 'He certainly moves fast!' one of the girls said. The youngest sister said, 'That's because he's Coyote!'

"I know what happened next!" Sparrow cried. "Coyote broke down the fish dam that the River People had made!"

"Aa-heh, Coyote swam up to their fish dam and tore it down, pulling out all the stones so the water rushed free over the falls," Kaya continued. "He jumped up and down on the stones and shouted gleefully, 'Look, your fish dam is broken!' The girls saw that it was so. The youngest sister said, 'I told you he was Coyote!'

"Coyote said to them, 'You selfishly kept all the salmon behind your dam. But now the salmon will be able to swim upstream to spawn. People will be happy because they can catch the fish, and they'll thank me for giving them food.' And that's how Celilo Falls came to be, and why salmon can swim up all the rivers and streams now," Kaya finished.

"Did Coyote really make those waterfalls?" Sparrow asked, pointing at the water rushing over black stones. Because he was thinking about the story, he was no longer frightened.

"You can see for yourself that the fish dam's not

there anymore," Kaya said with a smile. "And who else but Coyote could have knocked it down so that the salmon could swim upstream?"

She scratched Tatlo behind his ears and gazed at the distant hills across the river. Would Two Hawks and his people soon be riding over those hills? Would she be strong no matter what news he brought of Speaking Rain? And what of her beloved horse— would she discover Steps High in one of the many horse herds here at the falls?

"*Katsee-yow-yow* for telling the story," Kautsa said. "Come along now. We're ready to move on."

After Kaya and the others greeted friends and relatives, the women set up their tepees and unpacked their goods. Then *Eetsa* gave Kaya permission to join the other girls, all of whom were like cousins to her. Some girls had gathered on a flat stretch of ground to play a stickball game called Shinny. They'd formed two teams and were chasing a rawhide ball, hitting it to each other with curved sticks. As Kaya walked up, several of the girls waved to her.

"Play on our side, Kaya!" Little Fawn called to her. "You're a fast runner!"

"Play on our side!" Rabbit called. "Magpies fly fast!"

Magpie, again! As Kaya picked up a shinny stick, she tried to shrug off that awful nickname she'd gotten when she had neglected her brothers and all the children had been switched because of her forgetfulness. And as soon as she was running down the field with the others, she forgot about everything except the game. The girls batted the ball and passed it to each other, trying to hit it between two branches stuck in the ground at each end of the playing field. Some dogs, barking wildly, ran along with them.

Little Fawn knocked the ball to Kaya, and she raced down the field with it, Tatlo right at her heels. But when other girls charged after Kaya, Tatlo got caught in the middle of the action. Someone stepped on his paw, and, with a yelp, he tumbled head over heels. Kaya stopped playing and led her pup to the sidelines.

Rabbit was there, tying her moccasins more tightly. *"Tawts may-we,* cousin!" she greeted Kaya.

Little Fawn knocked the ball to Kaya,
and she raced down the field with it, Tatlo right at her heels.

"Tawts may-we! Have you been here at the river long?" Kaya stroked Tatlo's ears as she caught her breath.

"Not long," Rabbit said. "Only for two sleeps."

"I want to find Two Hawks," Kaya said. "Have you seen him?"

"Raven went looking for him yesterday," Rabbit said. "He told us that no Salish people have come here yet. They don't always make the long journey, you know."

"I know," Kaya admitted. Two Hawks had given his promise, but his people might have made different plans. Her heart sank when she thought that he might not be able to bring her news of Speaking Rain after all.

"Your pup runs fast," Rabbit said, holding out her hand for Tatlo to sniff. "But I think his rear legs run faster than his front legs!"

"Aa-heh," Kaya said. "I'm going to tie him by our tepee so he won't get trampled."

"Come back quickly!" Rabbit called after her.

When Kaya approached her tepee, an elderly, gray-haired woman Kaya didn't recognize was carrying her belongings inside. Brown Deer knelt by a travois, untying more rolls of tule mats. She beckoned for Kaya to come close. "Cut Cheek's parents have sent one of his aunts to live with us for a while," she said in a low voice. "Crane Song's here to make sure I'm a strong worker and will make a good wife for Cut Cheek." She looked pleased, but she seemed nervous as well.

"Everyone knows you're a strong worker!" Kaya assured her sister, who was so dutiful and so good.

Brown Deer shook her head. "A woman has to prove her worth," she said softly.

"You'll be a fine wife for Cut Cheek. His aunt will see that right away," Kaya insisted. She tied one end of a piece of cord around Tatlo's neck and the other end to one of the tepee stakes.

Brown Deer frowned. "Tie Tatlo farther away, will you? Sometimes he chews on the tepee coverings, and I won't have time to look after him."

Kaya led Tatlo to a stack of tepee poles and tied him there. He sat with his ears drooping, whining as if he were being punished.

"Katsee-yow-yow, Kaya," Brown Deer said gratefully. She picked up the mats and hurried into the tepee, where Crane Song waited for her.

Kaya patted Tatlo on his rump. "Don't whine," she told him. "I'll be back for you soon."

At the beginning of each new run of salmon, everyone honored and thanked the fish with a feast. Kautsa and the other women built big, slow-burning fires to roast the salmon. While the fish cooked under the open sky, the women spread rows of tule mats down the center of a lodge large enough to seat all their family and friends. Kaya stood with the other girls and women across from the men and boys while her grandfather led them in prayer.

"*Hun-ya-wat* made this earth," *Pi-lah-ka* said. "He made all living things on the earth, in the water, and in the sky. He made Nimíipuu and all peoples. He created food for all His creatures. We respect and give thanks for His creations."

All the people took a sip of water to purify their bodies before they accepted the gifts from the Creator. After everyone had taken a sip of the cold river water, each person took a tiny bite of salmon, giving thanks before beginning the rest of the meal.

The men and boys served the roasted meat they'd

provided. The women and girls brought forward the foods they'd gathered. With the others, Kaya placed bowls filled with roots and berries on the mats. Then the women brought large wooden bowls of the cooked salmon into the lodge.

Kaya watched Brown Deer moving quickly and quietly along the mats. It was a great honor to feed the others, and Brown Deer kept her eyes downcast, even when she offered Cut Cheek a bowl. But her face reddened slightly when he took it from her.

Surely Crane Song will see what a fine woman Brown Deer is, Kaya thought. And soon Cut Cheek would prove his worth by fishing well and bravely with the other men. If their parents approved, the couple could marry in the autumn.

That thought made Kaya's heart glad—and also sad. She wanted Brown Deer to marry Cut Cheek, but she was sad to think of her sister leaving their family. She'd lost one sister when she'd had to leave Speaking Rain with the enemies. Now she felt she might be losing her other sister as well.

CHAPTER
TWO
—
DANGEROUS
CROSSING!

When Kaya followed her mother and
the other women to the riverbank the
next morning, the men and boys were
already fishing. Some spearfished from rocky
outcroppings along the shore. Others stood on
sturdy poles lashed together to make platforms built
out over the falls. They held their long-handled dip
nets down into the crashing waters. When a
salmon leaped into a dip net, the force of the
current closed the net around it. But it took
great strength to lift a large, struggling fish, and
if a man was pulled into the rushing water, he
could be swept over the falls and drowned. For
safety, the men tied lines around their waists and

secured the lines to rocks. Kaya shivered as she saw
Toe-ta and the others leaning over the raging waters.

The men's work was difficult and dangerous,
but the women and girls worked hard, too. All
day Kaya helped carry the heavy salmon the men
caught to the women who cleaned the fish and
sliced them into thin strips. Other women hung
the strips on racks, to be dried by the sun and
wind. By the end of the day, Kaya's hands, arms,
and back ached.

As Kaya walked with Kautsa to their village
upstream above the falls, she wiped her eyes with
a handful of soft grass. "The wind makes my eyes
sting," she said.

"Aa-heh," Kautsa said, wiping her own eyes.
"The wind blowing up the gorge is a powerful force!
But it's another gift from Hun-ya-wat. With so much
wind, fish dry very quickly. There's no need to build
drying fires here at the falls."

Kaya looked back down the valley at the
villages that crowded the shore. "I've been watching
for Salish people to arrive," she said. "Two Hawks
might come with them."

"They could be on the other side of the river,"

Kautsa said. "Two women came across today in a canoe to trade with us. I don't speak their language, but Crane Song knows it. The traders told her that newcomers from the north were putting up tepees over there."

Kaya felt a shiver of hope. "Did they say anything about a blind girl?"

"About our Speaking Rain?" Kautsa asked. "If they had, I'd have taken a canoe to see for myself! But they said only that the newcomers had hide-covered tepees, not like ours."

"Two Hawks's people have hide tepees!" Kaya said. "Couldn't I cross the river with the traders and see who the newcomers are? I could cross back later with some fishermen."

Kautsa looked kindly into Kaya's eyes. "I know you won't be satisfied until you see for yourself," she said. "The traders tied their canoe upstream. Surely they'll have room for you. Take them some finger cakes as a gift."

Kaya ran to their camping place, where Brown Deer was sweeping the ground with a broom of sage branches. Her older sister looked tired and unhappy.

"Is something wrong?" Kaya asked.

"I think something's wrong with *me*," Brown Deer admitted. "I'm doing my very best to please Crane Song. I was the first one to waken, long before first light. I brought fresh water and built up the fire before she'd even stirred. Still, all she did was frown and shake her head as though I'm not working hard enough."

"You've always been hardworking and respectful," Kaya insisted. "And you're strong and good, too."

"I'm trying my very best," Brown Deer said. "I don't think my best is good enough for Crane Song."

"But of all the girls, Cut Cheek chose you!" Kaya said, her face hot with feeling. "And you chose him, too! That means more than anything, doesn't it?"

"It does to us," Brown Deer said. "But if Crane Song isn't convinced I'll make a good wife, Cut Cheek's family won't approve of our marriage."

Kaya couldn't believe what she was hearing. All her life she'd admired her older sister, and she feared she would never be as steady or as strong as Brown Deer. "What does Kautsa say about this?" she asked.

"Kautsa says these things take time," Brown Deer said. "She says to be patient, that Crane Song might seem hard-hearted, but she's fair. What do you think, Kaya?"

"I think Kautsa's wise in all things," Kaya said. "You can trust her judgment."

"I hope so," Brown Deer said. "Everything depends on Crane Song's good opinion of me." She set aside the broom and got her knife and workbag. "I've finished cleaning here," she said. "Now I have to join her. Wish me well, Sister." Walking fast, she took the path toward where the women were cutting up salmon and spreading the strips onto drying racks.

Kaya ran into their tepee and put a handful of kouse cakes into the bag she wore on her belt. Then she had an idea. She took Speaking Rain's doll from her pack and tucked it into her belt. If, somehow, she found her sister, she wanted to put the beloved doll into her arms—a sign that she'd never lost hope they'd be together again.

Tatlo was sleeping in the shade beside the tepee. When Kaya came out with the doll, she crouched and he jumped up and licked her chin.

Then he sniffed the doll and licked it, too.

"Do you want to come with me?" Kaya asked. Tatlo barked twice, as if saying Aa-heh! He ran ahead as she raced up the shore to where two women were putting bundles into a dugout cedar canoe.

Kaya threw the elder woman the words, *May I cross the river with you?*

With her hands, the elder woman said, *Come with us.*

Gratefully, Kaya gave her the kouse cakes and climbed into the canoe, with Tatlo jumping in right behind.

The young woman knelt in the prow of the canoe, and the elder woman sat in the stern. The elder woman expertly guided the canoe away from shore. Soon they were paddling across a place where the water was shallower and quieter than the rest of the river. This was a prized fishing place because it was easy to see salmon in the clear, smoothly running water. A fisherman could slip his net over a large fish, just like roping a horse.

Kaya saw the boys Raven and Fox Tail fishing together on a little island just downstream.

They'd tied their safety lines around the same rock, and they were taking turns using a big dip net. As Kaya watched, Raven dragged up the net with a large salmon twisting in it. Fox Tail helped him hold the long, heavy pole until they got the netted fish onto the rocks. Raven took his fish club and killed the salmon with a single blow. Kaya could see it was a good catch.

The many fish leaping and splashing around the canoe excited Tatlo. He put his feet up on the side and barked at them. "Get down!" Kaya said. "Down!" She grabbed the big pup by the scruff of his neck and tried to make him sit. But Tatlo was too excited to sit. When a salmon jumped right next to the canoe, he lunged and snapped at it—and toppled out of the canoe into the river! The surging current caught him and swept him downstream.

"Help my dog!" Kaya cried. The wind whipped her braids across her face and tore away her words. She watched in horror as Tatlo struggled to swim in the churning river. His paws thrashed the water, and his amber eyes looked about wildly. Each time he came up for air, the current dragged him under again. Surely he'd be swept down to the falls and

"Help my dog!" Kaya cried.

killed on the rocks below!

The elder woman turned the canoe downstream, and the young woman paddled hard and fast. But Kaya knew there was no way they could catch up to Tatlo. Already the current had carried him downstream almost to the island.

Then she saw Raven looking their way. He quickly thrust the dip net back into the river. Fox Tail leaned out and peered down into the wild water. Then, with a sweep, Raven raised the net with something in it. Fox Tail grabbed the handle, too, and steadied the heavy weight against his body as he helped lift the net. It took a long moment for Kaya to realize that it was Tatlo they lifted out of the swirling water!

The elder woman guided the canoe toward the island. By the time they beached on the stones, the boys had Tatlo out of the net and onto his feet. The pup was coughing water and shaking it from his coat. His legs were wobbly, but he managed to wag his tail when Kaya scrambled from the canoe and knelt by him, pressing her face against his drenched head.

"The current carried him right to us!" Raven yelled over the river noise.

Then Fox Tail leaned toward Kaya with a sly grin. He put his mouth near her ear and shouted, "Magpies don't know how to take care of dogs!"

That awful nickname again! *But he's right,* she thought. *I didn't take care of Tatlo. I should have held him every moment. It's my fault he fell in.* Instead of hanging her head, she looked Fox Tail right in the eye and flapped her arms like a magpie. They both started laughing.

"Katsee-yow-yow!" she shouted so the boys could hear her thanks. With Tatlo shivering against her legs, she climbed back into the canoe so that they could continue on to the opposite shore.

Kaya made her way through the many villages crowded along the shore. She saw people from the coast trading dried shellfish, shell beads, cedar-root baskets, and canoes. People from the south had brought bowls of black stone and baskets of water-lily seeds to trade. And the people who lived in the midlands, like Kaya's people, traded elk and buffalo robes, kouse and camas cakes, and horses. But Kaya wasn't interested in the trading. She had only one thing on her mind—finding the newcomers from the north.

Tatlo stayed right by her side, his nose twitching at all the new scents around them. If any of the dogs that roamed about came too close to Kaya, a growl rose in his throat and his ears went back. He was such a loyal friend—how terrible if he had drowned because she hadn't kept him in the canoe! "I'll take better care of you," she said, patting his shoulder.

Kaya's ears buzzed with all the different languages she heard. From time to time she stopped where women were cooking and threw them the words, *Where are the newcomers camped?* Always they pointed east, so she kept walking upstream. At last she saw several hide-covered tepees ringed in a small circle. Women were building fires and carrying bundles into the tepees. Could these be Two Hawks's people? She ran, with Tatlo loping at her side.

A young woman was unloading deerskin bags from a travois. Kaya threw her the words, *What tribe are you?*

The young woman cocked her head and studied Kaya closely. She signed, *I am Salish. What tribe are you?*

Kaya swept her hand from her ear down across her chin, the sign for Nimíipuu. *Is Two Hawks with you?* she signed. *He wintered with our people.*

Two Hawks told us about you, the young woman signed. *Right now he's fishing with the men.* She motioned for Kaya to follow her to where women were putting up another tepee.

A white-haired woman with a bent back was smoothing the elk-skin tepee covering. A round-faced younger woman was pounding tepee stakes into the ground. As Kaya and the Salish woman approached these women, Tatlo sniffed the air a moment, then bounded away and began ranging back and forth between the tepees. "Tatlo! Come!" Kaya called, wanting to keep him close to her. When he didn't come, she ran after him.

Horses grazed near the tepees. Tatlo ran between them, his tail wagging, and headed for some small pines. Kaya followed. She saw a baby in a *tee-kas* propped against one of the pines. Tatlo was sniffing the girl who sat tending the baby. The girl's back was to Kaya, who was so intent on catching her pup that she didn't realize until she was only a few steps away that the girl was Speaking Rain!

"Sister! My sister!" Kaya cried. She felt tears sting her eyes as she went to her knees in front of Speaking Rain and seized her hand. "You're alive!"

"Kaya?" Speaking Rain hesitantly touched Kaya's face, then threw her arms around her shoulders. "Aa-heh, I'm alive! How did you find me?"

"I didn't find you," Kaya said. "My dog did! Tatlo knows your scent from your doll." She took the doll from her belt and placed it in Speaking Rain's lap. "I mended it for you and kept it safe. I knew we'd be together again!"

Speaking Rain clutched her doll to her chest, her smile shining like sun on the water. "Katsee-yow-yow," she said softly. "I prayed for you every day."

"And I prayed for you," Kaya said. As she spoke, she looked closely at her sister. When Kaya had last seen her, Speaking Rain had been thin and frail and dirty. Now she wore a fine buckskin dress decorated with many beads and elk's teeth. Her cheeks were round, and her glossy hair was sleekly braided and tied with abalone-shell ties. She wore a pretty necklace of white clamshell beads. "Two Hawks' people have been good to you, haven't they?" Kaya said.

"Aa-heh, they've been very good to me," Speaking Rain said.

Tatlo was gazing intently up at Speaking Rain, as though he recognized her. Kaya placed her sister's hand on his head. "Tatlo likes you. He's a smart dog, but even if he hadn't sniffed you out, I'd have found you."

"If Two Hawks didn't find you first!" Speaking Rain said. "He told me he was going to cross the river to look for you at sunup."

Kaya took a deep breath. "Brown Deer will be so excited to see you! Our parents will be so glad to have you with us again!"

Speaking Rain's face sobered. "I have so much to tell you," she said. "But I smell rain in the air, and don't you hear the wind rising? A storm is coming, and I should take the baby inside. Help me, and we'll talk more later."

STRANDED BY
THE STORM

Kaya remembered that storms here on the Big River were often fierce ones.

She picked up the baby and hurried with Speaking Rain toward the women, where the baby's mother took him and carried him into her tepee. The wind quickly grew wilder. As the sky blackened, other women rushed to bring their belongings and coals for the fires inside. Tatlo whined, wanting to follow Kaya, then huddled up with the other dogs, his head buried in his tail.

The white-haired woman led the girls to her tepee. When they were inside, she fastened the tepee flaps securely against the gusts. The woman was plump-cheeked and very old, her shoulders bent as if she were carrying a heavy load. She unrolled an elk hide and motioned for Kaya to sit on it. Then she led Speaking Rain to the hide, and spoke quietly with her. Kaya was surprised to realize that Speaking Rain spoke Salish now.

"I told White Braids that you're my sister," Speaking Rain said to Kaya. "She's the one who found me and saved my life."

Thank you for saving my sister! Kaya signed to White Braids.

You are welcome here with us, White Braids signed to Kaya. Then she poured water from a rawhide bag into a cooking basket, and set about heating stones in the fire so that she could cook with them.

Kaya leaned close to Speaking Rain. "Tell me what happened after I escaped and left you behind," Kaya urged her. "Many times I've thought how hard it must have been for you. I should never have gone!"

"But I wanted you to go!" Speaking Rain insisted. She held her doll tightly. "I *couldn't* have kept up with you. Two Hawks told us how difficult your journey was."

Pelting rain began to drive against the tepee covering. "This storm reminds me of the night I escaped," Kaya said. "Was Otter Woman angry when she discovered I was gone? Did she whip you for helping me get away?"

"She was angry, but she didn't whip me," Speaking Rain said. "They were all hurrying to pack up and break camp. They wanted to get back to their own country before snow stranded them."

"Somehow you got away from them, too," Kaya said. "Or did they abandon you?"

Speaking Rain put her hand on Kaya's arm. "I don't know what happened, Sister. I found my way to the river to drink and wash. When I came back, everyone was gone. Maybe in their rush they forgot about me. I was alone."

"My poor sister!" Kaya breathed. "What did you do?"

"I tried to stay calm," Speaking Rain said. "I needed a place to sleep, to hide. I crawled through the thicket near the river until I found grass trampled where deer had bedded down. Low branches sheltered the nest. I decided to stay there. Even if I could have found a trail, I'd never have been able to follow it."

"Did you have any food?" Kaya asked.

"They'd taken all the food," Speaking Rain said. "I tried to eat grass, but I couldn't keep it down. After a few sleeps, I was so weak that I could scarcely walk. And the nights grew colder and colder."

As Kaya listened to her sister's story, her heart hurt in her chest. "You must have been frightened," she said softly.

"I knew I would die, so I tried to make my spirit strong," Speaking Rain said. "But I drifted in and out of swirling dreams—awake, asleep? I didn't know anymore. Then I heard steps in the grass, steady ones—not a deer browsing. Someone was walking nearby. I moaned. The steps came closer, and then I felt a touch on my cheek."

"White Braids found you there?" Kaya said.

"Aa-heh," Speaking Rain said. "She was with a small group returning north. She'd come to the river to get driftwood for a fire."

"What happened after she found you?" Kaya asked.

"For a long time I was sick—coughing, choking,"

Speaking Rain said. "Each breath burned, and my face flamed. White Braids brewed *wapalwaapal* for my fever. Every day she carried me into a sweat lodge and bathed me. She fed me broth, then mush. She treated me as if I were her own child, and slowly I got stronger. When the digging season came, I was able to travel with her to the root fields. That's where Two Hawks and his family found me."

A sudden gust of wind forced smoke back inside the tepee. Squinting, White Braids fanned the smoke away from Speaking Rain, then went back to tending the fire. When the stones were hot, she dropped them into the basket of water and added pieces of salmon to boil.

"When White Braids was a young woman, she had a daughter," Speaking Rain said. "But her little girl died. White Braids says that now she has a second daughter—me. I sleep by her side and warm her. When her shoulders ache, I rub them. I carry bundles of firewood for her. She trades the hemp cord I make for hides and other things we need."

"You've cared for White Braids, just as she's cared for you," Kaya said. "Who will help her now that we've found you again?"

Speaking Rain pressed her fist to her lips. Then she took Kaya's hand in hers. "Listen to me," she said slowly, as if she'd thought through carefully what she wanted to say. "It's true that White Braids brought me here to join my family again. But, Kaya, when she saved my life, I made a vow that I'd never, ever leave her. I can't break that vow. I can never live with you again."

Kaya couldn't make sense of what she heard. Speaking Rain was back, she was safe—but she could never live with them again? "Why do you say that?" Her voice trembled with disbelief. "Eetsa and Toe-ta have been so sad! Brown Deer missed you terribly, and so did the twins. You're my sister! You must come back to us!"

Speaking Rain leaned closer and squeezed Kaya's hand harder. "Please, try to understand," she said. "When White Braids gave me back my life, I vowed I'd repay her. It was a solemn vow, Sister, and I won't break it. I know in my heart this is right."

Kaya stared at her sister's serious face. She didn't believe what she was hearing—no, she couldn't believe that she had found her sister only to lose her again! "Surely White Braids won't let you give up your family," Kaya said. "She lost her own daughter—she knows how sad your mother would be to lose you."

"I haven't told her yet that I'll never leave her," Speaking Rain admitted. "But I'm sure she'll respect my vow."

White Braids took the fish from the cooking basket with tongs and divided it into two bowls made of horn. She placed one bowl in Speaking Rain's hands and gave the other one to Kaya.

Kaya tried to eat the delicious food, but her mouth was so dry, she couldn't swallow. Her thoughts whirled like smoke in the wind. She wanted her sister back, but how could she convince Speaking Rain that it was best to be with her own family? And was it right to urge her sister to break her solemn vow?

Someone was at the doorway. White Braids unfastened the flaps and pulled them aside. It was Two Hawks. In a burst of rain he came, drenched, into the tepee, and he started when he saw Kaya. "*Tawts*, you're here!" he said. "You see, I did what

I promised. I found your sister!"

"Aa-heh, you did as you said." Kaya was more grateful than she could say, and she was proud of him, too.

A powerful-looking man followed Two Hawks inside. He and the boy dried and warmed themselves with deer hides. Then, because Two Hawks could speak both languages, he acted as an interpreter. He told Kaya that the man was his father and that his mother had stayed behind in their own country. Then he told his father that Kaya was the girl who had fled with him over the Buffalo Trail.

Two Hawks' father put his hand on Kaya's shoulder. With Two Hawks interpreting, he told her he was grateful to her and her people. He wanted to greet her parents and unite them with their lost daughter again.

As Kaya listened, she thought, *They don't know Speaking Rain has decided not to come back to us. Though she sounds so sure, maybe she has her own doubts.*

Again Kaya thanked Two Hawks and his father. Then she asked if they'd seen her horse in any of their herds.

"No one has seen your horse yet," Two Hawks said. "But someone will have Nimíipuu horses—and yours. Don't give up hope."

"I'll try to keep hoping," Kaya said, keeping her voice steady. But could she?

Two Hawks' father spoke to him again.

"My father says you must stay with us tonight," Two Hawks told Kaya. "No one can take a canoe across the river in a storm like this. When it's over, my father will find some fishermen to take you to the other side."

Kaya didn't want to stay—she wanted to take her sister back to her own people. Once Speaking Rain was with them, she'd realize that it was right. But Kaya had no choice.

White Braids served the men the food she'd prepared, then sat down beside Speaking Rain. From time to time she removed a small bone from Speaking Rain's bowl of fish, or gave her more mashed berries.

After their meal, White Braids took out the fishing net she was mending and gave Speaking Rain shredded hemp to make cord. For a while they worked quietly. Speaking Rain kept an even tension on the strands of hemp as she rolled them together into a long cord. Kaya marveled at how expert Speaking Rain had become—her cord was smooth and strong. Praising her work, White Braids patted her shoulder.

As Kaya watched them work, her own feelings were as tightly twisted as the cord. She saw that her sister wasn't just helping White Braids—the old woman relied on her now in a way that Kaya and her family never had. It came to her that a part of Speaking Rain was already gone from them—and this time Kaya was the one to be left behind.

Tee-tew! Was that a bird call? Glad to be distracted from her painful thoughts, Kaya looked over her shoulder. Two Hawks had taken a flute from his bag and had played those sweet notes on it. Looking pleased with himself, he held out the flute for Kaya to examine. This flute was longer and more finely crafted than the first one he'd made. And when he put it to his lips, he could play a melody.

They all listened to Two Hawks play the soft, beautiful song. Then his father laughed and said something to White Braids that made her laugh, too.

"What did he say?" Kaya asked her sister.

*As Kaya watched them work,
her own feelings were as tightly twisted as the cord.*

309

Speaking Rain leaned close. "He said that when he was young, he could play love songs well because he got so much practice!" she whispered with a smile. "He says that soon Two Hawks will be old enough to serenade the girls as he once did."

Kaya studied her friend. He was no longer the angry, stubborn, skinny boy who'd crossed the Buffalo Trail with her. He was taller, his shoulders were broader, and his dark eyes were clear and bright. She realized with surprise that someday he would be a handsome young man. She wanted to tell him that she liked the tune he played, but suddenly she was shy. Instead, she took Speaking Rain's doll and with her finger showed her sister where she'd mended it.

Outside the tepee the storm howled, but inside it was dry and warm. When it was time to sleep, White Braids spread deer hides on both sides of the fire. Two Hawks and his father lay down on one side. On the other side, Speaking Rain lay on her bed of hides next to the old woman's. "Here's a place for you beside me," she said to Kaya, as though everything were just as it had always been. *Except that everything's different!* Kaya thought.

Kaya lay down and tried to sleep, but she was troubled and restless. She felt the familiar warmth of her sister's shoulder against her own, but in her heart she was cold and lonely. *Creator, spare my life from accidents, illness, and loneliness,* Kaya prayed silently. *Help me to face life with a strong will and without fear of man or beast—or change.*

CHAPTER
FOUR
—
A NEW PATH

By the time Kaya and Tatlo were taken
across the river the next morning, everyone was already at work. Kaya found her
mother kneeling on a smooth rock, cutting the head
off a large salmon and taking out the entrails, which
she put into a basket to take to the trash heap. Kaya
knelt beside her and used her hands to speak over the
roar of the falls. *Speaking Rain is alive! She's over there!*
Kaya pointed at the opposite shore.

Eetsa sat back on her heels, and her eyes filled
with tears. It was a long moment before she could
answer. *We'll cross the river tonight and bring her back,*
she signed. *Go tell your grandmother!* She pointed
toward the workplaces on the hillside.

Kaya found Kautsa on an upland rise, spreading salmon eggs to dry on tule mats. Here the smell of fish was especially strong. Attracted by it, bald eagles and condors circled overhead, riding the winds. The roar of the falls wasn't so loud on this side of the rise, and Kaya didn't have to shout to tell her grandmother about Speaking Rain.

Kautsa clasped Kaya's hand when she heard that Speaking Rain was alive. "I've hoped and prayed to hear this!" she said. "Tell me what happened to her after you two were separated."

Careful not to leave out anything, Kaya told all that had happened to her sister and about her life now with White Braids.

When Kaya was through, Kautsa handed her a basket of salmon eggs. "Hold this while I spread these eggs. When they're dry, you can have some for yourself to trade. Maybe you can get some beads, or a shell to hold them while you're working."

Kaya knelt in silence by her grandmother for a little while. Then she said, "Speaking Rain's different now, Kautsa."

"Do you mean she's grown?" Kautsa asked.

313

"She's a little taller, that's true, and her face is rounder," Kaya said. "But she's grown inside. She seems older. I always looked out for her. Now she doesn't seem to need my help anymore."

"If she can't see, she'll always need some help," Kautsa said. "That hasn't changed, has it?"

"She's still blind in her eyes," Kaya said. "But her heart sees things clearly."

"Everything you're telling me is good news, but you look troubled," Kautsa said. "Didn't you sleep well, Granddaughter?"

Kaya bit her lip. "I stared at the fire all night," she admitted. "But that's not what troubles me. Speaking Rain told me about an important vow she made, one she won't break, no matter what."

"A vow she refuses to break?" Kautsa asked. "Her spirit is strong, then. All that she's been through has made her that way. What was her vow?"

"She vowed she would never leave the woman who saved her life!" Kaya blurted out. "Because of that, she can't live with us anymore!"

Kautsa looked at Kaya long and hard. "Aa-heh, your sister is very strong. But listen to me, Granddaughter, you have strength, too."

"Do you mean the strength I needed to escape from the enemies?" Kaya asked.

"Not exactly," Kautsa said. "I mean you have the strength to make hard choices."

"Are you telling me I should let Speaking Rain go?" Kaya asked.

"I'm not telling you that at all," Kautsa said. "You wanted your sister to live. Don't you want her to have the life she chooses?"

"But I want her to choose to live with me!" Kaya said. "With us! I would miss her so. You'd miss her, too, Kautsa!"

"Aa-heh, I would miss her very much," Kautsa admitted. Her face was grave, and she looked sad. "Remember how you wanted Lone Dog to stay with you? But it wasn't her nature to do that. Perhaps now Speaking Rain must follow her own path—just as you must follow yours."

The heat shimmering up from the stones and the smell of the fish made Kaya dizzy. She swayed, and Kautsa clasped her shoulder, then handed her the water basket so that she could drink. "I know you love your sister," Kautsa said gently. "You love your parents, and all your grandparents, and Brown Deer,

315

and the twins—and others. You love many people. So does Speaking Rain. If she loves and respects two mothers now, she has her own hard choice to make. Do you understand me?"

Kaya wiped her lips on her wrist. "Aa-heh," she murmured.

Her grandmother patted Kaya's shoulder. "You need to rest," she said. "Brown Deer is working near the tepees. Stay with her for a while. She'll want to hear about Speaking Rain, too."

Kaya found Brown Deer kneeling in the shade of a tepee, pounding dried salmon into fine pieces in a stone mortar. Kaya sat down next to her sister and hurriedly told her all about Speaking Rain.

"I have split feelings," Brown Deer admitted after Kaya had told her everything. "One feeling is happiness that our sister is alive and well. The other is sadness that she won't live with us."

"Aa-heh, I understand," Kaya said right away. "It's just the way I feel about your hope to marry Cut Cheek," she went on, surprised to hear herself confessing these feelings, too.

"But you like him, don't you?" Brown Deer asked, startled.

"I *do* like him," Kaya said. "And I know you love each other. I want you to marry. But at the same time, I don't want to lose you. So I'm happy and sad at the same time."

Brown Deer set down the stone pestle and put her hand on Kaya's arm. "We'll always be sisters, no matter what happens. You'll never lose me, I promise. Now we should think about how we can help Little Sister with her choice."

Kaya scrubbed at her eyes with the back of her hand. Brown Deer's kind words helped ease the ache in her chest. "I just wish there was some way for Speaking Rain to choose *both* Eetsa and White Braids!" she said.

Brown Deer scooped the ground-up salmon from the mortar and put it into a basket lined with dried fish skins. "We're friends with the Salish," she said. "We trade with them, and we join them to hunt buffalo. White Braids could live with us for a time. Is that what you mean?"

"White Braids doesn't speak our language— I don't think she'd want to leave her own people," Kaya admitted. Then she sat up straighter. She wasn't tired anymore—and she had an idea. "But

"We'll always be sisters, no matter what happens."

Speaking Rain knows both languages now. Maybe
she could go back and forth between White Braids
and us."

"What do you mean?" Brown Deer asked.
She stopped working and looked closely at Kaya.

"I mean, what if Speaking Rain chose to live
part of the year with White Braids and part of the
year with us?" Kaya said. "That way she could keep
her vow to help White Braids, but she wouldn't
have to give up our family completely."

Brown Deer's eyes lit up. "That's a new path
to think about—a girl shared by two families and
two tribes. We'll have to ask Kautsa for her counsel.
But first I must finish this. Crane Song will be
coming to check on me, and I still have so much
work to do. Look, the sun is almost high overhead."

That evening Kaya and her parents tied up the
canoe on the far shore and started walking upstream
toward the Salish village. Eetsa carried a large
woven bag filled with dried kouse roots to give to
White Braids in thanks for saving her daughter.
"I've told you how Speaking Rain came to be our

child, haven't I," she said to Kaya.

Kaya hurried to keep up with Eetsa and Toe-ta. "We were both still babies, weren't we," she said. She'd heard this story many times.

"You'd learned to walk," Eetsa said. "And Speaking Rain had just taken her first steps when her mother grew sick and died. Her mother was my dear, dear cousin. We'd grown up together, and when we both gave birth to daughters, we became closer still. When Speaking Rain lost her mother, and her father was gored to death on a buffalo hunt, Toe-ta and I took her to raise."

"But at first Speaking Rain didn't like you," Kaya added. "When you went to pick her up, she tried to squirm out of your arms!"

"She couldn't see me, but she knew from my touch that I wasn't her mother, so she fought me," Eetsa said. "When she hit me with her little fists, I thought, 'Tawts! She's a strong one! She'll be an independent girl.'"

"And you loved her anyway," Kaya said.

"I loved her *more* for that strong will of hers!" Eetsa corrected her.

"Now Kautsa's told us that Speaking Rain's

320

made a vow she won't break," Toe-ta said. "That's her strength showing itself."

"But she can't leave us!" Kaya insisted. "Maybe she can live with White Braids—and with us, too. Do you think she'd do that?"

"We've talked that over with Kautsa," Eetsa said with a frown. "But live with two families? That troubles me."

"We'll hear what Speaking Rain has to say," Toe-ta said firmly.

As they approached the Salish tepees, Kaya saw Speaking Rain standing near the path. Her head was tilted as if she could hear their footsteps approaching, and she was smiling. Kaya's heart lifted all over again to see her sister looking so healthy and well. "We're here!" Kaya called out.

Eetsa hurried to her daughter and hugged her tightly. "I feared for you!" she exclaimed. "And how I missed you! Now you're back again!"

Not saying a word, Toe-ta picked up Speaking Rain. She put her arms around his neck while he held her tightly against his chest for a long time. Then he set her gently down. White Braids, Two Hawks, and Two Hawks' father waited a few paces away. With his hands he thanked White Braids for saving his child's life, and he thanked Two Hawks and his father for bringing them together again.

"White Braids has prepared a meal for you," Two Hawks said. "Come to our tepee with us."

White Braids opened the tepee flaps to let in the cooling wind. As they sat there, shadows lengthened and the evening star began to rise. With Two Hawks interpreting, the talk was slow and respectful, and there was much to say. Kaya watched Speaking Rain's face as she turned first toward one speaker, then toward another, as if she were reaching out to them all.

Finally Toe-ta said gently, "Little Daughter, you haven't said much. What are your thoughts?"

Speaking Rain swallowed hard, and she sat up straighter. "Toe-ta, before you came here tonight, I told White Braids I'd made a vow always to help her, as she's helped me. 'We need each other now,' I said. She argued with me—she wants me to go back to you. But I can't break my vow. I owe her my life. You understand, don't you?" She turned to face White Braids and repeated what she'd said in Salish.

Right away White Braids spoke with her hands,

322

I love this girl very much, but I never wanted to take her from you! I only wanted her to live, to be well, to join her family again!

I believe you, Eetsa signed to her. *But I also respect my daughter's vow and her need to keep it.*

Kaya could hold back no longer. Putting her hand on Speaking Rain's, she said, "Listen to me. I have an idea." Then slowly, carefully, she described how Speaking Rain could spend part of the year with White Braids and part with her own family. "If you do that, you can choose *both* of your mothers. Do you think that's possible, Little Sister?" As she spoke, Kaya heard her heart like a soft drumbeat, urging *Find a way, Find a way.*

"Do you mean go across the river with you for a few days, then come back here to join White Braids again?" Speaking Rain asked. "I could do that, but what would happen when the salmon fishing ends and we all leave the Big River?"

"Consider this," Toe-ta said. "You could go with us to Salmon River Country for the winter. Then, when it's digging time, we could take you back to the Palouse Prairie."

"You could meet White Braids there for the hard

work of the digging season," Eetsa added.

Two Hawks spoke a moment with his father. "My father says some of my people can meet you at the Palouse Prairie, then bring you here to the Big River again."

"Everyone will help," Kaya said.

Finally Speaking Rain said slowly, "I can follow the path you've shown, Sister. I believe I can keep my vow but not hurt anyone. That's more than I ever hoped!"

"Then you'll come to us now?" Kaya asked her sister.

"Aa-heh," Speaking Rain said. "Katsee-yow-yow, Kaya."

When White Braids put her wrinkled hand on Speaking Rain's shoulder, Kaya knew she, too, was saying *Katsee-yow-yow*.

Kaya got to her feet. She was so light with relief that she felt like floating up to the small clouds racing toward the setting sun. "I'll carry your things, Sister. Let's go now while it's still light. The others want to welcome you back, too."

A few days later, Kaya was walking with
Speaking Rain to their tepees when she saw people
gathered on the plain upstream from the falls. The
fishermen caught only as many salmon as the women
were able to clean—when they'd caught their limit,
they got together for games, trading, and races. Now
Kaya saw a group of men sitting in two lines facing
each other, playing the Stick Game. They were
drumming to distract the ones trying to guess which
hands hid the small bone markers. They kept track of
the score with sticks stuck upright in the ground. A
few women stood behind the players, singing loudly
to add to the confusion. Jokes and shouts and songs
echoed across the valley.

"I hear so much commotion!" Speaking Rain
said. "They're playing the Stick Game, aren't they?
Let's join them."

"But some riders are getting ready to race their
horses," Kaya said. "Let's go there instead. I'll tell
you everything that's happening with the races!"

They hurried toward the long, flat stretch where
riders raced their horses. Kaya loved to watch the
beautiful horses run, though it made her ache for
Steps High. As she came closer, she realized that one

of the riders on his spotted stallion was Cut Cheek. Brown Deer stood on the sidelines with some other young women. She had the twins with her.

"Is Cut Cheek going to race?" Kaya called as she and Speaking Rain came up to them.

"A band from the prairie challenged us!" Brown Deer said. Her eyes flashed with excitement. "They bet us that their best horse and rider could beat our best horse and rider. Our men chose Cut Cheek."

"I hear his stallion's fast!" Speaking Rain said.

"But look at that gray horse the other man is riding!" another girl said. "Those long legs, that sleek head! They say he's as swift as an antelope."

"But Cut Cheek's horse runs like a cougar!" Brown Deer said. "And Cut Cheek is a better rider, so he's sure to win. You'll see!"

The two men rode away from the others toward the far end of the race grounds.

"Cut Cheek's horse is straining at the bridle as if he can't wait to race!" Kaya told Speaking Rain. "The gray horse is prancing and snorting. He's ready to run, too!" Kaya held her breath as the starter raised his arm and brought it down. "There they go!"

326

Both horses leaped forward like arrows shot
from bows. The riders lay low, their faces close to
their horses' necks. The horses lengthened out,
running faster with each stride, their tails streaming.
Cut Cheek and his horse seemed to blend into a
single being, running easily, as if
they could race forever.

"Cut Cheek's ahead!"
Kaya said. "He's pulling away from the
gray! They're coming to the finish line!"

"Cut Cheek wins!" Brown Deer cried out.

"I want to ride like he does!" Wing Feather cried.

"Nimíipuu won the bet!" Sparrow hopped
around like a jackrabbit.

As the riders rode back slowly, cooling their
horses, Brown Deer waited, smiling. Kaya knew
her sister was struggling not to let her feelings show,
but her face shone.

"You're proud of Cut Cheek, aren't you!" Kaya
said.

"Aa-heh," Brown Deer said. "He rode well! But
I have something else to be happy about. Just before
I came to the race, Crane Song nodded at me!"

"Was her nod a good sign?" Kaya asked.

"It was only a little nod," Brown Deer admitted.

"But it must mean she's pleased with you," Speaking Rain assured her.

"At least a little pleased!" Brown Deer said. "I'm so glad! Would you two look after the twins for a while? I want to tell Cut Cheek—he'll be glad, too. I'll work even harder now!"

"Aa-heh, go tell him," Kaya said, giving Speaking Rain's hand a squeeze. "We'll take care of these bothersome little brothers of ours!"

As long as the run of salmon continued, Kaya helped Speaking Rain go back and forth across the river, staying a few days at a time with each of her two families. Now the season for fishing on the Big River was nearing an end. Speaking Rain would travel with Kaya and her family to higher country for berry picking and hunting, then down to Salmon River Country before snows came. But first there was work to be done while the men completed their fishing.

Kaya knelt beside Brown Deer under a tule mat lean-to they'd made on the hillside above the river. Speaking Rain sat beside them, a box-turtle shell filled with green paint in her hands. Brown Deer had soaked a buffalo hide in the river and had staked it onto the ground in the shade. Now she was going to paint a design on the hide so that she could make it into a parfleche.

"Remember, we have to work quickly so the hide won't dry out. Paint bonds only to a damp hide," Brown Deer said. "I'll lay out the shapes and outline them. Kaya, you help me fill in the larger spaces with paint."

The tule mat shelter they'd made was a small one, but Tatlo managed to creep into its shade. Kaya scratched him behind his ears, and he went to sleep with his head on the edge of her dress.

Brown Deer had already covered the damp hide with a clear mixture of fish eggs to make it smooth and waterproof. Now she laid peeled willow sticks on it in a design of lines and triangles. She dipped a buffalo-bone tool into the paint, then expertly traced the design she'd made, drawing the edge of the bone tool down the hide in long, steady lines.

Kaya dipped in another tool, letting the porous

329

bone soak up the lovely green paint made from river algae. Then she began spreading it where Brown Deer showed her.

"White Braids told me that soon she'll go back to her home country," Speaking Rain said. "I'll be sad to see her go."

"She's a fine woman to adopt you in this way, and you'll meet her again at the Palouse Prairie in the spring," Brown Deer said.

"Will Crane Song be coming with us for the berry picking, or will she go back to Cut Cheek's family when we leave?" Kaya asked her older sister.

Brown Deer's lips turned up a little as she drew. "Crane Song told me this morning that she'll be leaving us." She sat back and looked hard at the lines she'd made, then dipped her tool in the paint again. "She said I must work hard even when she's not around to keep an eye on me. But she told me she's satisfied I'll make Cut Cheek a good wife!" She sighed deeply, as if she'd been holding her breath for a long time.

"That's wonderful news!" Kaya exclaimed. "Why didn't you tell us?"

"I was afraid it might not be true," Brown Deer admitted.

330

"But it is!" Speaking Rain said. "I hear it in your voice. You're almost singing today."

"I feel like singing," Brown Deer said. "Cut Cheek said his parents will join us soon. They'll visit our family with their gifts. Then, in a little while, we'll visit them and give them ours. I'm making this parfleche for Cut Cheek's mother. I want it to be my very best work!"

"You've already made so many gifts," Kaya said. "Woven bags of beautifully dyed cords and grasses, and baskets filled with dried roots."

Brown Deer set aside her tool and picked up

a little buckskin bag of powdered pigment. She took the container of green paint from Speaking Rain and gave her a large mussel shell in its place. "Hold this for me now," she said. "I want to mix up some red."

Speaking Rain held the mussel-shell bowl steady in her cupped hands as Brown Deer mixed the dry paint with water. "What will happen next?" she asked.

"First, Cut Cheek will live with us for a while," Brown Deer said. "Crane Song says he has to show my parents he'll be a good provider." She took two fresh bone tools from her kit and let them soak up the beautiful red paint, the color of sacred power.

"And when he proves himself?" Kaya asked.

"Then we'll make our home with my family for a time," Brown Deer said. "In hunting season, my parents will need our help more than Cut Cheek's family will. So I won't have to leave you now, after all." Her gaze caught Kaya's, and they both smiled.

"Soon you'll plan your marriage," Kaya said. The words were good ones.

Tatlo's paws twitched in his sleep—he was chasing rabbits in his dreams. Kaya stroked his warm head as she watched paint seep into the bone tools. She'd thought she would lose Brown Deer when she married, but that was not to be. She'd thought Speaking Rain would leave them forever, but that wasn't going to happen, either. If only she could get her horse back, her life would be complete. As she picked up her bone tool, she felt as if her full heart were glowing like the crimson paint.

TO MY STEPDAUGHTER BECKY,
AND HER CHILDREN,
TONY AND ADRIENNE,
WITH LOVE

CHANGES FOR
Kaya

SMOKE ON
THE WIND

Kaya sat with Speaking Rain and some
younger children on the dry, yellowed
grass by the stream that wove its way
across Weippe Prairie. For the first time in a long
time, Kaya and her sister played with their dolls.
At the end of summer, *Nimíipuu* women and girls
worked hard to collect as much food as possible
before cold weather came. Kaya couldn't work with
the others because she was still mourning for her
namesake, Swan Circling, and her sad feelings
would spoil the roots and berries. Instead, she
helped in other ways. Today she'd been busy
carrying water, gathering wood for the fires, and
sweeping around the tepees. Then, as the sun had

grown hotter and hotter, she and Speaking Rain were given the job of looking after their little brothers and some other small children in the shade of the pines. "Let's pretend we're setting up a camp," Kaya suggested, and the children nodded happily.

First Kaya made split-willow horses so that the little boys could play roundup. Then she made a fire ring of pebbles so that the little girls could pretend to cook with their miniature woven baskets. After that she set up a small tepee frame of willow branches and covered it with several old tule mats. The play tepee was big enough to hold several little girls, and they crawled inside with their dolls.

Kaya and Speaking Rain lay at the tepee entrance. As Kaya smoothed the delicate fringe on her doll's dress, she caught a glimpse of Brown Deer digging camas with the other women. It had been many snows since her hardworking older sister had played games like this one. Kaya knew that someday she would be too grown-up to play with her doll. And although she wanted to be strong,

responsible, and a leader of her people, right now she was grateful to enjoy this game with the children.

After the salmon runs were over on the Big River, Kaya's band traveled here to the foothills of the mountains to dig roots, pick berries, and hunt. Speaking Rain would spend part of the year with her Salish mother, who had saved Speaking Rain's life when she was separated from the enemies who held her captive. But until spring the sisters would be together. Now Kaya's strongest fear was that she'd never see her beloved horse again. Although

Toe-ta told her to choose another good mount of her own, she was certain she could never love another horse as much as she did Steps High.

As Kaya thought of her horse, she put a toy horse made of a forked stick into Speaking Rain's hands. "Will you hold this so I can hitch up the travois?" Kaya asked. "Your doll can ride the horse when we've got the travois loaded."

Speaking Rain held the stick horse steady between the poles of the little travois, but instead of smiling as the other children did, she frowned. "The smell of smoke on the wind is growing stronger," she said.

"You've got a nose as keen as a bear's," Kaya teased. She thought that because her sister was blind, her sense of smell was especially sharp.

Speaking Rain lifted her chin and sniffed again. "It smells like a grass fire," she said. "Is a new one burning?"

Kaya shaded her eyes and gazed across the prairie. To the west, the sun blazed above red clouds massed at the horizon. To the east, a thick haze hung low over the Bitterroot Mountains, which she had crossed with Two Hawks after they escaped from their enemies. When she drew a deep breath, smoke stung her nose, too. She licked her lips and tasted ash on her tongue. In this hot, dry season, lightning set many fires in the fields and forests, but she didn't see any new plumes of smoke in the surrounding hills. "Fires always flare up toward sundown when the wind rises," she said. "Are you troubled, Little Sister?"

"*Aa-heh*, I am troubled," Speaking Rain admitted. "Fire is like a mountain lion—you don't know when it might attack."

"I'd be troubled, too, if our scouts didn't always warn us of dangers," Kaya said.

"But our scouts are on the lookout for many things besides fires these days," Speaking Rain reminded her.

Kaya knew her sister was right. The scouts always kept watch for anything that might endanger the people, but now they were scouting out game trails and salt licks, too, as the best season for elk hunting approached. When Kaya thought of the elk hunts, she felt a shiver of pride. Toe-ta was

341

one of the most experienced hunters, and the men had asked him to serve as headman for the hunts. Toe-ta's *wyakin*, a wolf, had given him strong hunting power, and the hunters needed to kill many elk to feed everyone through the long, cold season to come. The elk hunts would also be a chance for Cut Cheek to prove his worth as a provider so that he and Brown Deer would be allowed to marry.

Speaking Rain cocked her head. "I hear horses coming this way," she said.

Kaya heard the hoofbeats, too, and got to her feet. "They're coming slowly," she said. "The horses would be galloping if scouts were bringing a warning."

Soon Kaya could see a line of men riding out of the woods on the far side of the prairie. They were followed by women and children on horseback, pack horses, and other women whose mounts pulled loaded travois. Their dogs trotted alongside the horses, wagging their tails as the camp dogs rushed out to meet them.

"It's the hunting party that went over the

Buffalo Trail last year to hunt," Kaya said. "Come on, let's welcome them back!"

The children didn't need urging—they were already hurrying to meet the buffalo hunters and the women who'd gone along with them to run the camp and prepare the meat. Kaya grabbed Speaking Rain's hand and they ran to greet them, too.

After everyone had greeted the hunters, and the dried meat and hides had been distributed, the young men took their horses to the stream. When the horses had drunk their fill, the men splashed them with the cool water, then let them dry themselves by rolling in the grass. Kaya and Speaking Rain eagerly joined their young uncles, who always brought news and stories. Tatlo, growing big and long-legged now, left the milling dog pack and pressed himself against Kaya's legs.

Jumps Back tugged Kaya's braid to tease her. He was a short, easygoing fellow with a big grin. After Brown Deer turned him down in the courtship dance and chose Cut Cheek instead, Jumps Back had said he hoped she was happy with her choice. Kaya liked him for that generous thought. "We've been gone so long, you girls are almost grown-up!" Jumps

Back said. "I bet the boys serenade you with their flutes!"

"Not me!" Speaking Rain said with a giggle.

"Not me!" Kaya echoed her sister.

"Do your cousins still call you that silly nickname, Magpie?" Jumps Back asked, nudging Kaya's arm with his and laughing.

Kaya laughed, too. "Nobody calls me Magpie anymore—except once in a while," she said. These days she rarely heard the nickname she'd gotten when she neglected the twins, and Whipwoman switched all the children for her offense. But to change the subject, she pointed to a young stallion getting to his feet, bits of grass stuck in his black mane and tail. "I haven't seen that bay before. He looks fast."

"Aa-heh, he is fast," Jumps Back said. "I chased him hard on my best horse to get a rope on him. Four sleeps ago we came upon a few horses led by a rogue stallion. He drove off his herd before we could get close, but this young stallion hung back from the others, and I gave chase. He'd been driven off by the older horse, I think."

"I didn't know there was a herd of untamed

horses in this area," Kaya said.

"Some seem tame," Jumps Back said. "We think they're Nimíipuu horses. We're going to try to find them again before the snows come."

Kaya's pulse sped. "Nimíipuu horses!" she exclaimed. "The ones stolen from us last year? Was my horse one of them? Steps High has a star on her forehead, remember?" Hearing the excitement in her voice, Tatlo gazed up at her, his tail thumping against her leg.

Jumps Back rubbed his forehead as he thought hard. "I'm not sure," he said. "There were a few spotted horses in the herd, but I didn't get a good look."

"I guess I'm hoping for too much," Kaya said with disappointment. "I last saw my horse in Salish country. She couldn't be back in these mountains."

"Don't be too sure about that," Jumps Back said kindly. "A stolen horse can stray off if it isn't tied to another horse while it gets accustomed to the herd. Your horse could have strayed off and headed back this way, maybe searching for you. If we can track down those horses again, we'll find out."

But Kaya was almost afraid to hope—it would

hurt so badly to have her hopes dashed. Instead, she asked Many Deer, one of her uncles, "Did you make any good trades in your travels?"

"We met up with some hunters from the north," Many Deer said. He was known as a good hunter but was even better known for his short temper. "They wanted to trade for our best horses, but we refused. Instead, we traded a pack horse for three buffalo calfskin robes and some rawhide rope. That was a good trade!" His broad face flushed as he boasted. "And I got something they say came from the east, maybe from men with pale, hairy faces. Look here!" He opened his pack and took out a red-and-white bead, holding it out for Kaya to examine.

"It's pretty," Kaya said hesitantly—she remembered her grandmother's warnings about dangers from pale-faced men.

Speaking Rain was stroking Tatlo. Kaya took her sister's hand and guided her fingertip to the bead. "It's smooth!" Speaking Rain exclaimed. "Maybe Brown Deer could sew it on a gift she's making for the wedding exchange."

Kaya leaned forward to take a better look at the

pretty bead. "Would you trade it to me for a basket of dried salmon eggs?" she asked Many Deer.

At that moment Tatlo thrust his muzzle into Many Deer's pack, seized a small bundle in his sharp teeth, and shook it. Many Deer aimed a kick at Tatlo and caught the dog in the chest, sending him tumbling. "Stay out!" he hissed.

"My dog!" Kaya cried.

But Tatlo wasn't hurt. He lunged to his feet and placed himself between Kaya and Many Deer, baring his teeth and growling, ready to protect her at any cost.

Many Deer stepped back and put away the bead. "Forget it! Magpies have a lot to learn about making a trade!" he said scornfully.

"Aa-heh, you're right," Kaya said quickly. She held Tatlo firmly by the scruff of his neck and tried to think what Swan Circling would have done in a situation like this one. "I'm sorry my dog got into your pack," Kaya said after a moment. "Don't let that spoil your homecoming."

Jumps Back tapped Many Deer on the shoulder. "Come on," he said to the bad-tempered fellow. "We're tired and hungry. The boys will look after our horses while we eat." As they walked away, Jumps Back glanced at Kaya with a look of approval that said she'd handled the tense moment well.

Kaya took a deep breath to settle herself. More and more lately she'd been thinking about Swan Circling, the young warrior woman who gave Kaya her name. Kaya realized that her thoughts were now lighter when she remembered her hero. Perhaps sad feelings would no longer spoil the food that Kaya gathered. She wanted to talk over her thoughts with her grandmother.

Swan Circling

Toward sundown, Kaya found her grandmother and Brown Deer cutting tule reeds in a marshy place at the edge of the prairie. They bent low to cut off the tall reeds. "Here you are, Granddaughter," *Kautsa* greeted her. "Come bundle up these tules so we can take them to the village to dry."

Kaya carried an armload of tules to a sandy spot and wrapped cord around them. "Kautsa, I've been thinking," she said.

"Have you been thinking how to make your dog behave better?" Kautsa asked with a smile. "I saw

348

Many Deer kick Tatlo when he got into the pack."

Was there anything her sharp-eyed grandmother didn't see? Kaya said, "I was angry about that kick, but I apologized for Tatlo."

"*Tawts!*" Kautsa said. "You must treat everyone well if you want to be a leader like your namesake someday. It's easy to be kind to a pleasant person, but it takes strength to be kind to an angry one. Now tell me what else you've been thinking." As she spoke she cut more tules, passing them to Kaya.

"I've been thinking a lot about my namesake," Kaya said, careful not to say the name of the dead out loud. "I've mourned her death for many moons, and I think my heart feels lighter now."

"Are you sure?" Kautsa asked.

"I'm sure," Kaya said.

Kautsa stood up, put her hand on Kaya's shoulder, and looked into her eyes. "If the time of mourning has passed in your heart, will you join us to pick berries?"

"Aa-heh," Kaya said firmly. "My namesake was always a strong worker. I want to live up to her name."

"Tawts! Let's take these tules back to the

village," Kautsa said. "We need to fix our evening meal."

Brown Deer straightened and slipped her knife into the workbag on her belt.

"We need your help with the berries, Sister," she said as they picked up the bundles of tules. "Brings Word told us this will be the last time she leads us in the berry picking. She's getting too old and her eyesight is failing. She feels it's time to find someone to take her place. Who do you think would be a good leader?"

Kaya knew that for quite some time the women had been talking about who would replace Brings Word. She'd been thinking about it herself. "I think our mother would be a good leader," she said without hesitation. "*Eetsa* is very considerate of others, and she's a good judge of where berries are thickest and when they're ready to be picked. She always leaves some on the bushes so there'll be more the next season. But shouldn't the next leader be one of our chief's own daughters?"

"Not necessarily," Kautsa said. Though she carried a heavy load, she walked with vigorous strides. "To Soar Like An Eagle isn't the son of the old chief, but he's the wisest and the bravest among our men. That's why the council selected him to lead us."

"He showed his courage when he was very young, didn't he?" Kaya asked. She loved to hear stories about warriors and their deeds.

"Aa-heh," Kautsa agreed. "As a young man he was hunting buffalo when a prairie fire swept across the plains toward the hunting camp. The horses bolted and ran away. There seemed to be no escape from the rushing flames—the men were sure to be killed! But To Soar Like An Eagle quickly set a fire of his own and burned a patch of the dry grass. Then he and the others lay down on the hot ashes as the prairie fire passed around the burned-off place. He saved many lives that day!"

Kaya frowned in concentration. She tried to imagine standing her ground in front of a wall of flame in order to set a backfire—would she ever be able to think so fast and act with such courage? "To Soar Like An Eagle is very brave," she said.

"Aa-heh, he is brave, but above all else, he's just and he's generous," Kautsa added. She slid the bundle of tules off her shoulders and placed it near the doorway of their tepee. "Wait here a moment,

"Now it's time for you to wear this," Kautsa said.

Granddaughter," she said as she ducked inside.

Brown Deer and Kaya put down their bundles, too. In a moment Kautsa appeared again, the hat she'd woven last winter for Kaya in her hand. Kaya had planned to wear the new hat this past spring when she dug roots for her First Foods Feast, but because she was in mourning, she hadn't been able to dig with the other girls and women. Kautsa had kept the hat with her own things.

"Soon we'll start berry picking, and after that we'll go with the hunters on the elk hunt," Kautsa said. "You'll need much strength in the days ahead if you're to work as your namesake did to feed the people. Now it's time for you to wear this." She placed the hat firmly on Kaya's head.

"*Katsee-yow-yow*," Kaya said softly, touching the single feather that decorated the top. She was eager to join the others again. And when they went with the hunters farther into the mountains, she might find her horse again, too. She narrowed her eyes as the evening wind carried more ash from distant fires. "I'm ready, Kautsa," she said.

THE ROGUE
STALLION'S HERD

The days were growing shorter now. Kaya heard owls screeching at night and saw geese flying high—signs that the coming winter would be a hard one. But berries were especially thick and plump this year, and with Brings Word's leadership, the women and girls were able to pick and store a great many.

As the berry season came to an end, the band split up. Many journeyed down to Salmon River Country to set up their winter village in the sheltered valley there. Kaya traveled with her family and the hunting party higher into the mountains for the elk hunts. The men rode ahead, leading the way, the women and children following with travois and pack horses. Raven, Fox Tail, and other young boys brought up the rear, driving extra horses to carry back the meat.

As they ascended the trail, Kaya looked out across steep, rocky hillsides split by stony gulches. Whirring ladybugs swarmed around the horses. The mountainsides glowed with deep green heather and red-orange huckleberry bushes. All around, a blue haze of smoke rose from the valleys and tinted the sky gray with ash. Though cold weather was not far off, the days were dry with no sign of rain—it was still the season of fires. The scouts constantly scanned the mountains and skies for signs of danger.

As the women set up the hunting camp, Kaya helped raise the tepees, then took the twins to where Kautsa and Brown Deer were preparing a meal. The boys were hungry, so Brown Deer gave them some pine nuts to nibble on while the deer meat cooked.

"Speaking Rain was glad to go down to Salmon River Country," Brown Deer said to Kaya.

"Aa-heh," Kaya agreed. "The fires in these mountains trouble her."

"I'm not afraid of fire," Sparrow boasted. "It can't hurt me!"

"Speaking Rain knows better—fire *can* hurt you," Brown Deer corrected him. She placed heated stones into the water in the cooking basket, stirring them so that they wouldn't scorch the basket.

"You must always respect the power of fire, Grandson," Kautsa added sternly as she put deer meat into the boiling water. "Fire is a great gift, but it has its dangers, too. You remember the story of the boy who brought fire down from the heavens, don't you?"

"Tell it again!" the twins begged.

Kaya smiled at her little brothers—and at her grandmother. She thought Kautsa liked to tell stories almost as much as children liked to hear them. And although winter was the proper season for story-telling, Kautsa couldn't resist telling one now.

"Long ago, Nimíipuu had no fire," Kautsa began, sitting down on a tule mat and giving her full attention to the story. "They could see fire in the sky, but it belonged to *Hun-ya-wat*, who kept it in great black bags. When the cloud bags bumped together, they crashed and thundered, and fire flashed through the hole that was made."

"That fire was lightning!" Wing Feather knew this story well.

"Aa-heh, it was lightning," Kautsa went on. "How the people longed to get that fire! Without it they couldn't cook their food or keep themselves warm. The medicine men beat their drums, trying to get the fire down from the sky, but no fire came.

"Then a young boy said he knew how to get the fire. Everyone laughed at him, and the medicine men said, 'How can a mere boy do what we aren't able to do?' But the boy waited patiently. When he saw black clouds on the horizon, he bathed himself and scrubbed himself clean with fir branches to prepare for his task. Then he wrapped an arrowhead inside a piece of cedar bark and put it with his bow and arrow. He placed the white shell he wore around his neck on the ground, and asked his wyakin to help him shoot his arrow into the black cloud that held fire.

"The medicine men thought they should kill the boy so he wouldn't anger Hun-ya-wat. But the people said, 'Let him try to capture the fire. If he fails, we can kill him then.' The boy wasn't afraid. He waited until a thundercloud loomed overhead, rumbling and crashing as it came. Then he raised his bow and shot his arrow straight upward. Suddenly,

357

everyone heard a tremendous crash and saw a flash of fire in the sky. The burning arrow, like a falling star, came hurtling down among them. It struck the boy's white shell, resting on the ground, and set it aflame.

"Shouting with joy, the people rushed forward to get the fire. They lighted sticks and dry bark and hurried to their tepees to start fires of their own. Children and old people, too, laughed and sang.

"When the excitement had died down, people asked about the boy. But he was nowhere to be seen. There lay his shell, burned so that it showed the colors of fire. Near it lay his bow. Men tried to shoot with that bow, but not even the strongest man could bend it.

"The boy was never seen again. But," and here Kautsa touched the beautiful shells that fastened her braids, "his abalone shell is still touched with the colors of flame. And the fire he brought down from the clouds burns in the center of every tepee," she said, finishing the story. Then she fixed her steady gaze on the twins, and the sharp lines between her eyes deepened. "Listen to me. You two must try to be as strong and generous as that boy of long ago."

Kaya was glad to hear the old story another time, but she thought again of Speaking Rain's worry about fires. She vowed to keep a sharp watch for them as she searched the surrounding countryside for signs of her horse.

On the day before the hunt, Toe-ta hobbled the lead mare with a rope attached to her forelegs so that she couldn't wander away—he wanted the horses close by so that they could be easily rounded up before first light. He invited the hunters into his tepee to talk over plans for the hunt. Then the men gathered in the sweat lodge to make themselves clean. They thanked Hun-ya-wat for all His gifts and prayed that they would be worthy of the animals they needed for food. Kaya could hear their prayer songs rising up to the Creator.

sweat lodge

That night everyone slept only a short while. Kaya heard Toe-ta and Cut Cheek rising in the dark to join the other men. They took their bows and arrows and put on headdresses of animal hides to disguise their human

scent. Kaya, Eetsa, and Brown Deer quickly dressed
themselves. They rode away from the camp long
before sunrise while the elk were still out feeding or
returning to their bedding place from the salt lick.

Everyone dismounted near the valley where
scouts had discovered the elk herd. Raven and the
boys looked after the horses while the others went
forward on foot. Quickly and quietly, the hunters
took up positions at the narrow end of the valley,
downwind from the elk. At the wide end of the
valley, the women and girls fanned out in a broad V
to drive the elk ahead of them toward the waiting
hunters. They took care not to startle the elk
as they moved slowly forward.
If the elk started running, they'd
plunge right past the hidden men,
who wouldn't be able to get clear shots.

Kaya concentrated on the rustle of the elk
moving through the plumed beargrass. She could
make out the tips of their antlers, the flash of tan
rumps, and the flickers of ear tips. Even in the faint
light she could see their tracks on the worn game
trails. Birds flew up all around her, and from time
to time a woman added her whistle to the birdcalls,

making her position known to the others.

Then Kaya remembered that she should be on the lookout for fires, too. She scanned the mountain slope at the far end of the valley. There was no sign of smoke on the plateau there, but shapes moved among the pines, and she thought she heard a distant whinny. Holding her breath, she stood still and peered through the dim light. Gradually she made out horses emerging from the trees to graze. Kaya's heart sped. Could that be the small herd that the buffalo hunters had seen? Could Steps High be with them? Kaya stared hard, but the horses were too far off for her to see them clearly.

Kaya walked slowly forward again, but her racing thoughts tumbled ahead, one over the other. What if she slipped away from the others to get a better look at the horses? Couldn't she run up to the ridge for a better view and be back before the slow-moving elk herd reached the hunters? Or couldn't she get a mount and ride close enough to the horses to whistle for Steps High if she was with them? Maybe she could round up the horses by herself— think how proud of her everyone would be!

Then, right in front of her, a pair of magpies flew

out of their dome-shaped nest in a thorny bush. Crying boldly, they swooped upward among the other birds. Like an upraised hand, the sight of the magpies halted Kaya's racing thoughts. No, she must not act in such a way that she could be called Magpie ever again! It would be irresponsible to go after the horses by herself. She must follow in Swan Circling's footsteps and do only what was best for her people. She must work with the others so that there would be food for all. Whistling to signal her place in the group, she drove the elk forward to the waiting hunters.

The hunters' arrows were swift and their aim was true. Many elk gave themselves to Nimíipuu that morning. Then the women and girls prepared the meat to be packed back to the camp, where they would cook some of it and dry the rest. Kaya could tell by Brown Deer's shining eyes that Cut Cheek had hunted well. He'd given the elk he'd killed to her parents as a sign of respect.

Kaya couldn't wait any longer to talk to her father about the horse herd she'd seen at sunup.

362

She found Toe-ta lifting a heavy bundle of meat onto a travois. Quickly, she described the horses she'd seen. "Jumps Back thinks they're our horses, Toe-ta. Steps High might be with them," she added, trying to hold down her excitement.

Toe-ta put his firm hand on her shoulder. "Daughter, there's not much chance that your horse could be with that herd."

"But there is some chance, isn't there?" Kaya insisted. "Steps High could have strayed off and come back this way."

Toe-ta thought for a long moment. "That's possible. We'll go look for the herd," he said. "I'll ask Raven to come along—he's not needed here right now. Let's see what we can find."

Kaya mounted a chestnut horse and rode out of the valley behind Raven and Toe-ta. They followed a game trail that led upward toward the plateau where she'd seen horses grazing. The sun was high overhead, and heat waves shimmered over the stony hillside. She was sure she'd seen the horses near those pines ahead, but now there was no sign of them. Had the lead mare taken the herd where it was cooler?

363

The trail left by the horses curved around the mountain and angled down the northern side. Kaya's gaze swept across slopes dotted with stunted firs and hunchbacked pines, bent down by past winter snows. Deep gulches jagged down the mountain in every direction. The herd could be in any one of them. Would they be able to find the horses before they had to rejoin the hunting party, now a long way away?

The trail descended more and more steeply, and after a time they found themselves in a narrow canyon where a thick grove of tall firs grew. Spears of sunlight shafted down through the canopy of branches, and the shadowed air was a little cooler here. A small stream snaked through the trees. Toe-ta signaled Kaya and Raven to halt their horses and let them drink.

Kaya slipped off the chestnut horse she rode and knelt upstream from the horses, drinking from her cupped hands. The spring water was clean and cold, and she was very grateful for it. When she glanced up again, she realized that the patches of dappled light in the grove of trees were moving. Slowly and silently, as if in a dream, a few horses appeared in the grove—and then a few more. Coming to the watering place, they stepped around fallen logs. When the lead mare spotted intruders, she halted in her tracks, and the other horses came to a stop behind her.

Kaya got slowly to her feet. Toe-ta and Raven stood, too. Then Toe-ta pointed to a horse barely visible behind the others, a horse whose black forehead was marked with a white star.

"Steps High!" Kaya whispered, almost afraid to breathe. In the same moment that she recognized her beloved horse, a long-legged, spotted foal crowded against Steps High's side—her horse had a little one!

Toe-ta climbed onto his stallion Runner again. Raven jumped back onto his own horse, too. "Whistle for your horse, Daughter," Toe-ta said softly. "She'll recognize your whistle. Call her to you."

Kaya's heart thudded, and her lips were dry. She licked them and managed to make the shrill whistle with which she'd called Steps High so many times. Her horse's ears shot up. Kaya whistled again, and Steps High began to move toward her, the foal following closely. "Come on, girl," Kaya urged her horse. She whistled a third time—just as the air was split by a stallion's scream of fury. The rogue stallion had come down from the hill to claim his herd and protect it.

The rogue was a reddish bay with a black mane and tail. Swift as an antelope, he plunged through the trees and across the clearing to guard his mares. His nostrils flared and his eyes shone with defiance as he screamed his challenge at the intruders. Then he lowered his head almost to the ground, his neck outstretched as he dove at the mares, driving them into a bunch.

Toe-ta had his rawhide rope ready. Raven coiled his rope, too, and began to circle around the milling horses. "Whistle again!" Raven cried to Kaya. "Keep calling your horse! She wants to come to you!"

Kaya repeated her whistle. Steps High swung around, trying to elude the rogue, but each time she swerved away from him, he drove her back with the other horses.

Now Toe-ta on Runner circled the herd in the other direction to distract the rogue. The rogue pawed the ground, snorting and trumpeting to drive off the challenger, screaming fiercely that these mares belonged to him alone!

When the rogue's back was to her, Kaya rode around behind the herd. Steps High made another dash for her, breaking away from the other horses. Kaya swung her rope and swiftly threw it over Steps High's head—she had her horse again! In a burst of speed, Kaya on the chestnut horse rode away from the herd. Leading Steps High, the foal running right behind, they galloped off.

Raven on his horse quickly caught up to Kaya. "Let's race!" he called to her with a grin. "Is your horse still fast?"

Toe-ta came galloping after, and they rode up the valley, the rogue's shrill trumpeting echoing behind them.

Stones clattered from under the horses' hooves as they ascended the narrow trail that led over the ridge. Heading back to the hunting party, they made their way through broad canyons and deep gulches. As they rode, Toe-ta studied the sky and the puffy, misshapen white clouds that rose on the updrafts. He seemed worried. In a narrow canyon, he said,

"Wait here. I want to get a look at the countryside from the crest of that hill."

Kaya slipped from the chestnut horse and went to Steps High. Her horse shuddered, then pushed her head affectionately against Kaya's shoulder. Kaya ran her palm down the muzzle, soft as doeskin, and stroked the powerful jaw and sleek neck. She gazed into Steps High's dark, glistening eyes and felt her own fill with tears. "You've chosen to be my horse again," she whispered. "Katsee-yow-yow, my beautiful one!"

The foal nuzzled Steps High's flank. "Raven, look at her foal!" Kaya cried. She smiled at the foal's short brush of a tail, long legs, and big eyes. "Isn't he handsome with all the black spots? Won't he be—"

The sound of a running horse interrupted her excited words. Toe-ta reined in Runner, hooves plowing the sand, and motioned for Kaya to mount the chestnut horse again. "There's a fire just over that ridge. The wind is spreading it this way. We have to get out of this gulch." He kept his voice low, but she heard the warning in his tone.

Kaya glanced at the ridgeline. She saw a plume

"You've chosen to be my horse again," Kaya whispered.
"Katsee-yow-yow, my beautiful one!"

of smoke, but it was thin and white—it didn't look threatening. Three or four small spot fires burned near the top of the ridge, but the grass there was thin and sparse and the blazes no larger than cooking fires. What had Toe-ta seen that alarmed him so?

"Stay with me and keep close," Toe-ta said. He urged Runner ahead on the narrow game trail that ran down the gulch. Kaya jumped back on the chestnut, clasped Steps High's rope tightly, and followed her father, with Raven coming right behind. When she looked back again only moments later, more fires burned from sparks blown into the scrub brush. And now she could hear something hissing and growling in the distance—like a mountain lion, the fire was leaping after them!

TRAPPED BY FIRE!

The twisted gulch they rode down was narrow and steep-sided. Kaya rode as fast and as close to Toe-ta as she could, keeping Steps High right behind her. The foal ran, too, his head at his mother's flank. Across the gulch, small fires flapped along the ridge where two winds met, pushing the fire back and forth between them. That side, the north one, was thickly wooded with juniper and fir trees. Kaya knew fire would burn fiercely in the dense trees. The south side, where they rode, was covered with bunchgrass and a few pines scattered here and there. Fire would burn more lightly on this side, though in the baking sun, the air itself felt like fire. Her eyes stung and her throat burned with every breath.

In a gust of wind, the wavering fire across from them dipped down into the pines. Swiftly, it grew and grew. Kaya watched in alarm as burning pinecones began to swirl through the air, starting spot fires farther down the slope. The smoke blackened and boiled upward. Fire began to growl like a bear as it spread both up and down the slope. Could it keep pace with them as they galloped their horses down the gulch toward the open end and safety on the plain beyond? The frantic horses couldn't be held back—every fiber of their beings wanted escape.

Other creatures also sought escape from the windswept fire. Frightened deer, their brown eyes wide, leaped out of the thickets and bounded to the south side of the gulch, racing up toward the ridge. Jackrabbits came, too, and ground squirrels. Clouds of grasshoppers whirred up out of the smoke. Patches of brush under the trees burst into flame, flushing grouse and quail. When Kaya looked back, she saw Raven lying low on his

horse, one hand cupped over his nose and mouth. Kaya thought only, *Stay with Toe-ta! Take care of Steps High and her foal!*

Fearfully, she looked across the gulch again. Heat waves heaved and buckled above the spreading fire. Fiery pine needles rose up like sparks flying. Burning twigs snapped and cracked. Juniper trees began exploding in the intense heat. But the open end of the gulch wasn't far off now—was it? Kaya coughed and her eyes teared in the bitter smoke. It was almost too hot now to breathe, and fear was another fire in her chest. It was all she could do to cling to her horse as it bolted behind Toe-ta's along the narrow mountain-goat trail.

Then, with a roar, the ground fire on the north slope suddenly exploded into the treetops. Kaya saw the topmost branches become a crimson tent of flames. The trees burned from the tops down, like torches. A high wind gusted up from the burning trees, making the boiling fires hotter still. Wind snapped off branches with a sound like bones cracking. It lifted logs into the air. The fire swirl spun down to the bottom of the gulch and burst across onto the south slope below them. With a stab of pure terror, Kaya realized that now it burned ahead of them, too, blankets of black smoke covering their escape route. The panicked horses doubled back, bumping into each other, rearing and snorting in terror.

Kaya fought to stay on her plunging horse. Steps High reared again and again—would she fall backward on the slipping stones? Would the foal be trampled? Terrified, Kaya thought, *Have I found my horse only to lose her to fire?*

Toe-ta scanned the steep-sided gulch, looking for a possible escape route over the ridge above them, but rimrock created a barrier just below the top. Could they find a way through the barrier? Kaya saw there was no choice—they had to try.

"Stay with me!" Toe-ta shouted over the howling roar. "Don't fall back!" His face was black with smoke and fierce with determination. Did he see a way out of this fiery trap? He gestured for Kaya and Raven to follow as he turned Runner toward the steep slope above them and urged him upward. Raven's horse clambered up behind, its powerful haunches knotted with effort. Kaya forced the chestnut to follow and yanked on Steps High's rope to bring her along. The foal sprang over the rocks like a deer. But could the horses climb faster than the fire? Racing for their lives, they struggled upward.

Ashes, like flakes of snow, swirled across Kaya's sight. Burning embers fell onto her head and shoulders, stinging her hands when she brushed them away. On the loose stones, the horses' hooves slipped backward with each lunge until they gained a broad shelf not far below the rimrock barrier. Then the wind suddenly split the smoke, and for a moment Kaya saw the barrier clearly. Was that slash a crevice, a way through? Could they reach it? Again Toe-ta signaled for them to follow. Raven urged his horse after Toe-ta as the curtain of smoke swung closed behind them.

Before Kaya could follow, Steps High began to rear, whipping her head back and forth frantically. Kaya looked back—the foal wasn't there! Was it lost in the smoke, caught by the rushing fire? Frantic to find her foal, Steps High thrashed her head, tearing the rawhide rope from Kaya's grip. "Stop!" Kaya screamed. "Don't go back!" But, searching for her foal, Steps High had already plunged down the slope and vanished into the smoke.

Kaya tried to rein in the chestnut, turn it back after Steps High, but the panicked horse resisted. Without thinking twice, Kaya slipped off the chestnut, which pushed on up the slope where Toe-ta and Raven had disappeared. Kaya whirled around. Smoke surrounded her on all sides. Through the smoke, the sun was blood red. She stood alone. Her eyes felt blistered by the heat, and she cupped her hands over them. *I must be strong!* she thought. *I must not give up!*

When Kaya opened her eyes, Steps High was lunging out of the blackness, her foal again at her side. She'd reclaimed her young one! As Steps High came near, Kaya leaped to catch the rawhide rope still encircling her neck. With her horse pulling her, Kaya stumbled alongside as they started uphill again. Jagged stones tore at her feet. Her ankle twisted and she lost her footing. She fell uphill onto her stomach beneath her horse's legs. Kaya rolled onto her side. Would the hooves crush her? But Steps High curled her forelegs and managed to bring her sharp hooves down beyond Kaya's head. "Katsee-yow-yow!" Kaya cried. But she knew that on foot she couldn't keep up with her horse. Steps High would have to let Kaya ride if they were both to escape the fire.

When Steps High turned uphill again, Kaya saw her one chance to mount—if her horse threw her off, there would be no second try. Using all her remaining strength, Kaya scrambled onto a boulder, clasped Steps High's mane with both hands, and dragged herself onto her horse's back. Steps High shuddered but accepted Kaya's weight—her horse hadn't forgotten! Kaya rejoiced to be one again with Steps High. But which way should they go? She had no idea. The blowing smoke created a vast black cave with no opening. She'd seen a crevice in the barrier, but where was it? There? Or there? Which way might offer escape? If they went the wrong way, the fire would seize them!

Then Kaya heard a shrill whistle, one high, wavering note that cut through the roar. Could it be green wood singing in the flames? The whistle came again, more urgently. *Here! Here!* the whistle sang. It came to her that Toe-ta was whistling to her, signaling the way. She looked toward the sound but could see nothing. Then a gust of wind knifed through the smoke, and again she spotted the crevice, with a deep game trail leading toward it.

Kaya turned Steps High along the game trail toward the opening. With the foal pressing after, they gained the base of the barrier. Now Kaya felt wind pouring through the opening. Steps High felt the wind, too, and nosed forward, though she balked at the narrow passage. "Go!" Kaya urged her horse. Steps High moved one step, then another. Kaya's knees scraped the sides as they slipped through, the foal following. On the far side Kaya saw the ridgeline right above them. She clasped Steps High even more tightly with her knees and pressed her face into the black mane. "A little farther—we're almost there!" she cried. A few more steps and they had reached the crest.

Still panicked, Steps High started to tear down the other side, stones showering out from under her hooves. Toe-ta on lathered Runner was riding hard back up the hill, looking for Kaya just as Steps High had searched for her foal. He swerved Runner, grasped the rope around Steps High's neck, and brought her to a standstill before she could injure herself and Kaya. Steps High's chest heaved, and her coat was

378

"Go!" Kaya urged her horse.

drenched with lather. The foal's legs shook with fatigue. Kaya slumped forward. Her breath rasped in her throat and her lungs ached from the smoke.

Toe-ta threw his arm around her shoulders. "Rest a moment!" he said. "We're safe here."

Kaya gazed around. The fire didn't threaten them here because an earlier one had already burned off the hillside. Ash-gray patches of sage still smoldered. Juniper stumps smoked. In some places fire had swept by so quickly that it had left scrub brush only singed. Farther down the stony hillside, Raven on his horse made his way to the narrow river below, where deer and elk stood chest-high in the water. He glanced back and raised his hand to her—they'd made it to safety!

"You fell behind," Toe-ta said in his deep voice. "I thought I'd lost you."

"Steps High ran away from me to find her foal," Kaya gasped. "When I caught her again, I lost my way. But you whistled to me! I followed your whistle and found the opening. Katsee-yow-yow, Toe-ta." Her voice shook, and she thought she was laughing until she felt tears running down her cheeks.

380

Toe-ta wiped away her tears with his palm. "I'm so proud of your courage, Daughter," he said. "You saved yourself, and your horse, too. But what was that whistle you heard?"

"Your whistle," Kaya repeated.

Gazing into her eyes, Toe-ta slowly shook his head. "I was headed for the river when I realized you weren't behind me. Right away, I started back after you. But I didn't whistle to you. That must have been the Stick People. They showed you the way."

"The Stick People?" Kaya said.

"Aa-heh," Toe-ta said. "I think they saw you needed help, and they gave it."

Kaya's head was spinning, but she remembered she must leave a gift for the Stick People. "What can I give them?" she asked Toe-ta.

"We'll leave them many gifts," Toe-ta said. "Now let's get to the river. The horses need water, and we do, too." Still clasping Steps High's rope, he began to lead Kaya on her horse down the burned-over hillside, puffs of ashes rising at their feet.

GIFTS

As the hunting party rode out of the
mountains to join the rest of the band
in Salmon River Country, the skies
turned gray with heavy clouds. Soon the first
autumn rains began to fall. After the long, dry
season of fires, the rain was a blessing. Kaya pulled
her deerskin robe over her head, but she lifted her
face to the rain. It would soon turn to snow, but
now it bathed her cheeks and forehead with a soft,
light touch. The rain dripped from the branches she
rode under, raising sweet scents of pine and fir.
Drops of it beaded in Steps High's mane and on her
foal's eyelashes. Kaya stroked her horse's warm,
wet neck and smiled to see the foal, which she'd

named Sparks Flying, splashing through the shallow stream.

Even in the rain, the woods around Kaya were filled with color. She saw aspen trunks washed to pure white and the larch needles shining yellow. Ferns had dried to a dark orange, rosebushes were red-leafed, and gilded mosses hung from the fir boughs. A snake slithered across the trail with a green gleam. Blackbirds flocked together for their flight south. Red-sided trout leaped from the stream after insects, and on the opposite shore Kaya saw a brown bear gorging itself on fish.

Now deer and elk were coming down to lower country to forage. As she rode across a clearing, Kaya saw a bull elk running through the scrub brush. He lifted his legs high and tilted back his head so that his huge antlers could slip through the branches as he raced like a scout bringing a message. Kaya's heart swelled. She felt how strongly she loved her beautiful homeland and all the creatures that shared it with Nimíipuu.

When the hunting party reached the wintering place, Tatlo burst from the village dog pack and came running to meet Kaya. Bounding alongside

Kaya's heart swelled. She felt how strongly she loved her beautiful homeland and all the creatures that shared it with Nimíipuu.

Steps High, he barked repeatedly as if to say, *You're back, you're back!* And when Kaya dismounted, he licked her cheek over and over again with his warm, rough tongue.

Kaya turned out Steps High and Sparks Flying with the other horses. Then, with Tatlo at her side, she ran to find Speaking Rain. She had so much to tell her sister.

Kaya found Speaking Rain in the snug winter lodge, twining cord from shredded hemp. Kaya went to her knees in front of her and placed her hands on Speaking Rain's arm. *"Tawts may-we,* Little Sister," Kaya breathed. "I'm here again!"

"Tawts may-we!" Speaking Rain gently touched Kaya's fingers. "Is that pine pitch I smell on your hands? Did you get hurt?"

"My hands and arms got burned by falling embers, but I treated the burns with medicine that my namesake taught me to make," Kaya said. "You were right to be troubled about fires!"

Speaking Rain drew in a sharp breath. "What happened?"

Sitting close to her sister's side, Kaya told how she'd found Steps High in the rogue stallion's herd, and about their escape from the fire. "When we got back to the hunting camp, everyone thought we were ghosts—covered in black from the smoke. Before we left that country, Toe-ta and some other men rounded up the other Nimíipuu horses," Kaya finished.

"And now you're back safely!" Speaking Rain had been listening intently, as though she could feel, and hear, and even see everything Kaya described. "Whistles! Your horse came to you because she recognized your whistle. Then the Stick People saved your lives with a whistle."

"Aa-heh," Kaya agreed. "We left the Stick People a big gift of kinnikinnick."

Speaking Rain clasped Kaya's shoulder. "Tell me about Brown Deer and Cut Cheek. Did he hunt well?"

kinnikinnick

"Cut Cheek's a strong hunter!" Kaya said excitedly. "Our parents agree that he and Brown Deer should marry. Eetsa's going to visit Cut Cheek's mother soon to plan the wedding trade. We'll have the marriage feast and gift exchange before the snow gets deep. But come with me now! Don't you want to stroke Steps High again? I know you love her, too. And you have to meet her foal! They're the most wonderful horses ever!"

When the time came for the wedding ceremony, the frozen ground was covered with lightly fallen snow. Brown Deer and the other women put up a lodge for the celebration, then began cooking for the wedding feast. Soon the air smelled deliciously of roasting meats, kouse and camas cakes, and berry dishes. Kaya's mouth watered as she helped carry the gifts her family had made to the new lodge.

"Here's the last of the bundles, Granddaughter," Kautsa said. She placed a large bag filled with dried roots into Kaya's outstretched arms, put another under her own arm, and picked up a torch. As she walked ahead, she left shallow footprints in the dusting of snow.

Kaya's skin prickled with anticipation as she followed her grandmother inside the empty lodge. Now it was cold and silent here, but when everyone gathered today it would be filled with happy talk and laughter. They'd feast until they couldn't eat any more. Then Brown Deer's family would give woven bags filled with dried berries, roots, and camas to the groom's family—food the women had gathered and prepared. Matching them gift for gift, Cut Cheek's family would give parfleches filled with dried meat to the bride's people—foods contributed by the men.

parfleche

Kautsa stacked the woven bags on top of the large pile of gifts already resting on the tule mats. "There, that's everything," she said with satisfaction. "Now we're ready! Let me light one of these fires to warm up the place a little. I want to stay here for a while, don't you? We've been so busy lately that we haven't had time to talk."

As Kautsa knelt to light the fire, Kaya gazed at her grandmother's kind face. Her black hair was streaked with gray and her forehead and cheeks were deeply creased. Firelight glittered in her dark eyes. "Have I ever told you about the time I got lost on the mountainside—truly, completely lost?" she asked Kaya.

Kaya smiled. She loved her grandmother's stories. "When was that, Kautsa?"

"As you might imagine, it was when I was a little girl, about the age of the twins." Kautsa sat back on her heels as the fire began to crackle and held out her hands to the warmth. "I was walking back from picking berries with my mother when she discovered her workbag was missing. She was upset and wanted to go back to look for it. But she didn't want to carry the heavy berry baskets, so she put them down on the trail and told me to sit by them. She made me promise to wait patiently for her and not to move, not even a little bit. She said she wouldn't be long, and she started back up the trail.

"I sat there for what seemed like a long time. I was hot and thirsty and bored. Mosquitoes bit me, and deerflies buzzed around my head. After a while I got up and began poking around in the bushes, looking for something to do. I walked a little way into the underbrush, then a little farther, and a little farther yet. All of a sudden, I realized I didn't know where I was. I tried to get back to the

trail, but I couldn't find it. I was lost! Then I forgot
everything I'd been told to do if I got lost. Instead of
staying right where I was and waiting to be found,
I started to run.

"I ran downhill, thorns tearing at my dress,
twigs scratching my arms and my face. There were
no trails there, no sign that anyone had passed that
way. I thought I would never see my family again,
so I started to cry, 'Toe-ta! Eetsa! Help me, help me!'
I called to them until I couldn't run any farther.
Then I curled up under a bush and sobbed until I
fell asleep.

"That's where I was, asleep, when my older
brother found me. He was hunting higher on the
mountain when he heard my cries. He knew that
sound travels upward, so he rode down, following
my sobs. He took me to our camp. I was overjoyed
to see my mother again! She put willow bark on all
my cuts and insect bites. She washed my face and
fed me. Then she called Whipwoman to teach me
my lesson!" Kautsa laughed, and Kaya laughed
with her.

Then Kautsa put her hand on Kaya's. "I told
you that story for a reason. What lesson do you

think my mother wanted me to learn?"

"Not to disobey her," Kaya answered confidently.

"Aa-heh, that's one lesson," Kautsa went on, "but there was another one. She wanted me to learn to be patient—to wait, and to trust the wisdom of others. That's a very difficult thing to do, for it takes great strength to wait patiently." She thought for a moment, then went on. "Granddaughter, you've already faced many tests of bravery. Your next test will be one of patience, and of trusting the wisdom of our elders."

Kaya frowned. "What do you mean, Kautsa?"

"I'm speaking of your vision quest, Granddaughter—the vigil you must keep at the sacred place on the mountain," Kautsa said. "If your spirit is clear and you're prepared—and if you can hold on and not run away—then your wyakin will come to you there. But before that happens you'll be hungry and thirsty, and exhausted by fasting and praying day and night. Are you afraid?"

Kaya clasped her elbows, asking herself, *Am I afraid?* She had certainly been afraid when enemies captured her. She had been afraid when she escaped and found her way home. She'd been frightened to think she'd lost her sister, and her horse. And she'd been terrified when she was chased by the forest fire. But what she felt now wasn't fear—it was determination. "I'm not afraid, Kautsa," she said in a firm voice. "I'm ready to meet whatever comes."

"Why, that's exactly what your namesake would have said!" Kautsa exclaimed. "You're more like her than you may know. Soon, I believe, you'll use her name. It will be so good for her name to come alive again!"

Kaya's chest felt warm with gratitude when she thought again of Swan Circling's gift. Kaya wanted so much to take the name of her hero, and now her grandmother felt that the time was almost here.

From across the village, criers began calling out, "Visitors are coming! Get ready to greet them!"

"Saddle up your horse and go meet Cut Cheek's people," Kautsa said, getting to her feet. "I'll light these other fires and make the lodge warm for our feast. Go on now, be quick! We've talked enough."

Kaya ran to get the beautiful saddle she'd received at the giveaway after Swan Circling's burial. Then she hurried to the horse herd nearby.

Tatlo bounded along with her, snapping at snow-flakes and tossing up fallen snow with his nose. Steps High was pawing through the ice for grass with the other horses. When she heard Kaya's whistle, she trotted to her side, snorting white plumes of breath.

Kaya thought her horse seemed almost as excited as her frisky dog. Kaya pressed her cheek to Steps High's muzzle and stroked her horse's chest, feeling the strong, loyal heart beating there. In response, Steps High arched her neck and nudged Kaya's shoulder. As Kaya cinched the saddle tightly,

Sparks Flying crowded against his mother, head high and ears forward as though he were eager to welcome visitors, too.

Kaya swung up into the saddle and settled her feet in the stirrups. "Come on, girl," she said to her horse, and then slapped her leg to signal Tatlo to stay at her side. Urging Steps High into a run, Kaya galloped out to meet the visitors on their horses appearing over the horizon.

LOOKING BACK

CHANGES
IN THE
WIND

Beautiful Wallowa Valley, one of the best-loved places in Kaya's homeland

In the same way Kaya knew to be careful when she smelled smoke on the wind, many Nez Perce people had visions that warned them to be careful of the people with pale faces who were beginning to come to their homeland.

In Kaya's time, most Nez Perces had heard about these newcomers but hadn't seen them. The very first white people who spent time with the Nez Perces were the explorers Meriwether Lewis and William Clark, who first traveled through Nez Perce country in 1805. Chief Twisted Hair befriended these travelers, drew maps that showed how the rivers could take them to the sea, and agreed to care for their horses over the winter.

A Shoshone woman named Sacagawea helped guide the Lewis and Clark expedition.

The Nez Perces were very interested in the explorers' journals and the way white people "talked on paper." They wanted to learn this language, too, both to add to their own store of knowledge and as a way to bond with these new friends from the East. In 1831, a group of Nez Perces went to St. Louis to see their friend William Clark, who had become the United States Commissioner for Indian Affairs. They told him they wanted to learn his language and asked if he would send teachers to the Nez Perces.

Soon after that, Henry and Eliza Spalding arrived in Nez Perce country. The Spaldings were missionaries who would teach the Nez Perce people English, but mostly they had come to teach about Christianity. Nez Perces eagerly gathered to learn, until Henry Spalding began whipping Indians for what he considered unchristian behavior, such as men refusing to cut their hair. He was nearly driven away a number of times.

Traditional Nez Perce beliefs are symbolized in this drawing from the 1880s. Some Nez Perces viewed Christianity as yet another source of spiritual strength.

In the 1840s, white settlers and prospectors, or people searching for gold, began trickling through Nez Perce country on the Oregon Trail. Some were infected with smallpox, measles, or other diseases that killed thousands of Nez Perces. The settlers dug up rivers, cut down forests, and let their pigs eat the camas Nez Perces depended on for food. That trickle of white people became a flood in 1850, when gold was discovered in the Northwest.

In 1855 the U.S. government offered its first treaty to the Nez Perce people. Government officials said they would set aside land called a reservation for the Nez Perce people alone, where no whites could settle or mine for gold. The Nez Perces did not want this treaty. They believed that land was for everyone to share, and no one should be excluded from it. Eventually they agreed to sign the treaty because it became clear that if they didn't, there would be war.

Then in 1860, prospectors discovered gold on the Nez Perce reservation. They urged the U.S. government to redraw the boundaries of the reservation so all the gold sites would be outside it. In May 1863 the government

*Prospectors charged onto the Nez Perce
reservation to find gold, and the government
did nothing about it.*

offered another treaty to the Nez Perce chiefs, promising them money, schools, houses, and plowed land, but shrinking the reservation to a much smaller size. This is the treaty that tore the Nez Perce people apart.

At first, all the chiefs refused to sell their lands. Chief Hallalhotsoot, called Lawyer, told the white officials that the 1855 treaty was sacred. "I say to you," Lawyer told them, "you trifle with us. The boundary was fixed. . . . We cannot give you the country, we cannot sell it to you."

The government officials then met with the chiefs one by one. Many still stood firm. Lawyer, however, argued that if the new reservation was large enough, he would agree to it. Many other chiefs were outraged, but the officials ignored them. They made a new treaty with Lawyer and other Nez Perce men, many of whom were not chiefs.

WASHINGTON

MONTANA

OREGON

IDAHO

The 1863 treaty cut the reservation to one-tenth its original size (red area on map), giving nearly seven million acres to the U.S. government.

Nez Perce chiefs Timothy, Lawyer, and Jason (seated left to right). This photo was taken soon after the 1863 treaty.

The other chiefs called this the "Thief Treaty" and refused to obey it. They went back to the places they loved best. Old Chief Joseph led his people back to their beloved Wallowa Valley, the beautiful valley of winding waters. His son, Young Joseph, became the next chief for his band. He never forgot his father's dying words: "You must stop your ears whenever you are asked to sign a treaty selling your home. . . . This country holds your father's body. Never sell the bones of your father and mother."

In 1877, the government threatened the "non-treaty" Nez Perces with war unless they moved to the reservation. The non-treaty chiefs did not want to destroy their people any further, so they began the sad journey to the pitifully small reservation.

At this same time, several young Nez Perce men raided white settlements along the Salmon River. These raids set off several others. The anger that had been bubbling inside many Nez Perces finally boiled over. When the Nez Perce chiefs heard of these killings, some, including Chief Joseph and Chief Whitebird of the Salmon River Band, led their people to White Bird Canyon. They hoped to negotiate peace with the soldiers

Swan Necklace was one of the young raiders who started the Nez Perce War.

there. But the soldiers began shooting before anyone could talk of peace. The Nez Perce War had begun. The Nez Perces defended themselves and forced the soldiers out of the canyon. The chiefs then led about 800 Nez Perces toward Canada, where they hoped they could live safely forever.

U.S. Army soldiers chased the Nez Perces for more than a thousand miles, across the Bitterroot Mountains, twice across the Rocky Mountains, through Yellowstone National Park, and over the Missouri River.

Nez Perces carried all their belongings and drove a herd of hundreds of horses while they fled to Canada.

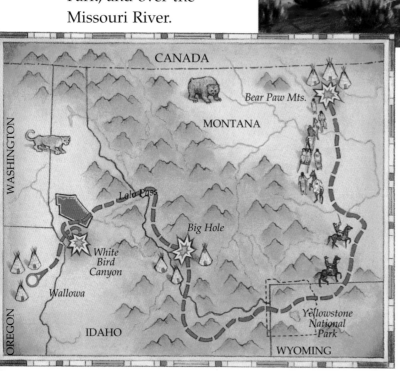

CANADA

Bear Paw Mts.

MONTANA

WASHINGTON

Lolo Pass

Big Hole

White Bird Canyon

Wallowa

OREGON

IDAHO

Yellowstone National Park

WYOMING

Chief Joseph's younger brother, Ollokot, was one of several key war chiefs during the Nez Perce War.

Warriors parading before the Battle of Big Hole. Their horses have honor marks on their flanks.

In the battle at Big Hole, a valley in Montana, showers of bullets tore through the tepees, pattering like rain. Women and children ran for their lives. Some soldiers killed them accidentally. Others killed them on purpose. The soldiers were told by their colonel to take no prisoners.

After four months of running, Nez Perce elders and children were having a hard time keeping up. The whole group was so grief-stricken, weary, and sick that they had to stop and rest in the Bear Paw Mountains, just 40 miles from the Canadian border.

Women watching the warrior parade. The woman in front may have scars on her arm, a sign of grief after losing a loved one.

It was there that army troops attacked them for the last time. After five days of battle, four chiefs and many other Nez Perces were dead. Others had escaped to Canada, to seek refuge with Chief Sitting Bull's people, the Sioux.

The army colonel promised the remaining Nez Perces that they could keep their horses and return to Idaho if they surrendered. With that promise, Chief Joseph said these words: "It is cold and we have no blankets. The little children are freezing to death. My people, some of them, have run away into the hills and have no blankets, no food; no one knows where they are— perhaps freezing to death. I want time to look for my children and see how many I can find. Maybe I shall find them among the dead. Hear me, my chiefs. I am tired; my heart is sick and sad. From where the sun now stands I will fight no more forever."

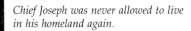

Chief Joseph was never allowed to live in his homeland again.

When a mountainside is swallowed by fire, the land looks as if it has died. But cooling rains do come, and small green shoots slowly bring new hope and healing to the land. The Nez Perce people, too, are trying to find hope and healing in their hearts. The Nez Perce War scattered them to different reservations and all over the world. Yet, as the Nez Perce saying goes, "Wherever we go, we are always Nez Perce."

Today, the Nez Perce people still reach out to new friends, just as Chief Twisted Hair reached out to Lewis and Clark long ago. Visitors from all over the world come to the Nez Perce National Historical Park in Idaho. Park rangers, both people of the Nez Perce tribe and others from the community, lead visitors on tours, teach them how to build tepees, introduce them to traditional foods, and demonstrate many other things.

At Nez Perce pow-wows, all people are welcome and are even asked to join in some of the dances. If Kaya lived among the Nez Perce people today, she'd be happy to see that many of them still live on the same land she called home. She'd be glad to hear her language being spoken, smell salmon roasting on the fire, taste fresh huckleberries, and step inside a longhouse to hear legends and stories. When a magpie alighted on a tree branch, she'd laugh quietly to herself. She'd be especially proud to watch the young girls, so much like herself, parade their beautiful horses in honor of their ancestors, whose inspiring spirits live on to strengthen and nourish all Nez Perce people, each and every day.

GLOSSARY OF NEZ PERCE WORDS

In Kaya's stories, Nez Perce words are spelled so that English readers can pronounce them. Here, you can also see how the words are actually spelled and said by the Nez Perce people.

Phonetic/Nez Perce	Pronunciation	Meaning
aa-heh/'éehe	*AA-heh*	yes, that's right
Aalah/Eelé	*AA-lah*	grandmother from father's side
Eetsa/Iice	*EET-sah*	mother
Hun-ya-wat/ Hanyaw'áat	*hun-yah-WAHT*	the Creator
Kalutsa/ Qalacá	*kah-luht-SAH*	grandfather from father's side
katsee-yow-yow/ qe'ci'yew'yew'	*KAHT-see-yow-yow*	thank you
Kautsa/Qaaca'c	*KOUT-sah*	grandmother from mother's side
Kaya'aton'my'	*ky-YAAH-a-ton-my*	she who arranges rocks
Nimíipuu	*nee-MEE-poo*	The People; known today as the Nez Perce
Pi-lah-ka/piláqá	*pee-LAH-kah*	grandfather from mother's side
Salish/Sélix	*SAY-leesh*	friends of the Nez Perce who live near them

Tatlo	*TAHT-lo*	ground squirrel
tawts/ta'c	*TAWTS*	good
tawts may-we/ ta'c méeywi	*TAWTS MAY-wee*	good morning
tee-kas/tikée's	*tee-KAHS*	baby board, or cradleboard
Toe-ta/Toot'a	*TOH-tah*	father
wah-tu/weet'u	*wah-TOO*	no
Wallowa/ Wal'áwa	*wah-LAU-wa*	Wallowa Valley in present-day Oregon
wapalwaapal	*WAH-pul-WAAH-pul*	western yarrow, a plant that helps stop bleeding
wyakin/ wéeyekin	*WHY-ah-kin*	guardian spirit

MEET THE AUTHOR

Each night when JANET SHAW was a girl,
she took out a flashlight and book hidden under
her pillow and read until she fell asleep. She
and her brother liked to act out stories, especially
ones about sword fights and wild horses. Today,
Ms. Shaw has three grown children. When they
were small, she often pulled them in a big red
wagon to the library, where they filled the wagon
with so many books, they had to walk back home.
Janet Shaw lives in North Carolina with her
husband. Their two dogs sleep by her feet
when she's writing.

MEET THE ILLUSTRATOR

BILL FARNSWORTH was honored to tell part
of the Nez Perces' story through his paintings.
He lives in Venice, Florida, with his wife, Deborah,
and daughters, Allison and Caitlin.

Meet the Advisory Board

American Girl extends its deepest appreciation to the advisory board that authenticated Kaya's stories:

Lillian A. Ackerman, Associate Professor, Adjunct, Department of Anthropology, Washington State University

Vivian Adams, Yakama Tribal Member, former Curator of Native Heritage, High Desert Museum

Rodney Cawston, Colville Confederated Tribes

Constance G. Evans, Retired IHS Family Nurse Practitioner and former Nez Perce Language Assistant/Instructor, Lewis-Clark State College

Diane Mallickan, Park Ranger/Cultural Interpreter, Nez Perce National Historical Park

Ann McCormack, Cultural Arts Coordinator, Nez Perce Tribe

Frances Paisano, Nez Perce Tribal Elder, Retired Educator

Rosa Yearout, Nez Perce Tribal Elder, M-Y Sweetwater Appaloosa Ranch